Daddy Soda

THE NEW HAMPSHIRE MYSTERIES
(BOOK ONE)

MIRA GIBSON

PROLOGUE

SPINNING TIRES KICKING up dust in a cloud that stung her eyes was the last thing that twelve-year old Candice saw before the van sped off and disappeared into the dark forest.

The slam of the van's door was still ringing in her ears, competing with the sounds of her own sobbing.

She gasped for air, as an incredible quaking panic rolled through her, distracting her from the sting of dirt embedded in her kneecaps, her palms, and every part of her that had landed hard against the earth.

Dust settled in her watery eyes, but the more she blinked, the harder it was to see. She made an honest effort to spit dirt from her mouth.

The pounding in her chest quieted.

She turned for the trail and started down it, one shoe coming off at the heel, the other nowhere to be found. That's how hard she had fought to keep her mother from getting yanked into the back of that van.

A crisp gust of wind blew at her sideways, causing her hair—long, stringy strands—to stick to her cheeks. Her face was damp with tears and sweat. Sheer panic was still seeping out of her.

As the wind died down, rattling the dead leaves that clung to branches overhead, a low growl emanated in the distance and gradually grew stronger.

The van had turned around.

No headlights. They were too smart for that. Tires crunched over gravel and twigs, as the van crept through trees and shadows, hunting for Candice.

She spied the van, her heart punching her chest cavity worse than before.

Maybe her mother had fought them. Maybe she had fought those men and seized the van. Candice hoped that was why the van was returning.

But in her gut, she knew that wasn't the case.

With a jolt, she started running along the trail. To her left, the trees were thin. The driver would see her as soon as he pulled the van alongside. But if she veered right, the ground would be too soggy with lake water for her to run. She wouldn't be able to keep her footing, pound on, and escape. She had no choice but to sprint along this thin clearing in the forest.

Candice pumped her arms. The brush underfoot threatened to trip her with every stride, but she tore through as fast as her legs would carry her.

As thin branches whipped her cheeks, arms, and legs, she ran with all her might, keeping on the balls of her feet and her gaze locked ahead.

But ahead was a sea of darkness, kissed by a razor's edge of moonlight.

Suddenly, the van surged beside her, swerving into the forest, bucking in front of Candice then veering away from her when a tree stood in its way.

She shrieked when the van surged at her again. The trees were thickening, slowing her pace. Her legs felt like rubber.

She stumbled and gasped for air when the van cut a hard left back onto the path. If it had gotten ahead of her, Candice would've doubled back, but they hadn't been so eager as to make a mistake.

Her socks sunk into muck. Had she lost her other shoe? This was where the lake met the dirt path. She recognized it. She had no choice but to cross over and risk full exposure or fall into the lake's murky depths.

She didn't so much run to the path as spill across it.

A sharp burst of pain sliced through her shoulder as she slid over dirt, her hair catching against the gravel. The van screeched to a skidding halt, as she rolled.

When she finally stopped rolling, she heard the van door click open.

The sounds of men's boots hitting the ground came next.

Candice's heart shot up her throat.

She was being hunted and the game was now even less in her favor.

She knew she had to keep fighting, keep running. Playing possum would result in her being kidnapped just like her mom, but when her gaze locked onto her right hand and she saw blood, Candice became petrified.

Get up, she ordered herself, *keep fighting.*

Without thought, without a second's consideration, Candice was on her feet, sprinting harder and faster than she ever had in her life. Her wet socks pounded the solid earth, as she tore down the dirt path. She didn't look back to see if she was being chased. She just kept going.

When she reached the house—*home!*—she shrieked for help, tumbled through the door, and fought to catch her breath.

"Mary!"

Her teenage sister, Mary, was standing in the kitchen. She held a can of beer in one hand, as she worked the burnt bits out of a casserole with a spatula.

"Why isn't Mom with you?" Mary didn't have to glance over her shoulder to know their mother hadn't returned with Candice.

Candice collapsed and Mary rushed to her, just as Candice lost consciousness.

The young girl's blond hair looked brown, Mary realized, and there was so much dirt encrusted in her hands that they looked stained. Her hands were also sticky, but from what? Mary's stomach dropped. It looked like blood. And where the hell were her shoes?

"What happened to you?" she breathed.

It had been a half hour since Mary had asked Candice to go out and fetch their mother. Kendra was supposed to have been on the dock getting some air. What the hell could have possibly happened in thirty minutes to have caused her younger sister to look like she had been beaten up?

Candice groaned and whimpered, as Mary carried her to the old sofa in the living room.

Her sister was dirty and bloody, and barely conscious.

Goddamn it that Mary had drank a few beers. It was impossible to mentally process this.

Forcing herself to snap out of it, Mary rushed to the sink, held a dishcloth under the faucet, and told herself to call the police.

But after stroking away the blood on her sister's hands, and checking every inch of Candice to confirm the young girl wasn't bleeding, she decided to get one of her father's guns first.

The handgun was stowed behind bottles of liquor in the top cabinet above the kitchen sink. A nine round GLOCK 27. The handgun had just enough dust on it that Mary was certain her dad hadn't messed with it.

She shoved it down the back of her pants, crossed the living room, and locked the front door.

Where the hell was her father, anyway?

When she returned to Candice, her sister's eyes were cracked open.

Candice was disoriented, but gaining consciousness.

"Are you hurt?" Mary asked. "Any broken bones?"

Candice groaned, "I don't think so, no."

Mary sat down on the sofa beside Candice and stroked the young girl's hair off her face.

"What happened?"

When the girl didn't answer, Mary pushed:

"Candice, you have to tell me what happened. Where's Mom?"

Candice touched eyes with Mary, but all she said was, "She's gone."

CHAPTER ONE

HANNAH WISHED she hadn't worn this blouse.

The number of things she regretted in life was low enough to count on her right hand—making out with Cody McAlister beneath the bleachers during prom twelve years back, growing up in Sanbornton, New Hampshire, which technically she'd had no control over, and this blouse. It was silky and loose and got caught on just about every item on her desk.

Her phone rang and when she reached for it, her sleeve, like a net sweeping the sea for tuna, knocked over her mug of pens and pencils. Writing utensils clattered to the linoleum floor before she could even announce the town and precinct she worked for. Embarrassment flared hot across her skin at the fumble, making her sweat.

At least no one on her floor noticed the clumsy move. But they had noticed others, all morning in fact, mainly because she was wildly overdressed, damn blouse and a pencil skirt, though the skirt seemed to be less of a culprit.

"Gilford Precinct, Homicide," she said absentmindedly into the receiver as she collected pens off the floor.

When the voice of a nervous-sounding woman came through the line, requesting Detective Barnes, Hannah placed her on a brief hold and transferred the call, being sure to alert Barnes that the woman was following up on her court date. Barnes grumbled a sigh into the receiver and reminded Hannah to direct these types of calls to the District Attorney.

Hannah knew that. She blamed her oversight on the blouse, but only in her head, and got off the phone fast.

It wasn't that she was trying to prove anything to the department by showing up dressed fancy. Lord knew she wasn't fancy in the first place. But as a twenty-six year old receptionist, she felt the twinge of her life's failings on a daily basis, and that morning, like a fool, she had thought looking a bit nicer might ease the sting. She couldn't have been more wrong.

Hannah kept her head down as she rolled her chair backwards to the fax machine, the spit of its wheels having alerted her to a report coming through. She said a silent prayer that she wouldn't have to walk it through the entire department and hand it to the Chief. Every walk through the office in this outfit, the heels of which were the cherry on top of her misfortune, felt like a walk of shame. She cringed at the thought then cringed harder when she saw the intended recipient in bold lettering across the top: Chief Holder.

Ugh.

The phone on her desk started ringing.

Thank God.

"Gilford Precinct, Homicide," she said on autopilot.

There was breathing on the other end, light and feathery, but not panicked, which was good. She hated when someone in crisis called the station instead of 911.

"Hi," a female voice came through, apprehensive. "Is this Hannah Cole?"

"Yeah. Who's this?"

Wind over the receiver as the caller exhaled.

"Look, if you're calling for personal reasons then make it quick," Hannah said. "The station is a madhouse today and my feet hurt too much to put up with any nonsense."

"It's Mary," she interrupted.

Hannah stiffened in her chair. The phone felt suddenly heavy in her grip and then an overwhelming sense of loss washed over her.

"How've you been?" Mary asked, but dryly, an edge of subtle resentment in her tone.

Hannah had nothing to say if not an outpouring of apologies, but she didn't dare break that dam, so she stated, "Good," as clinically as possible.

"I'm not sure if you're keeping up with what happened," Mary started, her tone even and responsible-sounding, not at all like her fifteen years. "It didn't exactly make headlines. We're not rich enough for that, I guess."

"What didn't make headlines?" Hannah asked, resting her elbows on her desk in a hunch of secrecy. Her stomach clenched.

"Mom."

The solitary word gripped Hannah's gut, but her ears were wide open.

"She disappeared a month back."

Disappeared? A *month* ago? And no one had contacted Hannah?

"No one knows what happened. Candice came home covered in blood. Now the town's done looking."

It was too much to process in a moment.

"Wait. What? Start over," she asked. "Mom disappeared a month ago and Candice came home covered in blood?"

"Yeah." Mary sounded exhausted. "There was a search party and the town kept looking for Mom for a few weeks, but then everyone gave up. Look, I thought you knew all this-"

"You thought I knew about this and I was sitting in Gilford on my high horse?" She shouldn't have snapped so she quickly offered, "I honest to God hadn't heard."

"Fine. The point is..." Mary's sharp tongue lost its edge and she softened. "Candice is doing really badly."

"Was she hurt? I mean what happened? She was attacked?"

"Would you listen?"

Hannah didn't even breathe, she was so poised to listen.

"Dale's been drinking *a lot* ever since. He's in a bad way, Hannah." Mary took a moment to swallow her pride. That much was clear when she had used his name instead of referring to Dale as her father. That's what he was, after all, Mary and Candice's dad, and nothing more than a stepfather to Hannah. "I need help over here."

"Hey, whoa, I'd love to help, but on my salary-"

"Not money." Again, there was another pause between them. "I need real help."

THE NEXT MORNING, Hannah was sure to put on a pair of soft, worn out jeans, which still fit her tightly enough that she wouldn't feel shabby, then she started off on the half hour drive from Gilford to Sanbornton. Her sweater was thin, but warm, and the coat she had decided to wear would keep her bundled well against the late October chill.

She didn't dare venture to speculate on the terrible circumstances surrounding her mother's disappearance, nor the harrowing tone in Mary's voice as she had hinted at how truly grisly life had become in Kendra's absence. She hadn't needed to explain. Hannah knew first hand. Dale's insertion into the family had been the reason she had left. In so many ways her stepfather had been a glaring cliché.

Hannah focused on the brilliant foliage beyond her windshield, rather than get sucked into dark memories.

Dark memories would catch up with her soon enough.

She had opted to take the back roads rather than hop on the highway. Deep down she wasn't about to lie to herself as to why that was. She knew. She could accept it. She needed to prolong her arrival, favoring the half hour route over a fifteen minute one. Her childhood home was close, too close, but there was a lot of land in-between. She needed to see as much of it as she could, let the picturesque scenery wash over her and give her some semblance of strength.

And it *was* picturesque. It was so God damn beautiful she could almost forget her family lived in it. Almost.

A thick forest of luscious maples lined the winding road that her Taurus was sailing over. The leaves were fiery shades of red and orange and subdued yellow, no different than the trees in Gilford, but things felt different here, like childhood, like home. That was the conflict brewing inside her. You always thought your childhood was great, until you grew out of it, and that was the problem. She had. She wondered if Mary was caught in the purgatory of having realized things at home were rotten, but unable to escape because she was still too young.

Beyond the flaming trees sat the mountains. A blue sky burned brightly overhead. Hannah rolled her windows down, all four, and drank in the scent of it. Fresh air, crisp and ever so slightly damp, filled her lungs. It brought her to her senses.

Breathing deeply, she savored the moment, shining as it was, suspended from time, the Gilford precinct behind her for the weekend to come, her family, as broken as they must be, waiting for her in the near future, but in this moment, it was just Hannah and the road, Hannah and the revitalizing air. If only this moment could last forever.

Mary hadn't elaborated on the phone. The teenager in her—in her? A teenager was what she was, but Mary had a way of denying it, ever ready to take on the world; hadn't shared much after Hannah had agreed to come. Stubborn, yet in need of love, that's how Mary had struck her during their phone call.

So, it became a real challenge not letting her mind wander into the dark territory of guessing what might have happened to their mother. And soon Hannah gave in. She didn't even see the smooth road stretched out in bends and curves before her. She was blind to the trees and the leaves rattling in the wind. She couldn't even smell the air anymore. She was consumed with Kendra: the woman Hannah remembered her to be and the woman her mother had become once Dale had entered their lives.

Before Dale, Kendra had been God-fearing. A woman who curled her hair and kept her nails clean, though the sheen of nail polish she wore would've hidden any dirt from prying eyes. She had been conscious of how she was seen from the outside as well as within. And Lord was she stern. She had watched Hannah like a hawk, never letting Hannah go off on her own, not even as a teenager, which Hannah grew to resent. But Kendra had had her reasons, the look in her eye said as much. Kendra had been the veteran of a silent war that had occurred before Hannah entered this world, and Kendra lived her life and went about her motherly duties as though a second war was on the horizon, waiting for her to be weak enough, waiting to take her life as it had failed to do all those years ago.

Kendra had never divulged what she had survived and Hannah hadn't asked. Instead, she came to respect her mother, though she fought her tooth and nail. Kendra had been strong, unlike anyone she had ever encountered.

When Hannah had taken her job as a receptionist in the homicide department, she came to realize the possibilities of what might have happened to her mother to make Kendra the way she was. The world was a very dark place.

As she veered right at a fork in the road, hugging Hermit Lake not far from the house she had promised to be at by 11 am, her childhood home, Hannah's heart ached for her mother. She truly had loved Kendra.

And now her mom had disappeared?

Her imagination ran wild, but she pushed it down until it felt like a ball at the pit of her stomach. Instead she hooked her mind around Dale.

The man was no good.

She nearly let the memory touch her, but she forced it down as well, taking in the scenery to get her bearings. Crushed beer cans that littered the shoulder of the road stole her attention. Why was it that the closer she got to her family's small corner of the lake, where the dock sat rickety like death on the water and the house sank into the soggy earth, did the side of the road have to be marred by Dale's hand? Not that he was the only one responsible for chucking empties out of his truck window, but he was certainly among the guiltiest.

Christ, the mere thought of him caused Hannah's hands to tremble. She reminded herself he wasn't her father, not her flesh and blood, which got her to calm enough to veer left at another fork. She glided over the weathered asphalt, the lake falling away to her right. She promised herself she wouldn't be late. Breakfast at the diner seemed reasonable, and all joking aside, she needed to pull over, thoughts of Dale driving her to drink.

Trying to forget, that's what alcohol amounted to.

A memory flashed in her mind, but she shoved it down, as she rolled her Taurus to a stop, dirt crunching under tires, in the parking lot of Gemma's Diner.

As soon as she killed the engine, she popped the glove box and grabbed a flask that she was proud to say she hadn't touched in months. Glancing around, she confirmed there wasn't a soul in sight then knocked back a long swig, feeling the sting of that silly outfit she had worn yesterday.

Look how fancy I am, she thought with a self-deprecating snort, as she took a long, hard look at herself—swigging booze at ten in the morning in a dusty diner parking lot tucked deep in the rural northeast.

She threw the flask into her purse and climbed out, locked her car out of habit rather than precaution, then ventured into the diner that wanted so badly to be a classic 1950s joint but so clearly failed on all fronts.

The bar stools were red and cracked. The mirror behind the bar was so tarnished it didn't so much reflect images as bounce hazy circles of them. The booths were just as dismal, but the wait staff took the cake.

Hannah spied two waitresses, as well as a tired looking cook in the back. She guessed he was a high school dropout. Who knew what that man had survived? The creases in his face had shadows that had shadows, like every inch of him was a dark story so sad you would die if you heard it.

She slid into a booth at the windows since it was her best option for privacy then buried her head in a menu.

"Well, I'll be, that's not Hannah Cole, is it?"

Hannah lowered her menu and feigned a smile at her fifty-year old waitress, who she recognized, of course.

Marjorie Abbott grinned at Hannah.

"It is," Marjorie decided.

"Hi, Marjorie," she said in a warm enough tone. "How've you been?"

Considering her answer, Marjorie sank into her hip. "I'm holding up," she said. "Christ, I'm so sorry about your mother."

Sympathy made her uncomfortable, but Hannah couldn't deny it felt good to drop her smile.

"Is that why you're in town?"

On a sigh, she admitted it was. "Need to check on the girls."

"Damn shame what happened to Kendra, and I feel pain in my heart saying that much, because the fact of the matter, no one knows what happened to her. Things like that don't happen in these parts." Marjorie was shaking her head and gazing out the window at the foliage as though if she didn't break eye contact she would shatter. "I was out there looking for her. The whole town was. I pray to the Lord, he keeps her safe."

Hannah felt the impulse to comfort her, but it left her feeling more awkward than endeared. She was itching for her flask.

"What can I get you?" she asked, pressing her pen hard against her pad. "And it's on the house. Don't you dare even reach for your wallet."

"Coffee for sure," she started and glanced down the menu. "And I suppose eggs. Hash browns and-"

"A few pancakes?" she brightened. "I know how you girls like your pancakes."

"Sure."

Marjorie collected Hannah's menu and angled her worried eyes down at Hannah, her stare lingering, as she added, "You got the same look in your eye as your mother, like you can do anything. Never lose that look, Hannah. It suits you too much."

Hannah smiled to herself and said thanks, but Marjorie was already walking away.

When her coffee came, Hannah was sly about pouring in a generous nip of whiskey, and when her breakfast arrived she was too consumed with the warm burn of her coffee to eat.

She kept an eye on her cell, noting the time at intervals, and reminded herself that drinking so early was excusable. This was her weekend after all, and venturing into the house she had grown up in would take the kind of courage she hadn't needed to exercise since the day she had walked out of it.

Hannah allowed herself to enjoy the sight of leaves fluttering down to the dirt parking lot beyond her window, as her whiskey-laced coffee warmed her stomach and sent a smooth rush of calm through her veins. The minutes ticked by, but she barely noticed. Some things about Sanbornton were undeniably beautiful, and she owed it to herself to appreciate them.

"Hannah?"

It was a man this time, and Hannah wasn't exactly eager to look up, but when she did, she almost didn't believe her eyes.

"Cody McAlister?" she replied, surprised. "Christ, I can't believe I'm running into you."

"It's a bit like seeing a ghost."

He gazed down at her, the same determined face ever-desperate to prove himself just as he'd always looked, green eyes lingering, but not wandering like they used to in high school, and an easy smile helped his lips curl, arching up on the right side, showing the imperfection of his gums in a way that used to set her heart pounding in high school and, she discovered, still did.

"Just call me the ghost hunter," she said, but the joke didn't land.

His smile remained, though his brow furrowed slightly, his eyes narrowing like he was trying to get it.

"Never mind," said Hannah.

He dropped it, glanced over his shoulder at Marjorie and asked for a coffee, black with two sugars, giving Hannah just enough time to take in the sight of him.

Damn if men didn't age well, she thought. Here she sat, her brown hair a mess of cowlicks that provoked her natural waves, and she didn't have a stitch of makeup on, except for the two strokes of mascara that she couldn't leave home without. Even her fingernails were a fright, chewed to the bone like a boy's.

Cody on the other hand seemed to have grown into his looks. The broad shoulders and pronounced jawline that had lent a goofy air to his overall towering appearance during high school now served to punctuate his muscular build. His hard chest, hugged by a dark tee where his jacket hung open, could only be the product of a lifestyle dedicated to manual labor, which seemed about right for Cody. He had been a smart kid, but hadn't exactly applied himself. She wondered if he was some kind of mechanic, maybe a contract laborer.

He angled his green eyes down at her along with a smile. Then an edge of awkwardness shined through. She hadn't invited him to sit. It was the unspoken conversation between them. It made her stiff and just as awkward.

"How've you been?" he asked to fill the silence.

Hannah shrugged, wondering how long their conversation would play out. It wasn't as though he'd found her on Facebook in all these years. Clearly, he didn't care. At the moment, he was enduring some kind of social obligation. He had run into her, now he had to ask.

"Fine," she said, keeping it brief, giving him an out. "I'm over in Gilford. It's not like I made it out of New Hampshire."

He shot her a crooked smile.

"You're over in Homicide, right?"

"As an administrator." The impulse to roll her eyes was a stretch to overcome. "I'm a receptionist. Not much to write home about. Our alumni newsletter wasn't exactly begging me to draft an exposé on my exciting life."

It got him laughing and Hannah remembered what a beautiful sound he made when he did that. They had been best friends in high school or close to it. Hannah a freshman, Cody a senior, two dorks that had been more or less shunned by the student body. Then he had gone and done the unforgivable. Cody had led her to believe he was actually interested in her, gotten her under those bleachers, kissed her, gotten her to think this was something real, *touched her*, and the next thing she knew a nightmare had befallen her, one that the whole school talked about. He had blabbed, revealing his true motives. He had only wanted to get out of the

18

dork circle and prove he deserved to be with the cool kids. And she had never lived it down.

He didn't ask to join her, but asserted as much when he wriggled his jacket off and tossed it on the seat across from her. She didn't have the opportunity to object either. He was focused on Marjorie, shouting his order for hash browns at her across the diner.

When he plopped down across from Hannah, he sealed her fate. They would eat together. She wasn't sure he deserved it, which was why she didn't ask how he was, what he was doing with himself these days, or why he had stopped off at Gemma's even though, as far as she had heard, he lived on the other side of the lake.

"So, tell me about Homicide," he said, smoothing his intrusion over. "Are you busy over there?"

Marjorie brought his black coffee, and Hannah wondered if he really expected an answer. He was focused on adding a packet of sugar. She took it as an opportunity to refresh her own mug with a splash of whiskey, which of course he noticed.

When his eyebrows rose, she took it as admonishment, but he was in no position as far as she was concerned.

"For the record," she stated, as she twisted the flask's top and tucked it back into her purse, "*I'm* not judging *you*." It was close enough to the truth.

"I'm not judging you, either," he said, grinning and glancing down. If his eyes widened, she would throw her mug at him. But they didn't. "Is that why you're here?"

"You think I need to drive thirty minutes to Sanbornton to swig booze?"

"No," he laughed then turned serious. "Because of Kendra, her disappearance. You work in Homicide now."

"First of all, stop saying I work in Homicide. I don't. Second of all," she leaned in close, as though he might be her best friend again for a moment. "No one called me. No one told me until yesterday."

"But that's what you're doing here? Going over to the house?"

It seemed to worry him, but she affirmed it none-the-less.

"So, what have you heard?"

"Not much," Hannah started, losing all sight of the man across from her in favor of envisioning Mary on their call. The pain in Mary's tone had been masked by her teenage pride. "Just that Kendra disappeared a month back."

Cody leaned in and looked at her. Her gaze locked on his mouth, as dangerous as it was to do so.

"No one knows what happened, Hannah, but people think she was murdered."

Hannah took a beat to absorb the magnitude of his statement. It hadn't even crossed her mind that her mother had been killed. Though she had to admit, she had done a soldierly job of not letting herself go there.

"Why do people think that?"

Cody's lips pressed together as he searched for words that wouldn't scare her, but there were few, so he came out with it.

"The blood. The scene."

"Scene? What scene?"

"Where she was abducted..." He trailed off as though there was no easy way to say it. "What happened to Candice, I mean all of it... It doesn't add up and at the same time, it does."

He punctuated the sentiment with raising his eyebrows. Hannah had heard enough. She didn't bother checking her cell. It was time to go.

"You're heading out?" he asked when she rose from the booth. "Want me to come with you?"

As busy as she had made herself thumbing through her wallet for cash, his offer halted her. "Why would I want you to come with me?"

"Are you planning on staying in town long?" He was deflecting, and she wasn't exactly happy about disappointing him a second time.

"No," she asserted. "I'm only here for the afternoon. Just until I know the kids are okay."

"I'll walk you out."

"Don't trouble yourself. I have to get going. Nice seeing you."

Cody was halfway out of the booth, but Hannah hadn't lingered to watch him start after her. She was already out the door.

Marjorie sauntered over with his steaming hash browns and grunted as she set them on the table.

"Did she take off?"

❄

THE HOUSE LOOKED worse than it had when Hannah had grown up in it. It looked like garbage. There was no other word for it. Years of harsh winters—rain and snow and sleet—had turned the side paneling to rot. The grain on the wood looked brittle like it would flake off if you dragged your nail over it. The tin roof was bent at strange angles and the porch sank low in front of the door.

There was vegetation surrounding the house, if you could even call it a *house*. In Hannah's mind it was a *shack*. Standing before it now was surreal. The bushes and trees didn't quite look as they had years ago, as though all the plants hugging it had swelled, wildlife bursting everywhere human life had shriveled. That was how Mary had sounded on the phone towards the end—shriveled up.

Hannah stalked over mud to get to the porch and hoped the memories wouldn't come flooding back the second she got inside. It was that hope which distracted her from watching her step.

When her left foot hit the wooden slats, she heard a crack then a snap, and gravity took hold. Her boot shot through, splintered wood slicing through leather, a sharp twist at the ankle as her palm smacked the door.

"Damn," she hissed, wincing as the sting of it reached her brain, but she claimed some balance, shifting her weight to her other foot and hoisting herself up.

There was a nasty gash in the porch where her foot had fallen through, and an even worse one at the side of her boot, which had saved the skin beneath.

"Christ Almighty, get me out of here in one piece," she grumbled.

Mary was quick to open the door when Hannah knocked. The young woman staring her in the face wasn't even an echo of the seven-year old she had left behind all those years ago. Except the eyes. Small and blue and screaming. Mary had made a solid effort of hiding her blue eyes, though, rimmed black around the lashes, which were thickened with clumps of mascara. Her once sandy, blond hair had been bleached into a coarse texture and cut sharp at the chin, and her eyebrows had all but been plucked clean off her forehead, penciled over with an arch that made her look surprised.

Hannah had seen that kind of expression so many times before in her day-to-day life, apathetic boredom staring back at her from a drive-thru window, but Hannah knew Mary had a hundred times the ambition. She had to, unless she truly had changed, inside as well as out.

"Sorry about the porch," Hannah said, indicating the hole.

"Yeah, I heard you trip."

"Thanks for the help then," she said dryly, as she tested her ankle, rolling it to investigate the damage. She would live.

Mary stepped back heavily on her bare heels in such a way that sent a jiggle up through her, as Hannah walked inside.

The house smelled just the same, the mudroom and the hallway not two feet deep. Nothing brought the past back like a distinct scent, but it wasn't memories that came to mind so much as the way she used to feel living here, weighed down and empty at times, yet so full of aspirations—lovely dreams that lifted her heart and made it ache just the same.

"Was the drive okay?" Mary asked her as she led Hannah into the living room.

"It was pretty enough," she admitted.

Watching Mary's bouncy step as she crossed to an old sofa and sat on its cloth-torn arm reminded Hannah of their mother. She had never seen much of Kendra in Mary when they had lived here together, but now their mother shone through

Mary's figure, her wide hips, the long legs that were a touch too thin to make sense beneath her large chest, a genetic trait Hannah hadn't received.

Mary fisted her hands around the hem of the white tee shirt she wore and munched on her lip.

Innocence mixed with pure trouble—that was what Mary looked like.

"Thanks for coming," she said softly, looking worried about having this conversation. She had been determined on the phone, but Hannah had to figure that being face-to-face with the sister who had abandoned them, Mary wouldn't have much to say until she let her anger go.

"Want to explain to me what happened?" she gently prodded. She made a point not to stare at Mary. Instead, she glanced around the living room, looking for a decent place to sit.

"I told you what I know over the phone."

"Then tell me about how I can help," Hannah suggested, settling onto a wooden chair she had found under a stack of old magazines.

Mary's voice cracked, finally showing her young age. "I just want to find Mom."

"You say it's been a month?"

She nodded, her lip quivering so she bit it hard, which forced her chin to wrinkle.

"Candice isn't talking. She hasn't said a thing, but she was covered in Mom's blood. Hannah, I checked every inch of her and besides a few bad scratches from running home through the woods, she was fine. I can't stand thinking that Mom is off somewhere she doesn't want to be... suffering."

Mary curled into herself and began crying.

Hannah was overwhelmed by the impulse to go to her, hold her, and yet something held her back.

Whatever touch of closeness they had once had, it was gone.

When Mary gained control of her emotions and swept the mascara from under her eyes, Hannah joined her on the opposite end of the sofa. Mary slid down to the seat, facing her, one leg curled beneath her, causing her jeans to pull taut.

"I'm pissed at Candice for not talking, and I mean, Hannah, she's not talking. She hasn't spoken a word. It's like she's trapped in her head."

"Damn," Hannah breathed.

"Things are falling apart over here and I can't hold it together. I just want her found."

It was Dale's job, if anyone's, to hold things together. Mary shouldn't have to take this on.

"What do you think I can do?"

"You work in Homicide," she pointed out, asserting the same misconception that Cody had assumed.

"I'll do what I can," Hannah assured her. "Make some calls."

"Thank you," she barked as though it had taken more effort than she possessed to get this far. She started shaking her head. "Being here..." She sighed and inhaled. "Living with Dad and Candice... the way he is now, the way Candice has dropped off into another dimension... I'm in hell."

Hannah was impressed with her use of the word 'dimension' until she remembered Mary was exceptionally bright.

"I don't know how to get through this."

"Are you telling me you're thinking about leaving?"

"I wouldn't leave Candice," she said. "But this past month without Mom…" More head shaking, her gaze fell. "I feel like I live with monsters."

Mary met Hannah's gaze and her cold blue eyes warmed as if the girl was having an honest go at connecting.

"We have the same eyes," she said, surprising Hannah.

Hannah felt examined, intrusively so, as Mary leaned forward studying her irises and the flecks of color all around.

"I could help you with your look," she offered.

"My look?" Hannah nearly snorted a laugh.

"Yeah, your makeup and stuff. You don't really have a look yet, do you?"

"Why don't you let me see your sister?" Hannah asked.

"She's out by the lake."

Mary padded into the mudroom. When Hannah reached her, Mary slid one foot then the next into a pair of beat-up Converse sneakers and threw her jacket on.

"Watch the hole," she told Hannah as they crossed the porch, as if her sister hadn't created it minutes ago.

There was something motherly about the command, and Hannah obeyed, stepping carefully around the weakened board and down the porch steps.

Hannah kept by Mary's side, trekking through the dying grass, which spanned the same fifteen yards that had always led to the lake.

As they approached, Hannah observed the lithe silhouette of a girl seated at the edge of the dock, facing out toward calm waters. The lake looked black other than the stark reflection of the sun on its surface.

When they reached the edge of the grass where the dock began, Hannah glanced at her sister for permission.

"Go ahead. It's not like she's talking to me," Mary shrugged, folding her arms and squinting through the sunny glare at Candice. "You might as well try."

As Hannah stepped along the dock that shifted much too easily under her weight for her to trust it, Mary shouted, "Don't be rude, now!"

Confused, Hannah shot a glance over her shoulder and saw that Mary's gaze was locked on their younger sister. Again, that motherly command, stern yet warm and so much like Kendra.

Hannah knelt beside Candice and stole glances at the young girl's profile. She hadn't seen her since she was four, Hannah eighteen, on the day she left home. And in so many ways the twelve-year old she was kneeling beside now was a stranger.

"Hi, Candice. Do you remember me?"

Candice stared vacantly across the water, her black pupils dilated as though she saw nothing at all.

"I'm Hannah. I'm your big half-sister. I live a few towns over. We have the same mother."

No response. Nothing. Not a breath. Not a blink, and certainly not a shred of acknowledgment. It was heartbreaking.

"I'm here to help you find Kendra," she went on. "It would be a big help if you could tell me what happened. Could you tell me everything you remember from that night?"

Hannah let that hang in the air knowing full well the girl wouldn't respond. Her knee was feeling raw against the wood so she stood and glanced across the water, felt the cold breeze on her face, and drank it in, trying in some sense to connect with Candice through the serenity that surrounded them.

Candice got to her feet and for one shining moment it seemed promising.

But then she turned and padded down the dock and crossed the soggy grass without so much as a glance at Mary.

As decisive as her direction had seemed, Candice suddenly began walking in circles next. She was staring at her feet, walking in circles, and flapping her skinny arms somewhat playfully, but to Hannah it was disturbing.

Mary locked eyes with Hannah, threw her hands up in the air, and shrugged as if to say, *that's how she is now,* so Hannah started for the grass.

When she reached it, Dale stalked out from a line of thick maples not eight feet from the lake.

He zipped his fly and stared hard at her.

The man was a grizzly bear, as broad and tall as she had remembered.

The look in his eye, steely and hardened, chilled her, and his tone was just as threatening:

"What do you think you're doing here?"

CHAPTER TWO

THE SANBORNTON Police Station's Missing Persons department was God's joke on the county.

The receptionist had passed Hannah from detective to detective. Henderson had referred her to Valkenburg who had told her she had to speak with Henderson, and it went on like this for hours, a virtual cat's cradle of administrative nonsense.

The silver lining, if there was one, was that Hannah no longer felt like the failure she had assumed she was, working at the Gilford precinct. At Gilford Homicide, Hannah handled her duties decently, and worked as hard as she could to keep her thumb on the pulse of each case so that civilians wouldn't leave the station house bald, having pulled their hair out in frustration.

Right now, she couldn't say the same for the Sanbornton precinct's receptionist, who had been causing Hannah a massive amount of frustration that morning.

"We're not holding the Kendra Cole case file anymore, I guess," said Sandy, the receptionist.

"You guess? Then why did you just send me running around from department to department as if someone had it?" Hannah asked.

Sandy frowned and suggested, "Try Homicide?"

"I was up there. Homicide said that they haven't received the Cole case file yet," she told Sandy.

"Well, then, the case must be archived."

"Archived? You mean *closed*?"

"No, we can't actually close the case," Sandy assured her. "Because the case hasn't been solved."

Hannah was far from assured. She hadn't a shred of confidence in this woman or her precinct.

"So, what are you telling me?" asked Hannah. "Kendra Cole's case is stuck in some kind of administrative purgatory?"

Sandy chuckled. "That's a great way of putting it, very humorous."

Christ, she was being serious.

"I don't find this funny."

"I wish I could help you, but I'm really swamped. If you leave your number, I'll have someone give you a call and help you further."

Hannah resigned herself to the fact that she had hit a wall. She grumbled and jotted down her phone number for Sandy.

She started for the lobby next, recalling the bench she had seen. She sat down on the bench and found her cell phone in her purse. Maneuvering was difficult since she hadn't bothered to take off her bulky coat. She racked her brain for a moment, trying to decide who she should call at the Gilford police station. A few people who worked in the Missing Persons department at Gilford had been friendly with her over the years, and might be willing to help. She decided to call Cranston even though it wasn't likely that he would be at the station on a Sunday.

Cranston didn't pick up.

Hannah left a detailed message, asked Cranston to call her back, and then tossed her cell phone into her purse.

"You're still in Sanbornton, what a nice surprise."

Hannah looked up to see who had addressed her and found Cody McAlister approaching. There was an easy smile on his face. His green eyes looked darker than usual, as he came to stand in front of her.

"I'm leaving tomorrow," she told him. "I figured I would stay the weekend. There's a motel on Route 12 that had a vacancy," she added.

Her gaze locked on the detective's badge that was dangling from a lanyard around his neck.

"The Super-8?" he guessed correctly. "I bet it's got a lot of vacancies."

"You work here?" she asked, shocked.

Cody glanced down at his detective's badge. "I didn't mention that I'm a detective?"

"No, you didn't. What department?"

He hesitated. "Homicide."

She popped up from the bench and said, "I was just up there. I didn't see you."

"Weird," he agreed.

"You know more about my mom's disappearance than you were letting on yesterday," she surmised.

"Not really."

"I doubt that."

"Your mom's case isn't being handled by my department."

"My mom's case isn't being handled by *anyone's* department, evidently."

"You came here to get the files?"

"I didn't come here for anything," she said dryly. "And I was just leaving."

"I'll walk you out."

Cody opened the door for Hannah and they started across the dirt parking lot. She had no idea why he was walking her out. He looked both ways as though a vehicle might speed through this deserted ghost town, and when they reached her car, Hannah turned to face him.

"I've learned a few things about the case," he told her, perhaps to keep the conversation going so she wouldn't escape into her car.

"Care to share with the rest of the class?"

"I've been keeping an eye on Missing Persons and their investigation. I've read their reports."

"Okay..." She waited for more. When he didn't continue, she said, "If you know something, you have to tell me. This is my family."

She felt herself getting choked up, but she shut her mouth before her voice could quaver.

He searched her eyes and asked, "You still feel like they're your family?"

"I can't believe you would ask me that," she snapped, offended.

"You left," he reminded her.

"You sound like Mary."

"Like a teenage girl?"

"Like someone who blames me for leaving. For the record, I didn't get very far. I only made it to the other side of the lake, so what's with your animosity?"

She touched eyes with him. There was too much history between them. He had been her friend at one point. But he had quickly turned into her enemy all those years ago.

"I left Sanbornton," she admitted. "But I never stopped loving my mother. I never stopped caring for and worrying about my half-sisters. I don't have to explain myself to you or defend my reasons for leaving."

"I agree."

"Something happened to my mother, and her disappearance broke my already-broken family. Help me out, Cody. Can you tell me what you know?"

"Kendra's blood was found in the woods near your family's property."

"Yeah, that's not a shocker. Candice was covered in it, according to Mary."

"There were tire marks and other pieces of evidence."

Hannah's brow furrowed. "I want to see it."

"The crime scene has grown over."

"It couldn't have grown over by much," she argued. "A month in autumn, when trees are drying up and the grass isn't growing, couldn't change the scene radically."

He eyed her Taurus and said, "Your car will get beaten to hell on the back roads. We'll take my truck."

A WALL OF SILENT tension rose between them, as Cody steered his Ford pickup and Hannah sat in the passenger seat.

The forest was dense all around them, and Hannah wasn't convinced that they were driving along a real road. It looked more like an old path—dirt and gravel that had been beaten down from years of trespassing.

The pickup truck bounced and bucked, as it tore deeper through the woods.

Through the trees, Hannah spied the lake she had grown up on. She had never journeyed down this particular stretch of wilderness in all the years she had lived here. In a sense, she felt betrayed by this hidden path in the woods, like her hometown had committed a lie of omission.

"The area is up a ways," Cody told her, his eyes locked on the terrain ahead. "The rains washed all the evidence away, but I can walk you through the scene."

"Thank you."

She had meant to sound gracious, but her tone had come across cold.

He shot her a sideways glance and she smiled, sort of.

Cody angled the Ford under a thick canopy of maples and parked to the wayside, clear of the dirt path they had been driving along.

After they climbed out, Cody said, "We'll walk the rest of the way on foot."

"We're not there yet?"

"Not by a long shot."

If Cody McAlister made sense anywhere, it was trekking through the woods.

Hannah couldn't picture him working a crime scene, canvasing a rural neighborhood to ask questions, or pouring over police reports, but in the forest, surrounded by trees, with a rifle over his shoulder maybe, he started to add up.

Cody had grown into a mysterious, burly creature. The way his eyes came alive in this setting and the way he inhaled deeply as though each lungful of oxygen was all the food he needed, told her that he would never leave this town, even if the only times he got to enjoy the great outdoors was when someone like her mother vanished in the dead of night.

As they walked deeper into the forest, Hannah noticed crushed beer cans and some littered trash. Then she heard voices in the distance. Boys. The sounds of their rowdy masculine laughter made her stomach clench. Too many men with too much freedom was a dangerous thing. She had learned that the hard way. Suddenly, Hannah didn't want to be there.

"This area has become a hangout for teenagers," Cody explained. During their high school friendship, Cody had been sensitive to Hannah's fear of drunk, teenage boys. "The kids that come here are harmless—as harmless as the boys we went to high school with," he added.

There was a chasm between them. Their memories of high school were at odds. As far as Hannah could remember, none of the boys they had gone to school with had been harmless. Quite the opposite, in fact.

"You're not nostalgic about our trashy upbringing, are you?" she asked.

"Sometimes I am," he admitted. "I have a fondness in my heart for those years. Why not?"

Hannah could think of at least a million reasons.

"We weren't raised in a major city where there are gangs and hard crimes corrupting the streets," he went on. "When we were kids, we got into trouble, sure, but look at all *this*..." He eyed the glorious autumn scenery all around them. "You can't beat this. You just can't, and we were raised with all this beauty."

Hannah shrugged, unconvinced, but she wasn't about to debate him.

"Come on, Hannah," he pushed, wanting or needing her to admit it. "Sanbornton is goddamn gorgeous. And you turned out okay."

"You're the one who turned out okay. I'm barely surviving."

"I doubt that. Don't downplay your life."

"Before I left Sanborton," she began opening up, feeling compelled to share a story from her past that would illustrate that her teenage years in this small town weren't worthy of nostalgia. "Dale and my mom got into it one night. Their argument was so stupid, I don't even remember the details, but I remember that my mom was cooking dinner and wouldn't acknowledge Dale. He was furious at her because she wasn't paying him any real attention, not more than replying when he yelled. Well, Dale flew into a rage. He pulled a gun on her. Pointed it right at her head. Cocked it. And you know what Kendra did? She looked him dead in the eye and said, *stop wasting my time*. Then she returned her attention to the dinner she was making as if nothing crazy had happened."

Finding that hilarious, Cody laughed. He threw his head right back and laughed and laughed, letting out good, hardy chuckles that boomed through the woods and sounded a lot like music to Hannah's ears. She was smiling too.

"That's just it, Cody. That's the problem," she went on, growing serious. "I used to think it was a good story, because it's funny and shocking. But it's not funny, and it's more than shocking. It's disturbing and very sad. It's downright dangerous how we used to live. And now my mom is gone."

His smile faded and he touched eyes with her.

"I know," he said.

Up ahead, a group of teenage boys came into view. They were laughing it up, drinking and smoking between the trees. Their car was parked nearby.

Hannah instinctively hung back, feeling intimidated.

"I know it's barely noon," she said, as she pulled her flask out of her purse.

"Hey," he allowed. "I think we've established a no-judgment dynamic."

"For the record, I'm not an alcoholic."

"For the record, I'm planning on flashing my badge and watching those kids scatter so that we can have the place to ourselves."

Now *that* was funny. She nearly choked, and snorted out her nip, but determined to feel the comforting burn, she swallowed hard then stowed her flask. With Cody here, maybe she wouldn't need to feel buzzed after all.

He didn't have to produce his badge. As soon as he swaggered through the trees and announced himself, the kids chucked their empty beer cans, climbed into their car, and drove off through the forest to God only knew where.

Cody waited for her to catch up. As she quickened her pace, approaching him, she felt self-conscious, but maybe in a good way. Cody watched her, and though she couldn't be certain that he was drinking in the sight of her, per se, she definitely sensed his attraction.

Cody had never made her feel this way during high school. Their kiss and all that had transpired between them under the bleachers and into the dreadful night that had followed, which she had worked so hard to forget, had never included this level of thrilling self-consciousness. Whether that was a good thing or bad, she had yet to find out.

"This is where it happened," he informed her, indicating a fifteen-foot circumference around him.

Hannah met him where he stood. He scanned the terrain, turning three hundred and sixty degrees around. She took in the surroundings—the dirt and gravel beneath her feet, and the brush that a vehicle had leveled. There were red and orange and pale-yellow leaves covering the ground, as well.

"The night Kendra disappeared," he began, "she wasn't in the house around dinner time, so Mary sent Candice outside to fetch her. This was around eight-thirty or nine in the evening. Why Kendra had ventured off is unclear, but according to Mary, she had grown secretive, aloof, and distant in general. First, Candice checked the dock to see if her mom was there. When she didn't find her, Candice began walking the trails that hug the lake in search of Kendra. One of those trails comes through here."

Cody's clinical-sounding explanation helped Hannah to stay unemotional, as she listened to the facts and tried to visualize the chain of events.

"We know a vehicle was here. We guess a van-"

"Wait a second," Hannah interrupted him, as she wrapped her head around this new tidbit. "Kendra was abducted?"

"We don't know that for certain. We only know that a vehicle was here. There were fresh tire tracks and blood on the dirt. Some blood droplets were over the tire tracks, too."

"Slow down," she said, feeling frustrated that she didn't already know everything. She forced herself to breathe and told herself to spread her mind wide open so that she could soak up every last detail.

"Okay," he agreed. "Kendra was up here with the van. We don't know if the driver had agreed to meet her or if the encounter was a bad coincidence—like a wrong place, wrong time kind of thing. It's also possible that the driver had been stalking her and knew about her evening walks. All we really know is that there was a vehicle, and an altercation occurred, which resulted in Kendra bleeding-"

"How could her blood be *over* fresh tire tracks?" Hannah asked, having fully grasped what Cody had explained so far.

"We think Candice found Kendra in the throes of being attacked. Kendra's blood saturated Candice's shirt and hands. We suspect that it wasn't until the van drove off that Kendra's blood, the remnants that were on *Candice,* fell to the dirt."

Hannah took a moment to mentally digest the information. She couldn't feel the crisp autumn air fill her lungs anymore. Her mind was racing and her heart was pounding out of her chest.

"Candice saw my mother get attacked..." she said to herself.

"Yes. And we think Candice fought with the attacker, or attackers, too."

Hannah wanted to sob and let the feelings that were roiling inside her burst out, just to release the building pressure and gain a shred of relief.

"We found Kendra's hair in some branches over here. We found her shoe, as well as both of

Candice's shoes, one here and the other near the lake," he explained, pointing out each spot except for the shoe at the lake. "We also found..." He trailed off, hesitating before sharing more information.

"What?" she pushed

"We also found an eight-ball of meth."

"Methamphetamine? The drug?" she asked.

Cody nodded.

Hannah stared at him in utter disbelief then offered her own explanations.

"Kids party out here all the time."

"We know that," he said.

"It could've been anyone's meth."

"We know that."

"My mother went to church on Sundays and read the bible," she added, fully convinced that if the police found meth near the crime scene, it could only be a coincidence. "Kendra wasn't a drug addict."

"Not when you knew her," he agreed.

"When *I* knew her?"

"The police can't rule out the possibility that Kendra started using drugs at some point, and it exposed her to a world of characters who connect to her abduction."

"There's no way that's possible, Cody," she insisted.

He studied her for a long moment, then compromised, "The drugs could have belonged to her abductor or abductors."

"That's what I would think."

"I'm telling you what Missing Persons documented, not what *I* think," he clarified.

"At this point, Cody, I would rather hear what you think. Kendra disappeared a month ago. Is my mother alive or dead? Yes or no?"

"When a missing person isn't found within the first seventy-two hours, then there's little chance..."

Hannah felt her heart split down its center. She was the one who had run away from Sanbornton. She was the one who hadn't looked back. She hadn't returned her mother's phone calls. They had lost touch.

She hated Cody for introducing her to the possibility that her mother, who she had known her whole life, might have completely changed in Hannah's absence. Changed into a drug addict.

Time could change a person, Hannah knew that, but it was still hard to swallow.

If Hannah had never left all those years ago, this tragedy would have never happened to her mother...

Understanding that fact and trying to make sense of it practically tore her mind in two.

Cody came near to her. He pulled her into his chest and held her, cradling her lower back and the nape of her neck. She melted into his arms, needing him and resenting him at the same time.

She released the hard emotions, letting out a breathy sob without making a sound.

Cody hugged her tightly and didn't say a word.

When her emotions subsided, she asked, "If Kendra was kidnapped by a bunch of random meth addicts, then how am I supposed to find her?"

"Candice is the key," he told her.

Hannah urged him and searched his eyes.

"She needs to see a child psychologist," he suggested. "She hasn't talked to anyone. Sometimes a complete stranger can get a kid to open up in ways their family can't."

"Why wouldn't she talk to Mary about what happened? Or Dale?"

"I don't want to speculate. I just know a psychologist could really help."

Hannah considered it.

"If there's anything you can do," he pushed.

She snorted a laugh. "Get Dale to sign off on that?"

"Hannah, I'm telling you. It could crack this thing wide open. Any detail can be a huge lead. Candice could've seen their faces, or remember tattoos, anything. Even a few digits of a license plate could help tremendously."

"There's no way Dale is going to allow a psychologist to talk to Candice."

"It's important."

Hannah shook her head.

"Hannah, it's our best shot."

"What aren't you telling me?" she asked.

Cody reached for her, but she backed away, staring at him.

"If there's more to tell me, I'm listening," she said, sensing he knew more.

Did he think that he could bring her here and tell her half-truths?

"There's only one other thing. Here, at the crime scene, the investigators found a message of sorts written in the dirt."

"What do you mean?"

"We think either Kendra or the kidnapper wrote it, maybe with their finger or a stick," he went on, unable to come out with it all at once.

"Wrote what? Just tell me, Cody!"

"The message said, '*Ask Mary*'."

CHAPTER THREE

MARY HAD NO shame nursing a Coors Light. Dewy beads of perspiration rolled down the side of the can, as she fried something Hannah knew she would never eat—fish. Mary had asked her to cut a cucumber. She had even provided Hannah with a cutting board and had selected the proper knife for her to use when at first Hannah had looked like a deer in headlights at the notion of helping to put dinner on the table.

"How's the salad coming along?" Mary asked, as she flipped the fish in the pan.

"Great, I would say." Hannah was saving face, of course. A fifteen-year old was one-upping her at every turn in the kitchen. Thank God the meal they were preparing didn't require use of the oven. Mary made frying look easy, but the fact of the matter was that Hannah's meals generally came from a drive-thru window, hot and wrapped and shoved at her while she sat in her idling Taurus.

Mary raised an eyebrow, her gaze lingering on the mess of badly chopped vegetables that Hannah had thrown into a bowl.

"Alright then," her half-sister said easily enough. "Throw a few grape-tomatoes in there then toss it with dressing. You made the dressing right?"

Made it? Paul Newman made dressing. All Hannah did was twist the top and feel satisfied when the paper wrapper broke easily.

"Well, I can," Hannah said, her confidence wavering. She mentally reassured herself that Mary was three beers deep and wouldn't know one way or the other if Hannah's portion of tonight's dinner was an eyesore or worse, a culinary disaster.

"Olive oil and balsamic," Mary began verbally listing between long gulps of her beer. "The seasonings are on the spice rack."

"Throw me a bone?"

"Try salt and pepper and basil," she suggested, sinking into her hip and stretching her long leg out, as the fish sizzled hard in the pan. Mary eyed Hannah, as Hannah fumbled through the cabinets in search of a mixing bowl. "I see you've done your hair a little better tonight."

"I washed it," Hannah said, which was partially true. She had driven to her dismal room in the Super-8, praying to holy hell that the shower would be hot. The water had been warm, and after she had washed up, she had blow-dried her wavy, brown hair straight. She had also lined her eyes black with eyeliner that she had bought at the local drugstore, trying to look better than she normally did. It wasn't until now that she realized it had been Mary who had inspired her.

"You look pretty," Mary told her as though she was an authority on the matter.

Honest to God, Hannah felt flattered by the compliment.

"Your clothes don't quite capture what your figure has to offer," she added, twisting the compliment a bit.

Hannah wasn't sure she wanted to highlight what her figure had to offer, because she wasn't offering it, but suddenly Cody crossed her mind.

"It's probably just a styling issue," Mary went on. "Sometimes a girl has all the right garments, but doesn't know how to throw a real outfit together."

An IQ of 140 tested when the girl was six and this was how she used it?

Hannah took a break from mixing olive oil with vinegar and glanced down at the clothes she was wearing. Her worn-out jeans hugged her well enough. Her black boots boosted her height and made her taller than Mary. The purple sweater she wore looked a tad moth-eaten, admittedly.

"What do you suggest?" Hannah met Mary's gaze as she poured the dressing over the salad, all the while dreading the next step of tossing it. Salad made her skin crawl.

"You really ought to wear a belt," she said. "It would pull the outfit together, but if I'm being honest with you, wearing only *tight* clothes isn't fashionable. If your pants are tight, your top should be loose and flowing."

Something about the advice endeared her to Hannah. Maybe it was because Mary didn't have the financial means to live up to her own advice. Hannah felt her heart turn to mush with sisterly affection.

She shot Mary a smile, thanked her, and said she would keep that in mind.

Mary returned her attention to frying the fish, which she flipped, seasoned with precision, and flipped again. All the while, she sucked down Coors and stole glances at Candice, who was sitting in a comatose daze on the living room sofa.

Hannah and Mary had both given themselves silent permission to feel okay about Candice for the time being since the TV across from her was blaring some kind of celebrity news program. It wasn't that Candice was staring off into space, they each told themselves. She was watching her show.

As Hannah studied Mary, she felt a twinge of something in her gut that almost resembled envy, and it was after the third twinge hit her that she wondered what it was all about. *Was* it envy? She could easily pluck her eyebrows away, too, until she looked perpetually startled, but that wasn't it.

It wasn't Mary's appearance that Hannah envied, nor was it Mary's ability to offer fashion advice.

Mary shined. Mary had a *way* about her. She had something special.

Then Hannah understood what it was...

Mary was becoming Kendra, and that was what Hannah envied.

Hannah had never, at any point in time, ever come close to being like her mother. The wilted salad she had thrown together was evidence of that. Mary and their mother, Kendra, loved cooking.

An idea struck Mary and she grinned at her older sister.

"We should bake a pie."

Hannah felt her jaw drop, but she quickly pressed her mouth into a hard line and hoped her expression passed for confidence. "I'm not much of a baker."

"I am," she said, as a wicked smile spread across her face. Hannah liked that smile. It awakened her inner teenager. "I'll pull the flour and sugar, you grab the rest."

The rest of what?

"The strawberries and rhubarb are in the fridge," Mary told her, reading Hannah's mind.

As Hannah grabbed the fruit and other ingredients from the fridge to place on the counter, rearranging the cluttered refrigerator as she went, she was struck with the significance of what it meant to Mary that she was there.

Mary had been hurting for her mother. She longed for a woman to share the kitchen with. And Hannah, as inept as she was, filled the void. Mary needed her, and was happy as hell to have Hannah at the house…

…which made Cody's disclosure in the woods all the more disturbing.

Ask Mary.

Had those words that had been carved in the dirt been Kendra's desperate plea for help? Or had they been etched by the kidnapper?

Ask Mary? So, Mary knew...

What did Mary know about a van full of meth addicts who had dragged their mother off, bleeding in the night, not to be found for a solid month?

"Well, don't just stare at it." Mary laughed. "Chop the rhubarb like celery. It's the same shape, and slice the strawberries."

Hannah went to work.

Mary knocked back the dregs of her Coors, maneuvered around Hannah to get into the fridge for a fresh one, and cracked the can open.

"I'll knead the dough," said Mary. "Daddy's going to love this pie."

Hannah cringed at Mary's use of the endearment. Dale was no 'Daddy,' except the dirtiest kind.

"When is Dale getting home?"

"He'll float in eventually." Whatever trouble Mary had been having with Dale now seemed like the farthest thing from her mind. "We do alright, the three of us, I would say." She stole a glance at Candice then beamed a smile at Hannah again.

And that was the problem—Mary's burgeoning optimism.

Hannah wasn't sure how long she would be able to stick around. Her work week started tomorrow. At best, she could stay at the motel tonight and drive Mary to school in the morning. Maybe talk to Dale to see if he would allow Candice to see a child psychologist. Then Hannah would have to return to Gilford and the life she had worked so hard to establish.

"Do you know Cody McAlister?" Hannah asked.

Mary shook her head, which caused her bleached blond locks to whip across her forehead.

"He works in the Sanbornton police station..."

"I've never heard of him," she said, as she pressed the dough into a pie pan.

"Cody has access to Mom's case," she went on, not entirely sure how Mary would respond.

Mary seemed to be shutting down a bit. Hannah didn't want to destroy the small steps towards bonding they had managed, but helping Mary find their mother was the reason that Hannah was there, so she continued talking:

"Someone dug a message into the dirt before Mom disappeared. It's possible that Mom, herself, was the one who wrote the message..."

She anxiously studied Mary. Any facial twitch or blink could give Hannah insight. But Mary remained neutral as though they were chatting about nothing more significant than the weather. That, in and of itself, was odd.

Hannah told her, "According to Cody, the message said: Ask Mary."

Mary stopped pressing the dough into the pan. She froze, tensing up. As her whole body stiffened, those surprised looking eyebrows went flat. She turned, her tone devoid of emotion, as she asked:

"What are you telling me?"

"Not telling. Just asking."

Mary glared at her. Hard. So hard that Hannah felt her bowels loosen just a bit.

"You're telling me that before Mom disappeared, she left a message in the dirt that implies I know what happened to her?"

"That's what Cody told me."

Mary looked furious. "Are you kidding me?"

"I thought I would ask." Hannah couldn't keep this up. She turned to the strawberries then quickly realized that she couldn't chop them. Mary's glare was burning a hole into the side of her head.

Hannah managed to excuse herself to the bathroom, quickly escaping into the hallway.

"I have to pee!"

She ducked into the bathroom and flipped on the light, remembering exactly where the switch was located. But when she reached for the lock, Hannah discovered that it had been removed. There was only a faded strip of wood where the lock panel had once been screwed into the door.

She didn't have time to scrutinize the matter, not with her need for the toilet, so she relieved herself. A jungle of undergarments dangled from hangers that had been hung across the shower rod. Mary's version of drying freshly laundered clothes, she deduced. She finished up by washing her hands at the sink.

For all the hanging bras and underwear, there wasn't a hand towel in sight, so Hannah blotted her dripping palms against the front of her jeans leaving slap marks, as she stared into the cracked mirror and studied her kaleidoscope reflection.

Her sister was right about Hannah's eyes, which were beady and blue like Mary's, and conveyed an edge of darkness. Her mother had the same darkness behind her eyes. Perhaps troubled eyes were the only feature that all the Cole women shared. Nothing else about Hannah looked much like Kendra, though.

Hannah's nose was long and delicate with a classic English bump. Her cheekbones were high and her jawline crisp—a handsome woman. She had told herself that she looked like her father. She had to. It was the only explanation, but Hannah had never met the man. She didn't even know his name. The way Kendra had guarded the information during Hannah's childhood had served as a warning that Hannah shouldn't want to know. But she *had* wanted to know who her father was, and the feeling had never left her.

She returned to the hallway, but chose to wander slowly in the opposite direction. The floorboards creaked underfoot, as she ventured towards Kendra's bedroom, which sat adjacent to the end of the hallway—Kendra and *Dale's* bedroom.

Hannah looked up and suddenly noticed a square of shiny metal on the upper lip of the doorway molding.

She stepped close and eyed it, realizing it was an aluminum cylinder lock, the kind that a turnkey fit into.

Why had a lock been placed high-up on the *outside* of the bedroom?

She started for her old room up the hallway, all the while curiosity was building inside of her.

The upper molding of the doorframe of Hannah's old bedroom didn't have a lock, she noted. She peeked around the door and discovered that Mary had taken her old room.

Band posters lined the walls. The glossy prints were tacked crookedly, their corners flopping over.

Taking a moment to peek inside, she scanned the messy room, but became fixated on the doorframe. Just like in the bathroom, the flip-latch lock had been removed, and overhead there was another cylinder lock... overhead?

Why had the old locks been removed?

Why had shiny new ones been installed on the upper edge of the doorframe?

From the kitchen, Mary called out, "Did you fall in?"

"I'll be right there!"

Hannah quickly ducked into Candice's bedroom to confirm that the locks had been changed in the same manner.

They were.

Ask Mary.

The message in the dirt and Cody's voice surged to the forefront of her mind.

Mary was out there, drinking openly and shamelessly, just like Hannah used to do when she had been Mary's age.

She inched deeper into Candice's frilly bedroom to have a look around and a funny memory struck her. Mary had been four or five at the time, always pattering around the house, always exploring, and trying to grow up fast. Back then, Mary liked to muscle the refrigerator door open and feel the cold air waft out. She had also liked to marvel at all the food and grocery items inside the fridge. One evening, when Hannah had been pouring over her homework in the living room, Kendra found young Mary standing in front of the open fridge. Their mother had educated the girl about what she could and couldn't have, explaining, *this is juice, and this is iced tea, and this is soda pop, but you can't have too much. And this*, Kendra had paused for emphasis, *this here is soda that only Daddy can have*.

Dale's beer.

And all Mary had learned that night was that the cans were *daddy soda*, which made them all the more interesting.

Daddy soda…

Daddy soda had been interesting to teenage-Hannah, as well. Sometimes, late at night, Dale used to pass Hannah a beer when Kendra wasn't looking. Their secret. His way of bonding, which had been a dirty trick.

Hannah pushed the memory out of her head, but a worse thought immediately replaced it.

Were the girls trying to keep themselves safe from Dale with those locks?

Without warning, Dale pushed the bedroom door wide open and Hannah jumped. She hadn't heard him come home.

"You don't live here anymore," he barked, his eyes blazing. "You can't snoop around like you own the place."

A six-pack of Coors was dangling from one hand, and there was an open can of beer in his other hand.

"I came to check on the girls." It wasn't an apology or an excuse.

"You checked on them yesterday."

"And I might check on them again tomorrow," she asserted.

He grinned, but Hannah knew it was a threat, like *watch yourself*.

"I didn't understand until I saw the girls yesterday that Candice literally hasn't been speaking," she began explaining. She used a reasonable-sounding, adult-like tone as she went on. "Candice needs to see a child psychologist."

"She'll talk when she's ready." Dismissing the notion, he waved at her to get out of the bedroom, and yet he was filling the doorway.

"You have to do what's right for Candice. It isn't healthy for her to be shut down like this for so long."

His gaze shifted, and for a moment it looked as though he was actually considering Hannah's suggestion. But he shook his head next and told her, "She's been through enough. I'm giving her time."

"It's been a month."

"She needs more time."

"Which she can spend with a psychologist." Hannah knew the second she had spoken that she had pushed Dale too fast.

"You want to talk?" he asked darkly, as he reached for the small of his back and produced a gun from his waistband.

Hannah's blood ran cold.

Pinching one eye shut, he glanced through the sight down the barrel. "Let's go talk."

DALE FIRED A round, and the tin can he was aiming at popped into the air. A perfect shot from fifteen yards away, and Dale didn't even have to set his beer down.

The deafening shot pierced Hannah's eardrums.

"Have at her," he said, passing the handgun to Hannah, though she had already declined several times.

It was dim behind the house. The floodlight that hung loosely from the tin roof wasn't exactly angled in their direction. Eerie shadows cut across the acreage. Whenever the wind rustled the dying vegetation, the hairs on the back of Hannah's neck stood on end.

There were three cans remaining on the wooden block in the distance.

Hannah chose to aim at the one farthest to the left. As she concentrated, Dale stepped in close to her, making her uncomfortable by invading her personal space. It unnerved her.

"Can you give me a little room, please," she said.

"Check your sight lines," he instructed, showing a softer side, which felt so wrong. "Squeeze," he told her. "Don't pull the trigger. Squeeze it."

"I know how to shoot a gun," she snapped.

He gave her some breathing room, pacing away, as he knocked his beer back, rattling the dregs down his throat.

Holding the gun, which she identified as a Smith & Wesson M&P 40 caliber—she had lived with Dale long enough to pick up the jargon and learn a thing or two—Hannah's arms strained from its weight and she reminded herself it would have a big kick. She didn't have a prayer in hell at hitting one of those cans, much less the one she was aiming for, but if this little charade was what Dale needed in order to agree to let Candice see a psychologist, then Hannah would play along.

She squeezed the trigger. Not one tin can blasted off the block, but a murder of crows surged up from the dark brush near the tree line and began shrieking as if she had shot one of them.

Dale burst out laughing.

Hannah rolled her eyes and tried to offer him the gun, but Dale keeled over, laughing hysterically.

When he sobered up, he pinched his thumb and index finger over his eyes and sighed. "I needed that. A good laugh. Man, you went soft in Gilford."

"Thanks," she said dryly.

Dale stalked over and relieved her of the weapon.

He stared down at the gun in his hands and his mood shifted. As he inspected the handgun, a faraway look filled his eyes.

"I miss her." He frowned and tucked the gun down the back of his jeans. "She changed, Hannah."

Because you changed her, she thought, but Hannah didn't dare say it out loud.

"That woman brought God into my life then abandoned the entire concept of him." Dale stared off into the burly nightscape, welcoming what revelations might come. "I've been going to church, you know? I started getting serious about regularly attending the Sunday services after Kendra disappeared." He turned dark, angling his eyes at her. "She's dead."

Hannah felt as though Dale had knocked the wind out of her.

"How do you know?"

"I just do." He returned his attention to the woods. "Thinking anything else is damn torture. But if I think of Kendra as dead… It's a huge relief."

Hannah wrapped her mind around his twisted logic and her stomach suddenly felt like it was filled with a lead ball.

"Do you think she's in heaven?" Hannah asked, hoping that Dale had meant to sound sweet and not creepy.

"She's not in heaven. She's in hell," he said.

Hannah's heart leapt up her throat. The guns. The locks. The bone chilling assertion that her mother was dead and in hell.

In an instant, she felt raw and vulnerable.

She was trapped in the woods with a dangerous man.

"Heaven is for me," he went on. "For us, me and the girls."

"Dinner's ready!" Mary called out through the back window. "Don't let this pie get cold!"

Dale didn't acknowledge her, didn't even feign a glance over his shoulder.

Moments passed. Dale continued ruminating. Hannah was on guard, not quite trusting the silence between them.

Angrily, Mary stomped towards them across the lawn and wasted no time grabbing Dale by the arm and yanking him inside. The fearless command she had over him was so familiar, it was jarring. It was like Mary had become a new version of Kendra.

"Easy, girl," Dale grumbled, stumbling a bit but chuckling.

Hannah followed after them across the dying grass, but paused when she felt a vibration in her back pocket. The call coming through wasn't a number she recognized, but she swiped the screen anyway.

"Hannah Cole," she answered.

"Hannah, hi. It's Cody." His tone sounded deep, deeper than it had in person, as though something was wrong. "Sandy gave me your contact info. I hope you don't mind."

"I'm listening."

"A man came into the station. Hannah, he had a human hand with him. He brought it in a box."

Suddenly, the dark forest was reeling all around her, swallowing her up.

Her voice was a thread. "Kendra's?"

"You might want to get down here."

CHAPTER FOUR

CODY DIDN'T WANT to be alone with it. No one did, which was why the rest of his department, the nose-to-grindstone and burn-the-midnight-oil types who found reasons to live here after hours and on the weekends, had converged with Missing Persons upstairs, as wildly disorganized as they were.

Cody wasn't upstairs with everyone else. He was downstairs with the hand.

Earlier, Sandy had freaked out when the man had stumbled in, his face covered in blood so thick and dark that it looked like motor oil. The mystery man had been the one to deliver the box that had a hand inside.

The evening had become very interesting after that.

Sandy had been holding down the fort this evening along with Robertson, whose method of finding missing individuals tended to be cautious, meticulous, and *contemplative*. If Cody didn't know better and hadn't known him for ten years and seen firsthand his capabilities, he would have thought the man just plain didn't care.

The real Achilles heel of their entire department, however, was that people in Sanbornton simply didn't go missing, not beyond the occasional teen who had made good on a threat to leave home, or a fed-up spouse who had checked into a motel, disconnected their cell phone, and claimed a Goddamn moment to breathe. Sure, those types of individuals had *technically* gone missing, and Robertson always shined in his ability to locate each individual, but their department had never seen a case like Kendra Cole's. The fact that they now had her hand in a box was a downright anomaly and cataclysmic at that.

The real kicker was that Homicide wasn't chomping at the bit to take over. Quite the opposite, in fact. Chief Marley had thrown his hands up and declared that until Kendra Cole was *actually found dead* this wasn't a *homicide* case. By the same measure, the Chief had also denied the glaring probability that wherever Kendra was, she hadn't a prayer in hell of staying alive for very long without her hand.

Tangled arguments had followed so Cody had isolated himself with the hand downstairs and tried not to pay attention to the ongoing argument they were still having upstairs. He could hear their muffled voices through the ceiling, though.

He felt his gut clench. The horror of the hand had been causing him waves of nausea all night. Several times it had crossed his mind to bolt for the men's room. Desperate to believe he had no weaknesses, Cody fought the urge to vomit. Doing so centered him in a way, and gave him a break from sorting through the nightmare in his head. Pain had the power to consume. Overcoming it was a real meditation.

He shouldn't have called Hannah.

He was sitting in one of the interview rooms. On the table before him was the box, the hand inside.

Cody planted his elbows on his knees and ran his fingers through his hair, trying to think. The heel of his right boot tapped the linoleum floor, making him jitter like a metronome, as he stared at the cracked tabletop and the side of the cardboard box that looked old and weathered, like it had been used for shipping multiple times. Cody, honest to God, couldn't fathom that a woman he had known had endured the torture of having her left hand removed.

It was unfathomable.

Kendra had been a beautiful beast of a woman. She used to hum while she cooked at the stove whenever he had come over for Hannah—Kendra would shove a hot plate at him as soon as he walked in the door, but Hannah would frown at her mother. A silent exchange between them would follow, one that told Cody that mother and daughter had talked about this and Hannah wanted no distractions from their studies. But Cody had always eaten, too intimidated by Kendra to yield to Hannah's annoyed glares.

Kendra had smelled like nail polish and fried food, but it was her physical presence that had been the most memorable. Her hair in curlers that were tucked under a net, her lips pursed but not so much that she couldn't smile at you, and those eyes, blue lasers angling on you with Old Testament judgment that made you certain you must have done something wrong. Cody had watched what he said and what he did when he was around Kendra. He had never wanted to get on her bad side, and luckily, he had stayed on her good side.

The year he had gotten close with Hannah in high school, Dale had long since warped the family. Inserting himself and breaking it wide open, the extent of which Cody had no clue about until years later when stories upon stories had passed through town. But there had been so much gossip that he couldn't discern fact from fiction—kids and guns and screaming matches heard only by the wilderness surrounding their dark corner of the lake. Dale had kept getting worse and worse. Cody had ignored the rumors, though. Hannah had stopped talking to Cody at that point, shut him out, and treated him as though he were dead to her, which he had deserved.

The muffled argument overhead fell silent, causing Cody to tense up. He held his breath and hoped nobody would come down to check on him or give him an update as to which side of the fence the Cole case had landed on, assuming that the department heads upstairs had come to a decision. As far as he was concerned, he was going to solve this case himself. It didn't matter whether the Homicide or Missing Persons department ended up claiming it. In fact, his gut told him neither would.

When they started arguing upstairs again, he let out a rocky breath and his thoughts began drifting into the past.

Hannah.

Back in high school, Hannah had been sprightly, her hair akimbo, her eyes as discerning as her mothers. She had lips he couldn't help but lust for. Hannah had exuded wisdom, not intellect or street smarts, per se, but the kind of wisdom that came with sensing the pain in this world and knowing only pure-hearted love could cure it.

In high school, she had been reserved but aware. She had always known where the bullies were in the hallways between classes and she kept her distance, spying them from afar and avoiding their cruel activities.

The day Cody had noticed her, it had been because she had swooped in on Timmy Baumbach. The skinny high schooler had been beaten silly. Bullies had slammed his head between a locker door and its frame a few times. As soon as the coast had cleared, Hannah rushed over to Timmy and wrapped her arm around his shoulder. She had a fistful of tissues ready for him.

Watching Hannah help Timmy that day had cracked Cody's heart wide open. The way she had helped him and how she had changed the subject so that he wouldn't be embarrassed had been so sweet. She had turned into a chatterbox, going on and on about how well Timmy had done in a recent school debate. She had asked him how he had done on his chemistry test, yapping on and on so Timmy wouldn't fall into a pit of despair. And it had worked.

After that, Cody had initiated a friendship with Hannah, not because he wanted to be her friend. He had wanted so much more than that. But he had decided that being friends was the best place to start.

But in the end, he had messed their friendship up so badly that Hannah didn't talk to him for years… until now.

There came a loud knock on the interview room door, which jarred Cody from his memory. He sprang from his chair and cracked the door open.

Hannah was standing on the other side.

"Cody?" she said. "You look white as a ghost."

"I thought you said you would call when you got here."

"I did call," she said, as she planted her fist on her hip, causing all kinds of dangerous angles to take shape in her figure. "You didn't pick up so I went upstairs where everyone was arguing. Sandy told me you were down here."

He was having serious doubts about showing her Kendra's hand, so he urged her back into the hallway and slipped out from the room, too. He pulled the door closed behind him with a gentle click, not that Hannah gave him much room to do so. She was holding her ground.

"You have the guy in custody?" she asked. "You caught him?"

She looked desperately hopeful. Her eyes pleaded up at him, as he stammered, thankful only that she hadn't demanded to see the hand.

"It's not cut and dry," he managed. "Thanks for coming down."

"Don't thank me. Tell me what's going on. Do you know where my mom is?"

"No."

Hannah must have realized their proximity, because she took a step back, as if she needed some air.

"Want to have a seat?" he offered.

He didn't wait for her response. He walked her into the bullpen, steering her towards his desk, and found the switch to his desk lamp.

Cody felt a brief stab of embarrassment at the clutter on his desk—a mess of reports, tchotchkes he had ordered from EBay collecting dust, and the most mortifying of all, a framed photo of Hannah and him from their senior prom.

He quickly flipped the photo face down on the desk before she noticed it and pulled the chair out for her to sit.

When she did, she crossed her arms and legs, fortifying herself. Cody took a moment to overcome the historical longing he felt for her. He pushed from his mind the fact she was damn easy on the eyes, and wrapped his head around the best way to explain what had occurred.

"The man who came in, we don't know his name yet-"

"How is that possible?"

"Let me explain." Cody said, pulling another chair up and sitting down beside her. He stole a moment to mentally process which details he should omit in order to spare her the horror of it all.

"Stop filtering everything," she insisted, reading his mind.

"The guy who delivered the box... His tongue was cut out. He couldn't talk."

She gasped and slapped her hand over her mouth. Then she exhaled, and her breath came out like she had been punched in the chest. Her eyes, widening and misting over with tears, told him that he would most definitely need to filter himself.

Despite her shock, Hannah indicated he should go on.

"The guy stumbled into the station, drunk from the pain," he told her. "I won't describe the scene that unfolded here next, but I will say that it was shocking to the few of us who saw. He had a box with him, like I mentioned on the phone. Right now, he's at the hospital. It looks like he was a victim, a pawn of sorts, to get Kendra's hand here. But we'll know more in a day or two when we talk to him. If we threaten him with charges, I'm sure he'll communicate."

He studied Hannah as she struggled to process that much. The information seemed to stun her. Her brow knit and he couldn't tell if she was breathing. She had the look of someone overwhelmed and dissociating. When she spoke, her tone was low and raw, but laced with hope.

"Maybe it's not my mom's hand?"

It was then that Cody knew his job as an investigator would ultimately upset Hannah. There were some things he wouldn't be able to tell her. Others he could, but if she pressed him for the details of how he had arrived at a conclusion, he wouldn't necessarily be able to tell her. Or, he would have to lie. So, he focused her on what he was authorized to discuss.

"It was Kendra's hand," he said definitively. Before she could ask why he was so certain or demand how he knew, he cut in with, "According to our medical examiner, Kendra was alive at the time her hand was removed."

For a moment, Hannah looked optimistic that her mom was alive, but then a fresh wave of anguish took hold. He could see her attempting to comprehend that her mother was being tortured, which was a very dark road to travel, so again he focused her.

"She's a hell of a fighter." He searched her eyes to see if his encouragement had landed. "She's alive,

Hannah. After a month. That's incredible." Vacancy and stunned silence sat in front of him. "We're going to find her."

"Ok," she breathed.

"Hannah?"

He wasn't sure if she was still mentally processing the information, or maybe the effort to do so had rendered her incapacitated. Cody rolled his chair closer, fitting his legs around hers and planting his elbow against the edge of his desk so he could offer her a shred of human connection. He laid his hand over her knee, and placed his other hand on her shoulder. She seemed to relax a bit.

She demanded, "Tell me, how do you know it's Kendra's?"

The horror of it all was hitting her. An explosion would follow. He rolled in closer, but wasn't sure what to say.

Finally, he offered, "I trust the experts."

Hannah couldn't hold the emotions in any longer. She lowered her head and began crying. But she was quiet about it, just as she had been in the woods when he had held her.

He pulled her in and hugged her again, holding her as closely as their damn chairs would allow. It crossed his mind that maybe she had trained herself to cry without making a sound and without the world knowing.

He eased back when he felt her palm on his chest. He felt the impulse to kiss her and hated himself for it. Now was hardly the time.

Her voice a thread, she uttered, "I have to see it."

"No."

"I have to."

"No, Hannah." He cursed under his breath. "I shouldn't have called you."

"But you did."

She turned to stone.

He explained, "Your mother is alive out there, but as soon as you see her severed hand, you're going to feel like she's dead."

"That's not for you to say, Cody."

Hannah sniffled and stood up from the desk. She started for the interrogation room door, intuitive enough to know that if he had kept her out of that room, surely that was where she would find her mother's hand.

He followed after her and opened the door. The fluorescent lights stung his eyes, as he neared the table and stood over the box.

Hannah lingered midway between the door and the table.

"You don't have to do this."

As if her soul had been fractured, she asked, "Why is her hand still in a box like a piece of trash?"

"Because no one has reached a decision upstairs," he explained.

She stepped forward, boots striking on linoleum as she neared the table. She gazed down into the box.

The moment her eyes saw the hand, she turned suddenly hollow like her spirit had been flushed out.

Cody stood ready to catch her if she fainted, but she didn't collapse. The effect of seeing her mother's hand laid out on torn newspapers in a ratty old box didn't liquefy her like it had Cody or make her crumble like it would any other woman. Hannah just seemed empty.

"So, Homicide has her case now?" she asked, exercising remarkable strength.

"We're figuring that out. Like I said, she isn't dead, but I think all hands will need to be on deck for this case."

"So Missing Persons is still working this?"

Cody had excused himself from the unproductive debate upstairs about an hour ago. He couldn't say one way or the other, but in his mind he had already committed himself to this case.

"I'm not doing anything but finding Kendra."

"Good."

When he dared to look at her, Hannah struck him as stoic.

Cody touched Hannah's hand with his. First a brush—the back of his hand against hers. Then he ventured to graze his palm around, sensing if she had spread her fingers for him. He lingered, hoping or needing her to let him offer comfort by way of this small gesture. He felt her respond. Cody slipped his fingers between hers, slid his hand in, and held her hand tightly. With purpose.

He didn't trust his voice to come through so he cleared his throat then said:

"Remember..." He swallowed the lump in his throat, taking a beat to get the memory right. "Remember the rainstorm? November? It was the weekend before Thanksgiving and everyone was planning on going to Mitchell's party on the ball field?"

She squeezed his hand a bit tighter, which told him that she did.

"It was so dumb of him to think that he could throw a party on the ball field, but the whole school bought it. It was going to be the biggest deal."

"And we knew we weren't invited," she supplied. Her gaze was vacant, though her attention remained fixed on the box.

"Because we weren't cool enough." Cody wanted to laugh at his remark.

"But we showed up out of sheer defiance," she added, merging into the same memory.

"Then the rain came. It poured. I was waiting for you on the field. There wasn't a soul in sight. And you came running. Your hair was soaked. You couldn't even see, you were squinting through the rain so hard. And those big stadium lights were bright as hell. It was our party, Hannah. No one was there but us. But we didn't care. We started singing loudly, some terrible song, while the pouring rain drenched us." Cody fell silent, stole a glance at her, and his heart warmed when he saw the faintest smile on her face. He whispered, "I'm here."

"Thanks."

CHAPTER FIVE

HANNAH IGNORED the justifiable twinge of embarrassment that came with accidentally letting Cody glimpse the inside of her motel room at the Super-8.

"Thanks for seeing me home, Cody."

He nodded, but didn't turn to go.

Good.

Hannah didn't want to be alone.

"Want to come inside and keep me company for a bit?" she asked, inviting him in.

She crossed the little room and turned on the nightstand lamp, causing an amber glow to illuminate the room, making it less bleak. The only downside was that the light brought attention to the mess she had managed to make in just two days. Toiletries were strewn across the dresser, the drawers of which were ajar to varying degrees. Her suitcase was lying open with shirts, pants, and panties spilling out.

Worst of all was the nest of bedding and covers on the floor, which was where Hannah had been

71

sleeping. She had a thing about beds. She didn't like them or trust them, and she wouldn't sleep in one.

Cody entered and his eyes widened at the mess.

"There was a recent tornado..." she joked.

Perhaps sensitive to her sudden insecurity, he turned for the door and took his slow time fixing the locks in place so that Hannah could quickly stuff her undergarments into her suitcase and muscle the heavy thing under the bed. She managed to sweep her toiletries into the top dresser drawer and shove the drawer closed as well as the lower ones. By the time Cody turned back around, the place looked a little better.

"Are you going to be okay here?" he asked.

"It's just one more night."

"You're still planning on heading out?"

Hannah sighed as though she didn't have a choice. "I have a job. People need me. I keep the Gilford police station organized."

She was torn up over seeing Kendra's hand, which had chilled her to her very core.

She felt freezing all of a sudden. She went to the windows and made sure they were closed then pulled the tattered curtains across, figuring that would do it.

As Cody studied her, she found her flask in her purse. If ever she needed a stiff drink, it was now.

He was making her feel self-conscious, but she knocked back a gulp of alcohol anyway, as she sat on the bed.

"I think you should reconsider going home," he said. "Take some serious time off until your mother is found."

"I agree."

Hannah stole another nip from her flask, and Cody sat down on the bed, too. First he sat down next to the nightstand, but that felt too far from her so he began inching closer.

The whiskey-burn melted any self-consciousness she had been feeling, and she studied him right back. The amber glow from the lamp had him backlit, but his green eyes pierced through. How many times had they sat beside one another like this all those years ago?

Cody seemed to take some pleasure in her company. Tension rose between them, but she ignored it and told herself that Cody wasn't attracted to her. He only felt bad for her.

"I'm going to be straight with you, Hannah," he said, as she tucked her legs under her and stared at the flask between her hands. "I don't want you to be alone tonight."

"Don't worry about me."

"I am."

"You want to stay the whole night?" she asked, but it wasn't an invitation. It was an honest question.

He searched her eyes and the look on his face was unmistakable.

"Did you call me to the police station to look at butchered body parts just so that you could insist you sleep over?" she challenged with an edge in her voice.

"That can't be what you think I did," he replied, taken aback.

"No, that's not what I think you did," she allowed.

"You wanted the inside track on the investigation," he pointed out.

"I'm not blaming you." Knocking back another swig helped her think. "But years have gone by. You don't get to pick up where we left off."

"That's not what I mean."

"Then what do you mean?"

He looked a bit nervous to be put on the spot, but he had made his bed and she had a perverse curiosity to see if he would lie in it, or run from the motel room screaming.

"You've been through a lot in the past two days. Things could get worse. I know you're strong. All I'm saying is that you shouldn't have to be so strong and you shouldn't have to be alone."

Mary came to mind. Hannah had thought the exact same thing about her half-sister. Why was it that you could easily see when someone else's burden was too great for them to bear, but be blind to your own hardships that were destined to crush you?

He placed his hand on her knee, which felt more natural than Hannah cared to admit to herself. Maybe she *would* like him to stay the night. She hadn't realized how badly she needed company, and to be touched—human touch, *his* touch.

But accepting his emotional support would be dangerous in the long run. She didn't like it when men didn't stick around.

"So, when that *man*..." she started to say, but her stomach twisted at the thought of him. "When he recovers in the hospital, you'll talk to him and find out where my mom is?"

Cody nodded. His eyes were glued to her, as if his gaze was holding her together and if he blinked, she would fall apart.

She had already fallen apart. Part of her had died seeing Kendra's hand.

"More likely than not, he's a victim in all of this, too," he said, thinking out loud. "But let's just say I'm confident he'll be eager to talk and tell us what he knows, and put whoever's behind this in prison."

Feeding her more positive news to keep her going, Cody added, "There's also a lot Forensics will be able to tell us about the actual..." He trailed off, mentally searching for a better word than the one that came to mind, but couldn't find one. He swallowed hard and said, "Forensics will be able to tell us more about the removal of her hand, which should shed light on what happened and maybe even on where she is. To my untrained eye, the cut had looked relatively clean. If it was a surgical removal, that could greatly narrow our list of suspects."

"Who's on the list of suspects at the moment?"

"Well, at the moment… no one."

"No one," she murmured. "Of course, there's no one. Kendra had no reason to be caught up in this."

"What do you make of the message that was carved into the dirt? The one that said, '*Ask Mary*'?"

It felt like he was pushing her and she wasn't sure if she could take it.

He added, "I think Kendra carved it."

"That's crazy, Cody. How would she have time to do that when she was being abducted?"

Cody held her gaze and she could see the gears turning deep within his fast-working mind. There was a hint of electricity between them, stronger than it had been in high school and more thrilling than it had been in the woods the other day.

"I've been thinking about it," she went on, "there was blood. She might have been stabbed. At best it was a struggle. Even if her captors had wrestled her down to the dirt, you think they would let her carve some words out? I think the abductor or abductors wrote it to confuse the crime scene."

He considered her point for a moment, but withheld his response.

"To me it doesn't add up." She let that hang in the air between them, as she internally debated whether or not to tell him about the rocky exchange she'd had with Mary. Seeing Cody's kind eyes, it dawned on Hannah that Cody was the closest thing to a friend that she had right now, and realizing this tipped the scales. "I mentioned *the message* to Mary."

"And?"

"And let's just say it didn't go over well." She snorted a laugh, shook her head, and settled into drinking loosely.

There should've been more to the conversation, but Cody fell into deep thought and was silent. He didn't share his insights.

After a long moment, he asked, "Why did you lose touch with me?"

"Why did *I* lose touch with you?" she said, taken aback. "Why did you lose touch with me? It's a two-way street, my friend."

"I thought you hated me."

She shrugged. He wasn't wrong. She *had* hated him. On some level, she probably still did. But she was also attracted to him.

"For the record," he said, "I was a dumb kid. I was on cloud nine when you went to prom with me, and not just because I had no chance of going with anyone else. I mean I was actually thrilled. I was a nervous wreck, and not just because Dale scared the crap out of me and made picking you up at your door a nightmare. That night meant a lot to me."

"You've been keeping records?" she teased.

Now it was Cody's turn to brush it off, but his responding shrug was half-hearted. This was serious to him. "I guess I have."

She had been keeping records, too. And everything that had happened to her after he had abandoned her that night, satisfied with himself that he had scored, was so knotted up in Hannah's memory of him that she couldn't help but blame him for all of it. Then when he had blabbed to the entire school the next week, and she was branded a slut as a result, she hadn't been able to handle it, emotionally.

The passage of time hadn't changed much—not her animosity towards Cody nor her desire for him. That was the trouble. She still felt attracted to him, even now. Nothing she had ever done in all the years since that night had successfully helped her to cut Cody clean out of her heart.

"I need you to go now," she told him.

"Okay."

He remained for another moment, looking like he might say something. But instead, he found her hand and laced his fingers through hers like before, and Hannah lost sight of why she was fighting whatever this was.

Cody released her hand, stood up, and unlocked the door to let himself out.

Part of Hannah wanted him to stay and to hold her and to prove to her that the world wasn't a cruel place, if only for a night. But another part of her felt as though she didn't deserve it.

There would be no solace until Kendra was found.

IF HANNAH HATED anything, it was her own head-to-toe reflection in a dressing room mirror. Her system of buying clothes generally amounted to throwing a hanger over her head so the garment would drape down her front, as she eyeballed it to assess if it would do; see if it flattered her shape and would fit her well enough to serve its purpose. Jeans were the easiest to buy. She would just hunt through the stack and find her size. Coats and shoes were her favorite. Throw them on and they would be the ones who told her if they fit.

Hannah was shopping at the K-Mart off Route 12 for something nice to wear. She already knew that driving back to the Super-8 to change wouldn't make a lick of sense, so there she was in the K-Mart dressing room, juggling tops and bottoms and angling her naked body away from her reflection in the mirror.

She clamped her cell phone between her ear and shoulder, listening to a blaring ringtone and hoping someone at the Gilford police station would answer her call.

"Holder?" she asked, startled to hear the Chief's distinct voice come through the line. "It's Hannah Cole."

The sound of his heavy sigh came through the line, like she had done something foolish.

"Where are you?" he barked.

She should've been handing him his coffee by now, black with one Sweet & Low.

She launched into the twisted tale. "I had to head over to Sanbornton for the weekend. I'm in the midst of a family emergency, to be honest. And, well, to refresh your memory, I never took my five vacation days this past summer…"

The Chief fell silent, and Hannah figured he was beyond aggravated with her.

"I have to ask for those days now," she concluded.

Another sigh. Hannah pictured him reclining in his squeaky chair, the thing straining to support his girth, as he worked his jaw and considered the most brutal way to rip her a new one.

"You have to call Human Resources," he grumbled.

Right. She knew that. This was the blouse all over again.

"Will do," she said, but something kept her on the line, perhaps a need for his approval. "It's my family-"

"Call the request in to Jenny."

"My mom's gone missing-"

"If you don't have the extension you can find it on the website."

The line went dead.

Hannah caught sight of herself in the mirror, but she didn't like what she saw, so she wasted no time getting dressed in the new outfit she had bought.

She sat down on the sorry excuse for a bench, being sure to keep her back to the mirror, and gnawed on her lip, as she pulled up the Gilford precinct website on her cell phone. She found Jenny's extension and made a vacation request.

Jenny was nice enough about it. She even went the extra mile and allocated Hannah's remaining sick days, which extended her impromptu vacation a few more days. After the bad phone call with Holder, Hannah hadn't bothered to tell Jenny the real reason she needed time off, and Jenny didn't ask.

By the time she hung up, Hannah had secured ten full days off. She would have to do a little math to see if she would be able to financially swing the Super-8 for that long, but all told, it had been a productive phone call.

Then it hit her.

Ten calendar days in Sanbornton. Ten days with Dale. Ten days of searching for her mother and trying to forget the past and wrestling with her feelings towards Cody…

Would she survive?

Eager to get the hell out of K-Mart, she threw on her shoes and coat, and climbed into her parked Taurus, as soon as she got outside.

Once she was buckled in and driving, she dialed Cranston at the Gilford station, hoping he had listened to the voicemail message she had left him. Hopefully, he would be able to help her in some way.

When the ringtone cut out and she heard slurping on the other end of the line, a surge of hope filled her heart.

"Cranston?"

He swallowed loudly and said, "Hi, Hannah, you caught me drinking my protein shake. The wife says I have to lose a few."

"Did you get my message?"

"I did, Hannah." His tone sounded warm, but concerned. "I had no idea anyone had been abducted in Sanbornton. I'm going to do everything

I can to help you from my end. You just tell me what you need."

She fixed her attention on the road ahead, driving through red and orange leaves that were fluttering down across the hood of her car.

"Thank you," she said, as tears stung her eyes. She blinked them back.

"How the hell are you holding up over there?" he asked.

"Barely," she admitted. "But I got some time off from the department. The Sanborton police have a witness. Did you get around to looking into anything?"

She heard the sounds of papers rustling on Cranston's end of the line. "I did. Give me a second."

More rustling, then Cranston began reading out loud:

"I was able to access Kendra Cole's police record. I'm going to give it to you straight, kid. Your mom has been arrested several times. Four times in the last year alone."

"What!"

"It looks like the majority of arrests were for methamphetamine possession. She never did time, but she did have to do community service. However, the judge agreed that Kendra could fulfill her community service hours at her church."

Hannah literally could not believe what she was hearing.

And yet, Cody had introduced her to the possibility that Kendra had intersected with a circle of meth addicts.

"That's all I got," said Cranston, breathing heavily into the receiver.

"I really appreciate it," she managed to say.

"You just let me know anything else you need, you hear me?"

"Yeah, thanks. I owe you one."

"Hey," he added before she could get off the line and fall apart now that she knew for sure that her mother was a drug addict. "You okay?"

No, no she wasn't okay. Not by a long shot, but she didn't tell him that.

"Focus on finding your mother," he suggested. "Have faith, Hannah. That's what it's for."

HAVING FAITH, AS a way to endure or a strategy to overcome, had never made sense to Hannah.

She spent the next hour in her car, trying to make sense of things, as she compulsively applied eyeliner. Not that it could mask what she had seen—her mother's hand in a box.

Drinking helped, but only slightly. She kept ingesting alcohol, forcing booze down her throat, and hoping her brain would shut down because of it.

Daddy soda.

It wasn't lost on her that she was attempting to dig herself out of the hole Dale had put her in by using the very tool he had introduced to her—alcohol.

Whatever.

She was already drowning in a catastrophe, her whole family was. Why not drown out the feelings with booze?

She couldn't stop thinking about those locks. The ones she had seen at the shack, fastened to the upper edges of the door frames.

Something wasn't right about them.

Hannah closed her eyes and rested her head against the headrest. Her eyelids felt heavy.

Hours later, she woke up with a start.

She wasn't in her car. She was in her motel room at the Super-8.

The room was cold. Experience told her that the boiler must have broken. It was the kind of wisdom she had earned during her upbringing with Kendra and Dale at the shack.

Keep fighting was the mantra that motivated her to get to her feet, throw her coat on, and haul herself outside to her parked Taurus. She needed to get to the house.

The drive was only a shy mile through the woods.

When she pulled to a stop in front of the house, she knocked back the dregs from her flask, not because she had a craving, but as a precaution. She didn't want a headache.

Mary was out on the porch when Hannah arrived.

Approaching the teenager, Hannah realized that Mary was trying to fix the hole that Hannah had made when her boot had cracked through the wooden slats.

Mary held a hammer in her right hand. Nails poked out of her mouth. She kicked a pile of two-by-fours that were stacked on the highest step, separating the boards to find the best one.

Hannah felt bad. She had accidentally created a chore for her half-sister, which Dale should've been handling.

Mary used her fingers to remove the line of nails from her mouth like a row of cigarettes. She brushed her bleached hair off her forehead with her woolen sweater sleeve, a garment from the local army-navy store no doubt, and said, "Hand me that board, would you?"

"Where do you want it?" Hannah asked once she had it firmly in her grasp.

Mary shot her a crooked smile. "Where do you think? Over the hole."

Hannah laid the board over the hole, making sure it was aligned properly, and held it in place, while Mary began hammering one nail after another.

"Did you make it to school today?" asked Hannah.

Mary snorted a laugh then hit at the nail harder. It took three thwacks before the nail was flush. She angled the next nail against the board and thwacked it hard as hell.

Hannah supposed that had been the girl's answer.

As Mary hammered one nail after another into the board along the perimeter, Hannah watched her closely, and admired her skills. Then she became a bit lost in the sight of Mary's youthful complexion, the arch of her eyebrows, and the delicate lines of her nose, mouth, and jawline. She could finally see through the makeup to the girl beneath. Mary was beautiful.

"That ought to do it," Mary said, straightening up and marveling at a job well done.

Mary shot Hannah a crooked grin that looked playful and thanked Hannah for helping.

Hannah, honest to God, felt praised, and it stirred her slumbering self-esteem just a bit.

"You do all the handy work around here, don't you?"

Mary shrugged with the kind of self-awareness that said she didn't mind wearing the pants.

"I'm the best man for the job, you could say. Whenever I catch Daddy trying to fix something around here, I put a stop to it. He can fix the sink a hundred times." A laugh erupted out of her. "But I'd rather fix it once."

Mary started off around the house, while Hannah took a beat to recover from how impressed she was. Then she caught up. It was clear they were headed for the dock.

Candice was seated at the edge of the dock just like she had been the other day.

"So pretty, it kind of hurts to look at, right?" said Mary, taking in the view before them.

The lake was so still that it looked like a sheet of glass, and the trees surrounding the lake were dark silhouettes, though the sun lingered low on the horizon, turning the sky shades of red and rose and lavender.

"Candice, scooch," Mary ordered, as she sat next to her sister and tucked her legs sideways like a mermaid so that she was leaning into the younger one.

Hannah ventured to sit down on the rickety dock on the other side of Candice.

She wriggled her coat off, feeling a sudden urge for the cold air to hit her.

"Nice top," said Mary, complimenting the outfit Hannah had bought at K-Mart. "It fits you nicely. See what I mean about loose and flowing tops? It looks good with your jeggings."

"Jeggings?"

"Your tight, skinny jeans," she explained. "That's what they're called—jeggings. Kill me before I get old."

The way Mary smiled at her reminded Hannah of their mother, Kendra.

"What do you have in mind for dinner?" she asked, feeling hungry.

"Daddy is going to handle it tonight. He insisted," Mary said with an eye roll.

"Dale's home?"

"Yeah." Mary chucked a blade of grass into the water and Candice didn't even blink. "He heard you were coming and he wanted to do something nice, I guess."

Out of nowhere, Candice began humming. She held a single note, but her tone grew louder and louder as she sustained the note.

To Hannah, it sounded disturbing.

Hannah and Mary touched eyes.

Candice continued the sustained hum until she ran out of breath. It was a long twenty seconds before she was quiet.

"She's been doing that," Mary explained. "It's the closest she's come to talking, so I consider it a good sign."

The entire situation was twisted. Candice was the only one who knew what had happened to their mother that night. She was seated right beside Hannah, but there was nothing Hannah could do. She couldn't reach into Candice's brain and pull the memories out.

"He's the reason you took off, isn't he?" asked Mary, referring to Dale.

Taken aback, Hannah searched for words that wouldn't come.

"That crap you asked me the other night," Mary went on, jumping topics so easily that Hannah felt suddenly afraid of her. "I don't know what that was, but I know my mother. I know her in a way that maybe you don't." Mary locked eyes with her. "She didn't write that *message* in the dirt."

"No, I agree," Hannah told her. "I'm sure it was some sick... ploy. I'm sorry I even mentioned it to you."

Mary's eyebrows lifted and she narrowed her eyes on Hannah.

"You know something, don't you?" Mary guessed. "You found something out?"

Hannah didn't have much of a poker face, she would be damned if she told her younger sister that the police had received a box with Kendra's severed hand inside.

"Christ, you have to tell me," she demanded right in front of Candice, who was the last person who should hear the answer.

"I found some things out about Mom earlier today," Hannah admitted, but she decided to ask Mary about Kendra's drug use, or at least try to, instead of telling her about the hand. "She became aloof? She started wandering off a lot?"

"Not a lot."

"Did you notice her personality changing? Was she turning into someone you didn't recognize?"

"I never said that," Mary snapped. "But she did change. She did start going off on her own and none of us knew where she went. I didn't necessarily mind. All I thought was that she was finally off my back instead of always watching me. She was too strict before."

It sounded familiar.

"But then one day, she wasn't strict at all." Mary stared at the lake. "Look, you're here to help, not blame me."

"I'm not blaming you."

She let out a disgruntled moan. "I don't care what you have to do or how you have to do it." She went on, but her tone was resigned. "Just find her."

"I will."

"And if you think I can't handle knowing what's really going on. You're wrong. I want to hear it." She rose to her feet and told Hannah, "Bring Candice in with you when you come. I'm going to make sure Dale hasn't burnt dinner to a crisp in there."

Mary padded down the dock, crossed the yard, and disappeared in the house, leaving Hannah with Candice.

Candice looked up at her and met Hannah's gaze. The young girl wasn't vacant, but totally cognizant.

Hannah waited on baited breath, poised for Candice to speak.

But she didn't.

Hannah tried to encourage her by saying, "How are you doing, Candice?"

The girl parted her lips, exposing teeth too big for her head. She sucked in a clipped breath. Hannah eagerly waited for Candice to say anything.

Candice let out another humming tone. An awful tone that pierced Hannah's ears and made her blood run cold.

"Shh, honey," Hannah said, but Candice only hummed louder.

The tone sliced through Hannah. This was a nightmare. She didn't have Mary's patience, command, or strength. She had to get away from the little girl.

So she fled.

She rushed off the dock and used a brisk pace to cross the yard, her boots trekking over the soggy grass.

Mary would have something to say to her about leaving their baby sister out there, but Hannah had to escape. And she hated herself for it.

CHAPTER SIX

BLAKE'S WORK BOOTS cracked into a thin crust of frost and sank into the mud with every step. Feeble suction fought him each time he pulled his foot loose. The marsh smelled like death, leaves and animal carcasses decomposing alongside one another. Where nature came to die was how he thought of this place, the bad side of the lake.

He checked for snappers when the vegetation got particularly gnarly, but for the most part he kept his eyes peeled looking for tracks no matter how faint, anything that would tell him just what in the hell had gone wrong with Dalton. The kid got blasted so often, it was no wonder he had messed everything up. But seriously, how hard could it be to drive into town and buy some sandwiches and two cases of beer?

Dalton had left for town a day ago and never came back.

Unbelievable.

When Blake came to a cluster of birch trees, he realized that he had already searched this stretch of the marsh. Man, it was dark as hell out here, nothing but moonlight bouncing off the water and a hazy glow from the shack up the way. Not that the glowing lights from the shack did him a damn bit of good. The floods dangling off their tin roof barely illuminated their withering backyard, much less did their flood lights reach all the way over to where Blake was trekking beside the marsh.

He would be a fool to keep going. He had gotten too close to the shack already. Yet something caused him to linger there. He squinted through the darkness at their windows, curious.

He shoved off before he could sink so deep into mud that lake water would seep through his laces, then he doubled back, trekking hard until the earth leveled off solid. Quickening his pace, he stalked through the underbrush, burs grabbing hold of his jeans, cattails waving at him as he passed by. It was minutes before he came to the site.

The old foundation protruded through a tangle of bushes. Corroded cinder blocks and rotten wood outlined the area where a house had once stood. A pipe or two, rusted out and bent, shot up from the brush. In the moonlight, the area looked like the setting of a horror film. Goddamn it that they couldn't get a TV down there. This entire operation was interrupting Blake's whole rhythm of life.

Movement up ahead caught his eye, and as he locked his gaze on a hunched shape that shouldn't have been there, Blake reflexively unsheathed his knife, ready to kill whatever was there.

But a billow of cigarette smoke told him the figure up ahead was no wild animal. Well, it wasn't the kind of wild animal he had thought.

"I told you to stay in the cellar," Blake shouted. "What's the matter with you?"

"I can't take the smell," said Travis, who was seated on an old stump. He looked like a giant, hunching vulture in the moonlight.

Travis sucked on his cigarette and twitched. Most people thought he looked like a caricature—his small head and big ears were to blame for that. But his eyes, man. Travis' eyes were a warning not to mess with him. Black as sin. You could see your own reflection in them, and that's how you knew God had forgotten to give him a soul.

Blake should have never involved his cousin, Travis, in this job. Trouble had a way of finding Travis. But Blake had figured it would be better for Travis to get wrapped up in Blake's kind of trouble than his own.

Of course, that was before Dalton had failed to return.

Travis stood up when Blake reached him. Travis towered over his cousin like the grim reaper. He crushed his cigarette butt under his boot and asked, "You didn't find Dalton?"

"He's not out there."

"Where do you think he went?"

Blake had no idea, but he feared Dalton had ended up with the cops. Deep down in the pit of his stomach his ulcer stung him. It was his body's way of telling him what his one-track mind wouldn't. Dalton's disappearance was the beginning of the end.

"Go down into the cellar," he told Travis.

His cousin glared at him with those black, soulless eyes of his. Then he obeyed, muscled the steel door away from the foundation, and flung it back. The steel sheet bounced off cinder blocks with a few clatters, and Travis lumbered down the stairs.

Blake scanned the marsh and listened out for a moment. He turned, studied the tree line in the distance, and watched the long dirt path beyond it. It was quiet except for crickets and the occasional belch of a bullfrog. The coast was clear.

Hiding in plain sight was working.

He stepped heavily down the stairs and closed the cellar door above his head. He continued farther down the rest of the stairs until he reached the concrete landing.

The cellar, which Blake figured had been a bomb shelter back when the house had been constructed in the 40s, was now divided into two rooms.

The front room, which was where Travis, Dalton, and Blake had been holed up since taking this job, was a cramped twelve-by-ten-foot square. There was nothing but concrete for a floor and bricks for walls on all sides, though metal shelves flanked the walls.

Travis, Dalton, and Blake represented everything that had gone wrong in this quiet corner of New Hampshire. They had no ambition, too much free time, and an affinity for smoking chemical drugs to help the years go by faster.

Again, Travis sat hunched like a vulture, this time sitting on his air mattress and sleeping bag.

"So, what do we do about Dalton?" Travis' knee was bobbing and Blake couldn't decide if it was nerves or withdrawal.

"Nothing we can do."

Travis looked extremely worried.

Ordinarily, wearing an expression like that on his face would warrant Blake smacking Travis upside the head, but Blake decided to go easy on him.

Dalton should've been back by now. Feeling concerned was healthy. But until they got further instructions regarding this hellish job they had taken on, they were in no position to make any moves on their own.

"Are you low on meth rocks?" he asked Travis, and the kid eased, a crooked smile forming across his face.

"I thought you wanted me to stay straight for the night."

Blake frowned, implying a change of heart. "Do your thing."

Travis shoved his fingers down his pocket, stretching and shaking his leg to jostle the bag loose. He pinched a pebble of meth from inside the plastic then dropped the pebble into a glass pipe.

As his cousin got high, Blake enjoyed the sweet sound of silence coming from the back room.

His thoughts quickly turned to the skinny woman who he had spied at the shack a number of times.

Blake didn't like unexpected variables, so he took it as a bad sign that a strange woman had arrived at Dale, Mary, and Candice's home.

The fact that she had caused his anxiety to ratchet up. He didn't like it. He had a sixth sense for these things and he knew that the woman was going to mess things up.

Travis asked, "When do you think we'll get paid for this job?"

Blake watched Travis exhale smoke through his teeth, and he instantly regretted allowing his cousin to get high. Smoke was filling Travis' side of the cellar room and wafting over towards Blake.

Meth smoke smelled like burnt bleach and day-old dog crap.

"We'll get paid when the job is done."

"When will that be?"

"Your guess is as good as mine."

Travis turned angry and he stared at Blake, itching for a confrontation.

"You want me to be high so I don't know what's going on, is that it?" Travis yelled.

Blake laughed.

"What's so funny?"

"You wouldn't know what was going on if you were stone cold sober and it was broad daylight."

Travis let the argument go. He would rather take another hit from his pipe. When the smoke filled his lungs, he held his breath, absorbing as much meth as possible, before he slowly released the hit.

"I didn't sign up for this," said Travis. "Helping remove her hand… That's some seriously messed up stuff, Blake."

"You think I don't know that?"

Holding gazes, the memory of who they used to be as kids struck him. White trash, but too young to realize, swinging off tires on a hot, humid day, their world no bigger than Hermit Lake. Blake had been tubby, and was often teased for it. Travis had been all limbs and gangly. Clothes hadn't fit either of them correctly until Blake grew up, evened out, and the girls started noticing him. Travis hadn't been so lucky.

"Why do you keep drifting off like that?" asked Travis.

"I'm not drifting off." But Blake had. He had been spacing out more and more. It was the hand. Ever since, he couldn't seem to keep anchored to his immediate surroundings.

"Are we going to get our money at the end of all of this, Blake? Or are we going to be tortured and killed, too?"

He didn't have to answer Travis. They both knew how this nightmare was probably going to end. But the money that had been promised was way too much. They couldn't pull out now. If there was even the slightest chance they could get away with this job…

Blake got to his feet and crossed to the stairs.

"Where are you going?"

"We haven't eaten since yesterday," he said. "I won't be long."

"I don't like being alone with her, man. She moans. It gets under my skin."

"I won't be long, Trav."

But Blake already knew he would be gone longer than the amount of time it would take to buy sandwiches at the 7-Eleven.

He emerged from the cellar, lowered the door onto the foundation, and locked his sights on the shack in the distance.

CHAPTER SEVEN

CODY ANGLED HIS pickup truck next to Hannah's silver Taurus and parked in front of the Cole house.

Damn, look at that place, he thought.

It had been well over ten years since Cody had seen the house. Back when he had been here last, it wasn't like the house had been in peak physical condition, but now it really looked run down. Dilapidated. It was hard to believe a family could survive inside unless it was a family of raccoons.

He killed the engine, pocketed the keys, and climbed out. The cool, damp air filled his lungs. A thick cloak of fog covered the lake. Cody walked through the mist to get to the house.

The porch looked precarious at best. New boards sat flush beside old ones. Cody watched his step as he came to the front door.

He felt a strange conflict brewing inside him. He had been downright elated when Hannah had called to tell him that she would be sticking around. She hadn't said how long. He got the impression she knew, but was keeping it to herself for the time being. He was excited about that, but she had also rejected him the other night, asking him to leave her motel room.

That was probably a juvenile way of putting it, but that was how he felt. He wouldn't describe his feelings for her as yearning, per se. Yearning, pining, and longing—those words were too small.

What he had been feeling since he had set eyes on her at Gemma's Diner, was something akin to love.

He felt compelled to do something, anything that might bridge the gap between them, or at least he wanted to. But Hannah had rejected his last attempt and had thrown a wall up to shut him out.

When she had called this morning, he told himself that nothing had changed between them and that Hannah hadn't changed her mind about him, either. She wanted to keep her distance and he would respect her wishes.

He gave the front door a knock and hoped like hell Dale wasn't around. The last time Cody had seen the man, Dale's fist had made contact with Cody's left eye, filling him with shame and a deep sense of satisfaction. Cody had deserved to get punched in the face.

He heard Hannah shout from inside, "We're just bundling up! We'll be out in a sec!" Next came the muffled sounds of Hannah helping Candice into her coat, "Shoot your arm through. Your laces aren't tied. I got it, zip up."

The door opened and Hannah stepped outside with Candice. She was holding the frail, little blond girl by the shoulders.

The sight of Cody seemed to make Candice hesitate.

"Come on, sweetheart," Hannah told her, as she led Candice across the porch, following Cody.

He was quick to open the passenger side door, but felt awkward and useless for the most part.

Hannah urged Candice into his truck. She scooted over to the middle seat.

"She's had some odd behavior," Hannah told him in a quiet tone so that the child wouldn't overhear. "Nothing violent, but definitely… bizarre."

Cody noticed that Hannah's eyes looked darker than usual. She climbed in and sat beside Candice, and Cody closed the truck door after he was sure Hannah had tucked herself neatly into the passenger seat.

As he rounded the front of his truck, coming to the driver's side, he realized why her eyes looked darker. She was wearing black eyeliner. He wondered if he should tell her that she looked pretty.

When he opened his door, Candice was staring at him with unblinking eyes, her face squared on him at such an angle it reminded him of the Exorcist. Odd behavior to say the least, he thought as he turned the key and checked the side mirrors. He wondered if Candice was going to stare at him the whole drive. Christ, he hoped not.

It wasn't until he got to the main road where the asphalt was smooth that he introduced himself.

"I'm Cody," he told the girl. "I'm Hannah's high school sweetheart."

"High school *friend*," she corrected him.

"We've got a fun day planned. You're going to meet my friend, Judy. She's heard all about you and she's impressed. You're going to love her. Then, I was thinking we could get some ice cream and play a round of mini-golf."

Hannah wasn't sure about that.

"A buddy of mine manages Pirate's Cove. You remember Hamilton? He said he would let us play mini-golf even though the place is closed for the season."

"That was nice of him," she said. "What do you think, Candice? Do you want to play mini-golf later?"

The girl didn't respond.

Cody felt the urge to tell Hannah that she looked nice, but he held his tongue. He didn't want to come off too strong.

Before long, they pulled into a strip mall where the child psychologist's office was located.

The strip mall looked dismal. There was a dentistry practice of questionable repute, a grunt lawyer no one needed unless they had been arrested for the worst varieties of petty crimes, and a holistic healing establishment that smelled weird. Judy St. Clair's office was dead center amidst the depression.

While Hannah brought Candice inside the anteroom of Judy's office, Cody locked his pickup truck. When he joined them inside, he neared the receptionist's desk, and Hannah got the girl situated on one of the chairs in the waiting area.

He tapped the dingy bell on the counter and spied into her office. The door was ajar but he didn't see Judy inside. He rang the bell again and waited, wondering why there never seemed to be a receptionist.

Behind him, Hannah tried to get Candice to take her coat off, but the girl preferred to stay insulated.

No one had explained to her that she was here to see a psychologist.

Candice needed to talk. She needed to tell Judy everything that had happened the night her mother was taken. How had her mother's blood gotten on her hands? Did she see the man, or men, who had taken Kendra? Cody hoped all of the details were still fresh in the girl's mind.

Finally, Judy St. Clair burst out of her office with gusto. Her brown eyes locked on Candice like a pair of heat seeking missiles.

"Good morning! Hello, Candice! McAlister, how are you?"

"Just grateful you can meet Candice," he said. "Thanks for being willing to work with us."

"Of course!" Judy turned to Hannah and shook her hand. "Nice to meet you, too."

Judy had the kind of energy that made her seem three times her natural size, and the way she leaned over and came nose-to-nose with Candice was cause for more than a little alarm. Judy didn't exactly have a *gentle* demeanor, But Cody trusted her. In Belknap county, Judy was a hero of sorts. She had a gift for interviewing traumatized children and helping to put guilty abusers behind bars.

Hannah began explaining, "She hasn't spoken for about a month."

"Cody mentioned," said Judy. "She's dissociating. It's good and it's bad. She's learned to tuck herself into her imagination to protect herself. So, we've got to coax her out."

Hannah and Cody exchanged a look, as Judy stooped in front of Candice to get a good look at the girl.

"Has she been acting like an animal?" Judy asked Hannah.

"What?"

"Barking? Meowing? Squawking like a chicken?"

"Ah, no."

"Good to know." She took Candice by the hand and said, "Alright, kiddo, up and at 'em."

"She's been walking in circles, staring at her feet," Hannah offered.

"Sounds adorable," said Judy, as she turned with Candice and started for her office.

Hannah added, "She sometimes hums a loud tone. Like she's holding a note for as long as she can."

Judy seemed interested in that, thanked her, then continued leading Candice towards her office.

Cody assured Hannah, "Judy is the best in the Tri-State area. Candice is in good hands."

Hannah looked skeptical of that, so he changed the subject and asked her:

"Are you hungry?"

HANNAH FEIGNED interest in their waitress, Marjorie's long winded anecdote about keeping her azaleas flowering into late autumn.

Cody and Hannah were seated at Gemma's Diner.

Marjorie went on, and the next thing Cody and Hannah knew, Marjorie was complaining about her son, Blake, and all the trouble he had caused her. How Blake had a damn thing to do with Marjorie's gardening was entirely lost on Cody, and by the looks of it, Hannah as well.

Hannah was polite and smiled when Marjorie finally wrapped the weird story up. Hannah ordered coffee with half-n-half and a stack of pancakes then handed her menu to Marjorie.

"I'll have the same," said Cody.

When Marjorie walked away, Hannah commented, "Judy seems like a firecracker. I hope she can get Candice talking."

"I hope so, too. I wouldn't have recommended her if I didn't have the highest confidence in her."

Hannah nodded but then the same worried look came over her that he had been catching glimpses of all morning.

"You look nice," he said to lighten the mood.

"Thanks," she said but then quickly changed the subject. "Any developments with that guy who brought the box to the police station?"

Marjorie returned and Cody waited for her to place their coffees on the table. When Marjorie paced away, Cody reminded Hannah of the big picture. "He's still recovering. It's been a day, barely. He'll come around."

She searched his eyes, which never lied.

"It's more complicated than recovering, isn't it?"

"We have him in the ICU with two officers standing guard. Plus the hospital security has been briefed. No one gets in without first being carefully scrutinized and we assured him of this, but at the moment, he's still too terrified to communicate."

"He told you he's terrified? He could say that much?"

"He communicated it." Cody stiffened under the magnitude of it all. "Not that he needed to. It's in his eyes. When I looked at him, I could sense that he wasn't scared to die. He was scared not to. He was afraid if whoever's behind this got to him, he would suffer a fate worse than..."

Hannah pinched her eyes closed, but he knew what she was thinking. She had mentally finished the point he had begun to make. The man at the hospital didn't want to suffer a fate *worse than Kendra's*.

When she opened her eyes, she began rummaging around her purse, and Cody knew what would come next.

Sure enough, Hannah produced her flask and poured an ounce of liquor into her coffee.

"Kendra is definitely alive out there," he promised.

Hannah gulped her coffee. Steam wafted up her cheeks, causing her eyebrows to knit together.

"Did you know my mom was on meth?" she boldly asked.

He hadn't exactly been eager to tell her about that, which was why he had kept that detail to himself.

"Yeah, I knew," he said.

"Did you know she was arrested a bunch of times?" Hannah poured more liquor into her empty mug and knocked it back. "It's crazy."

Beyond their window, a torrent of red maple leaves fluttered across the parking lot, but Cody couldn't take his eyes off Hannah.

"My mom was an addict." she realized, and Cody was just glad she didn't blame him for withholding the truth in that regard. "I feel like my head is spinning, but in the last year, that's what she was—a drug addict. You found meth at the scene. Is the guy at the hospital also an addict?"

"We think so."

"Why keep her alive?" she wondered. "And why torture her by removing her hand?" Hannah thought for a moment. "Who would do this? And why? Even if she owed a drug dealer a ton of money, they wouldn't retaliate like this. Whoever is doing this to her really hates her."

On the other side of the diner, Marjorie was sharing her woeful tale about her garden and her son, Blake, with the cook.

"I reached the same conclusion," he agreed. "The only question is, who?"

Hannah locked eyes with him. "I wonder if Dale is behind this."

Cody thought about it, but was interrupted when Marjorie angled their breakfast plates onto the table.

IN THE TOY-CLUTTERED bowels of Judy St. Clair's office, Cody and Hannah sat down on a shabby sofa where a family of puppets once sat, while Judy sat on a nearby chair.

All eyes were on Candice, who was making a pretend snow angel on the floor. Lying on her back, Candice moved her arms and legs, as if she had no concept of what was happening around her.

Judy told Hannah that Candice had been at it for well over ten minutes.

"Is that good?" asked Hannah.

Proudly, Judy asked Candice, "What are you making, dear?"

"A mess," said the girl.

Hannah's jaw dropped. Candice had spoken! Hannah smiled at Cody.

"Are you making a mess, Candice, or are you making a snow angel?"

Candice didn't reply, but that was alright. Hannah was over the moon that she had said anything at all, and Judy had more good news for us.

"There were three men," said Judy.

Hannah looked dumbfounded. "She told you there were three men?"

"Yes," said Judy. "This was in the forest. I'm using Candice's words, mind you. I haven't endeavored to draw connections and I won't."

"Yes, I understand," Hannah said.

"They wore masks and the van was white. Candice described what they were wearing, work boots, jeans, long shirts, etcetera. Candice says that Kendra was stabbed."

"How did you get this out of her?" Hannah was in awe of the whacky woman.

Judy hesitated in a manner that told Cody the answer would be so simple, it would break Hannah's heart.

"Candice might not feel as though she's very important at home," she explained. "If she's not listened to anyway, or respected, then why would anyone care to hear her speak?"

Judy let that hang for a moment then elaborated.

"A child's trauma can be impacted detrimentally if they assume they won't be believed. It's the bottling up of emotions, the silence they give to horrendous events that locks them into a shell, if you will. It's not enough that her needs are being met at home. Yes, she's fed and bathed and clothed and there's a roof over her head, but she must also be nurtured."

"When can we bring her back? How often should she come? I want her to get back to her normal self."

Judy looked at Cody for his directive.

Turning to Hannah, he said, "We'll work it out. Maybe two, three times a week?"

Judy smiled as though that would work for her, and he hoped that she wouldn't reveal to Hannah the arrangement that they had worked out prior. Cody planned to pay for all of this.

"That certainly works for me," Judy said, flipping her calendar open. "I can see her next on Tuesday? Or Thursday?"

"Let's plan on Tuesday." Cody looked at Hannah for the green light.

"Sure, definitely."

Smiles all around, and Hannah helped Candice up from the floor. "Come on, girl. Time to go."

As Hannah collected her younger sister, Cody took the opportunity to approach Judy, thank her, and reiterate under his breath that she should send the bill to his email address and he would pay it.

When they gathered at the door, Cody pulled it open and that's when Judy remembered a critical detail.

"One of the men had a snake tattoo."

Cody's heart skipped a beat.

"On his forearm. His sleeves were rolled up. Bear in mind this is Candice's impression," she warned. "A snake tattoo. That's all she said."

AS ENCOURAGING AS Candice's time with Judy had been, she spoke not one word when they stopped for ice cream, and seemed disinterested in mini-golf. She spent the half-hour game balancing on the wooden perimeter of each hole, experimenting with how far she could walk, heel to toe, before falling off. Cody did what he could to keep Hannah's faltering spirits up, but they plummeted none-the-less. She hadn't had an appetite for her triple chocolate scoop and seemed to lob her golf ball apathetically at every hole.

By the time he drove them back to the house, Hannah's mind was somewhere out the window and Candice had started staring at him all over again.

To Cody, she seemed like a girl who might only come alive if she was far from home.

When they reached the house, he shifted his truck into Park, and left the engine running.

Hannah climbed out with Candice.

"Today was fun," he said.

"Want to check out the lake?" she asked.

"Sure, I have time. Why not?"

Dusk gathered across the sky, as Cody and Hannah walked across the frost-covered lawn towards the lake.

Candice had darted ahead for the dock. She padded down the dock so fast, he thought she might run right off the end and into the water.

"The snake tattoo is going to help, right?" asked Hannah.

"Absolutely," he assured her, stealing a glance or two at her as they neared the shore. "Tomorrow I'll run through the Police Database to see if anyone with a snake tattoo has been arrested. It's a starting point. Today was a big victory."

She seemed to breathe easier, as she gazed across the water. She also watched Candice. The girl was on her knees on the dock, slapping the surface of the water with her palms and humming loudly in the manner that Hannah had mentioned.

Hannah wondered, "Why didn't the kidnappers take Candice, as well, that night?"

He didn't have an answer.

She shook her head, mentally analyzing the fragments.

The next thing Cody knew, a bullet zinged past his head.

Cody ducked. Hannah yelled and scrambled away. Cody whipped around to see who had fired at him.

Dale stood with his rifle aimed at Cody, ready to fire another round.

"You took my daughter?" Dale barked.

Hannah yelled, "We talked about this!"

"I didn't know you were going to go with Cody!" said Dale, drunk and furious.

"I took her!" Hannah yelled. "Put your rifle down! Have you lost your mind?"

Cody's hand was on his holstered handgun, but he knew if he drew it on Dale, this would turn into an all-out war.

"Have I lost my mind?" Dale barked. "My wife's gone missing and you think I take kindly to my littlest girl disappearing?"

"She didn't disappear. She was with me."

"You think I don't know who you are?" he asked Cody. "Cody McAlister."

"That's right."

"You work for the police now."

"Yeah."

"You're not welcome here."

"Yeah, I noticed," Cody said.

Cody started off for his truck.

The front door slammed open and shut, and Mary appeared, having stomped around the side of the house. Furious, she charged at Dale and grabbed the rifle out of his hands. Dale didn't fight her for one second.

"Get in the house!" Mary ordered him.

"Get him off my property. I don't care how you do it," he yelled at Mary.

"In the house!"

Dale obeyed. What struck Cody most about the exchange was that it seemed strangely loving. Dale was grinning, and then he was inside the house.

Hannah had never seen anything like it, and she wasn't alone.

Cody was just as surprised by the display as Hannah.

Mary approached Cody with the rifle in her hand, but she wasn't aiming it at him.

"Why does my dad hate you?"

Hannah answered on Cody's behalf and told Mary, "It's a long story. I'll tell you later."

"He doesn't usually shoot at trespassers," she went on, ignoring her sister. "What did you do?"

Flummoxed at the prospect of being candid with the girl, Cody offered, "Hannah and I went to prom together and it turned into a bad night."

"Cody!" Hannah snapped.

Hannah pulled him away and they started for his truck.

Mary called out after them, "Warn me the next time you come."

Yanking his truck door open, Cody realized he was furious. A teenage girl had saved him, while he had frozen in the face of danger.

CHAPTER EIGHT

CAUTERIZED.

That was the word for it.

Kendra couldn't remember where she had heard the term, cauterized. Had to have been from Mary, her smart one.

She could still feel her left hand. A phantom on fire every time she wiggled fingers that weren't there.

Kendra tried not to glance at it—the stump. She tried to be grateful. His precision, the sterilization, the drugs he had fed her before and after, the foggy echo of which zinged through her bloodstream even now.

She knew their names.

Blake and Dalton and Travis.

But she didn't know the man who had taken her hand. She hadn't seen his face and he hadn't come back.

Kendra hadn't seen Dalton in a few days. He was the nice one. He had been reading Paradise Lost to her. Dalton also opened up to her about things when Blake and Travis weren't around. He had given her a taste of what it might have been like if she'd had a son. She knew he was lonely. The essence of his loneliness had come through as he had mispronounced words then realized his mistake sentences later, correcting himself. It had endeared her. So, where the hell was he?

She prayed that Dalton would come back. She hoped he wasn't off somewhere, suffering. Maybe he didn't deserve her sympathy. Maybe none of them did.

It was impossible to make sense of this.

She didn't even know what day it was or how many weeks had gone by. Had it been months? Without sunlight, time moved slowly.

Thinking their names gave her a sense of strength. Blake, Dalton, Travis, *Kendra*. She had never liked the sound of her name. The consonants sounded too pointy, and didn't roll smoothly off the tongue. The vowels sounded aggressive. That's why she had given her girls soft names, ones that sounded feminine.

She felt safest in the fetal position with her back to the wall and her eyes on the door, but the angle at which her hip met the sleeping bag was causing her a dull ache at the moment. Pain swelled in her joints and radiated down her legs and up her spine.

Digging her heels into the cement floor and pushing her shoulder against the wall, she inched her way up to stand.

Her arms were bound tightly behind her back with cable ties. Her feet were bound at the ankles just above her boots. *Hogtied* was the name for it, or maybe that was only when the feet and arms were bound together. If she made it out of this, she would ask Mary.

The only light she had came through a crack under the door, but her eyes had long since adjusted.

Kendra said a silent prayer that if she ever got out of this, she would live a clean life and be genuine about her church attendance, and not just use the hour to let her mind wander. And she would do better with her girls. She would reconcile with Hannah and they would be a family again.

She wished to God she had a little fight left in her. She had wasted most of her energy in those first few days. She had kicked and screamed and spat in their faces. Damn kids. She had only wanted to score. They had tricked her into this nightmare.

Then the man had come and surgically removed her hand. Kendra had tried to make sense of it, but it made her mind reel. So many weeks lost down here.

She had never seen his face.

He hadn't spoken.

But she knew he would come back.

How the hell had Blake, Dalton, and Travis gotten roped into this?

She should've never met them in the woods.

Kendra scanned the room like she had done a million times before—the thin sleeping bag beneath her, nothing but bare cement for a floor, and a few metal shelves so rusted out you would probably get Tetanus if you touched them. The walls were brick, as bare as the floor. She didn't have a hope in hell for a weapon.

Her best bet was to wait until only one of the kids was standing guard, lure him in here, and kill him. But, Christ, how? Could she use her teeth like a wild animal?

The way she was sitting caused the surgical stitches in her lower abdomen to strain, pull at the skin, and pinch. The man had stitched up the stab wound and she didn't want to pop any stitches before she healed.

She muscled her way up to her feet and stretched her legs. She felt a touch light headed, but soon the feeling passed.

Inching like a penguin she cleared her sleeping bag and made her labored way to the shelving unit. She inspected the metal rungs closely, one then the next, working from the highest shelf then further and further down.

When she reached the rung third from the bottom she saw something shiny.

A flat metal head jutting ever so slightly out from the brick wall.

It was a nail!

She breathed deep and stilled her mind as though the kids beyond the door might read her thoughts if she got too excited.

Memorizing its exact location and attempting to visualize how she could grasp hold of the nail head with her good hand, Kendra was imbued with a fresh wave of her fighting spirit.

She pivoted, shifting her weight between her feet in a shuffle until her back met the metal shelving. Then she lowered down, knees bending, and thighs burning. The metal rungs dug into her back as she lowered, all the while feeling for the nail.

The angle was awkward and painful, but she felt the bricks, sweating hard in the effort to locate the nail.

Eventually the rough brick texture gave way to a smooth flat head.

She clipped her fingernails under its head and began prying the rusted nail out of the wall.

It did not want to come.

But there was no way in hell she would give up. Just feeling the head of the nail at her fingertips sent her heart racing. She could tell it was a big nail meant to lock in support beams behind the brick.

She pinched it, pulled, but her fingers slid off. Again, she felt around for it and pinched the nail, her fingers aching, and pulled. Was her mind playing tricks on her, or had the nail loosened?

Keeping at it though her fingers cramped, Kendra thought of her girls.

Mary.

Christ, she was a pretty girl no matter how much she wrecked her hair, and she was so damn strong, too. A lion tamer. Wouldn't any daughter of Dale's have to be?

Lord, the circumstances she had survived before she brought Hannah into this world—soul-murdering conditions, the kind that kept scarring even after you got out. And here she was again, like life was an endless cycle that she had no hope of escaping.

Hannah had tried to find out about Kendra's former life, the one she had lived before having Hannah. Hannah had asked. But Kendra had refused to tell her. It had been her way of protecting Hannah.

Kendra scraped at the nail and it eased out a good inch then jammed as her fingers slipped off.

The nail was stuck tight.

Again, she pinched it between her thumb and forefinger, and tried pulling. If the brick was old enough and corroded, it would crumble and turn to dust in the wake of the metal nail, so she kept at it. And kept at it.

CHAPTER NINE

SUNLIGHT HAD HER room at the Super-8 ablaze.

Stark orange, the light from the setting sun sliced in through the windows sideways, reminding Hannah she needed to hustle.

She squinted through the glare, as she pressed down on a heap of tangled clothes, forcing them into her suitcase. If she could flatten them to the rim she would have a prayer at zipping the suitcase closed all the way around and not just the one side she had managed. This battle had been going on for too long.

The door to her left was wide open in case the maid needed to get in and fix the motel room up for the next guest.

An icy breeze blew in, teasing her hair out from behind her ear. She tucked her unruly hair back, cursed at her clothes for not submitting then had another go at forcing the zipper around.

Knuckles rapped on the doorframe and without glancing up she said, "Do your thing. I'll be out in a minute."

Then she heard Cody's distinct voice, "It's me." His gaze bounced from the bed, which she had made, to her suitcase as she finally shut it successfully, to the dresser and counter tops that were no longer littered with toiletries and lady products. "You're leaving?"

"I am." He looked confused, so she clarified, "I can't afford to stay at the motel for the rest of the week."

"So, you're staying a week?" he asked, trying to pinpoint her exact date of departure. "Where are you going to sleep?"

As she sat on the bed, Hannah looked him over and noticed a black satchel hanging from his shoulder.

"Why are you here?"

"Stop deflecting," he ordered, his tone a bit stern for her taste.

"I don't have an extra fifty-five bucks a night to stay in a crappy motel. I already burned a hundred bucks or so. It's not like I can pull another four hundred out of savings. I don't even have savings."

If Hannah wasn't mistaken, Cody was doing mental mathematics, trying to get an idea of when she would be heading out of town for good.

"Until Wednesday?" he guessed.

"Thursday morning. It was as much time as Gilford would give me."

Cody wrapped his mind around that, adjusting to the timeline, perhaps coming to terms with the fact that she would be gone soon. His hands were planted on his hips, causing his shoulders to square at her, making him appear a bit bigger. He searched her expression, maybe trying to figure out how she might feel about leaving when the day came.

"It is what it is," she explained.

"You're not staying at the house, are you?"

Hannah sighed and wondered why she would prefer his approval. "Mary offered."

"Dale shot his rifle at us," he said, staring at her like she suddenly had two heads.

"He took shots at *you*," she corrected. "And he wasn't trying to hit you, just make a point."

"Well, I received it. Loud and clear. He's dangerous."

"I know." Hannah watched the light shift over him, creeping across his handsome face and down his piercing green eyes. Then the sun sank behind the horizon far beyond the window and the room went dim. "I can't explain this in a way you'll understand, but I have to be there, money aside. It was hard to hear Judy break it down how she did, but she's right. Candice isn't getting what she needs. I feel like if I'm there, she'll get used to me, open up, and maybe tell me more."

Cody's face flushed. The very idea of her in the house with Dale probably made his blood boil. He seemed to keep a lid on it and countered with, "Three days a week with Judy isn't enough?"

She didn't feel like arguing. "Candice needs someone around her who has the care and stamina to make her feel safe and get her to open up. What are you doing?"

Cody had smacked his satchel down on the foot of the bed and was roughly tearing it open. As the lid fell back to the comforter, she joined him and stared down at the contents inside the satchel. There was a small arsenal of weapons—handguns. She counted five, noting two GLOCKS of varying calibers, a revolver, and a few handguns she wasn't familiar with.

"You've got to be kidding me."

"Hannah, I'm dead serious. I was going to insist and that was before I knew you were reckless enough to volunteer yourself to live in that house." Cody selected one of the GLOCKS and put it in her hands. "Is that too heavy for you?"

She didn't properly hold the gun by the handle, but rather cradled it in her palm to feel its weight.

"Come on, grasp it. Is it too heavy?"

"It'll have too much kick," she commented, gradually getting on board. "Pass me that revolver."

"It won't kick back like you think," he argued. "Plus, it's got twelve rounds. You can miss a few times and still manage to protect yourself."

She snorted a laugh, "Miss a few times... I wouldn't want to actually *hit* him."

Cody frowned.

She released the clip, letting the long magazine slide out for her to briefly inspect then slapping it back up into place. Hannah shook her head. "The recoil on the larger calibers takes too long to recover from. A 43 is no good." She shoved it back at him then selected another GLOCK, examined it in the same discerning manner, noting, "The 45's no good." Shoved it at him, selected a third option, eyed it. "This pistol is better," she said with an air of approval. "19mm Walther P99?" she asked when she recognized the handgun. She shot him a smile and realized that Cody was both impressed and slightly horrified. "I don't like the Germans enough," she said, denouncing it, as she passed the gun back.

120

Cody kept returning weapon after weapon to his satchel, trying to keep up. "Ah," she said, an edge of humor in her tone, "38 Special, seven rounds, no risk of jamming, barely a breath of recoil." She tucked it down the back of her pants. "Thanks for the revolver."

Baffled, he said, "No problem."

She pulled her suitcase, lumpy as it was, to the floor and rolled it to the doorway.

"How do you know so much about guns?"

"I grew up with them," she shrugged. "When Dale came into the picture he brought more than a few with him. I was eleven at the time. Mom didn't want me accidentally blowing my head off or hers so she made him teach me to respect and handle them."

"And you never mentioned it to me?"

"What? Brag? Build myself up to look cool in high school? I didn't want the attention."

It wasn't the easiest pill to swallow—that she had kept something like that from him in high school—but Cody choked the realization down and closed his satchel. Then he offered her a box of ammo, which she found funny. She wasn't going to war, but she took it nonetheless, dropped it in her purse, and told him she needed to check the bathroom in case she had overlooked an item.

The sink was bare, the shower stall empty except for the motel's tiny shampoo and conditioner bottles and a flat bar of soap that had cracked when she had run it over her body that morning. When she returned, Cody was ready at the doorway.

"Leave it open for the maid," she said, as she passed through with her suitcase in tow.

He did, then he took over the task of carrying the bulky thing down the stairs. The wheels clanked against the landing and Hannah stepped down. She told him she needed a minute to settle her bill.

She held her breath when the clerk swiped her debit card, and didn't start breathing again until he gave her a confirming nod and handed her card back. After thanking him she met Cody, who had been waiting with her stuff just outside the door.

"Did you get a chance to look into convicts with snake tattoos?" she asked, grabbing her suitcase handle and starting for her Taurus.

"That's the other reason I stopped by," he said. "I pulled up seven."

She wasn't sure how encouraged she should be. "That's not a lot, right? Can you look into them?"

"Yeah and it shouldn't take long." He didn't sound thrilled. "We can't get our hopes too high. It's possible our guy isn't in the system."

"A meth addict not in the system?" She screwed her face up. "I doubt that. Even Kendra came up." She fished the keyfob for her car out of her purse and unlocked the trunk, and Cody hoisted her suitcase and set it in the trunk bed for her. "Keep me posted?"

"I don't want you at that house."

"See you later, Cody."

He lingered. His gaze lowered to her mouth and she realized he was standing a bit close, but with dusk falling all around them it didn't feel intrusive. It felt right.

He stepped in, but seemed to think better of it. He softly said, "I'll call you." Then he opened her door and waited for her to get settled behind the wheel.

After shutting her door, Hannah held his gaze.

She started backing out. She kept her eye on him in the rearview as he climbed into his truck and turned the engine.

Damn if it wasn't getting hard not to reach for him when he stood near her like that. Hannah squeezed the brakes and assessed the stream of traffic flowing down Route 12, tapping her thumb against the wheel as she waited.

Hannah leaned forward into the steering wheel and pulled the revolver out. This was nuts. She shoved the handgun deep within her purse and drove off.

She felt a knot twisting in her gut.

It would be a long six days at the shack.

NO ONE knew where Dale was.

Mary worked her magic, making dinner and nursing her beers, while Hannah struggled to pull her weight. Her sister told her which ingredients Hannah needed, but Hannah was still totally lost. She hunted through the cabinets for them, feeling the urgency.

From the living room, Candice made that weird sound, letting out low humming tones at intervals that seemed to underscore the pressure Hannah was under, as she scrambled to bread chicken that was too damn slippery.

All the while, Hannah stole glances at Mary, trying to see through her thick veneer of foundation. The girl beneath hadn't been acting like the one who had called her days ago. The anxiety she had conveyed for how rough and unmanageable Dale had become wasn't lining up quite right compared to the girl who had smacked Dale, snatched his rifle, and basically conquered him. Mary held a distinct command over the household. She didn't seem to need Hannah's help with her father.

But the inconsistency didn't lessen Hannah's awe of Mary. If anything, it strengthened it.

Sitting on the sofa, they ate bread-baked chicken, creamed corn, and salad, which Hannah had done a better job on. The TV was blaring some show about rich ladies who were married to important men and kept ripping each other's weaves out because of it. Candice was mentally present enough to keep shoveling food into her mouth and when a furious Italian woman overturned a table, grunting like the Incredible Hulk, she laughed right alongside her sister.

After dinner they migrated to Candice's room where Hannah sat cross-legged on the bed and watched Mary curl Candice's long, blonde hair with a curling iron.

Mary twirled the curling iron, sucking up their youngest sister's hair until the iron was tight against Candice's scalp. Mary looked like she was silently reflecting on the evening they had shared. It had seemed so normal on the surface, but felt so sad deep down.

Letting the ringlet fall, Mary moved on to the next lock, as Candice felt the warmth of her curly side.

"Looking good, mama," Mary told her, as she brought a canned beer to her mouth, taking advantage of the pause.

Candice smiled, a big toothy grin. She was gradually coming out of the thick shell she had been hiding in.

Glancing at Hannah, Mary said, "I can do you next," as she released the ringlet.

"My hair is curly enough."

"It's wavy," she corrected, setting the iron on the nightstand to maneuver Candice towards her so that she could get the final bits without craning around. When she resumed her work, she told Hannah, "You could use a trim around your face. Maybe get some bangs going with shorter fringe along your cheeks."

Curious, she asked, "What would that do?"

"Your eyes angle up at the outer corners, see? Just like mine, but you got those high cheekbones. Good lines. But the way your hair is all one length, it hides the shape." Finished with Candice, Mary looked at Hannah, her gaze passing through her like an anvil. "Whose face do you have?"

Her odd phrasing seemed to carefully conceal darker interests and Hannah felt her heart rate quickening in response.

"You don't look like Mom," she clarified, "except for your eyes."

"My dad, I guess. I mean of course."

Mary's expression turned to ice.

"What's he like?"

It occurred to Hannah that the girls hadn't heard about her father through Kendra, and hadn't been warned not to ask about him like she had been.

"I really don't know. Never met him."

"Is he in New Hampshire?"

"I have no idea."

"You never went looking for him?"

"I don't know his name."

Mary leaned back, started rocking her leg, and eyeing Hannah with God-like power.

"Does that bother you?"

It did. Immensely. But Hannah had never had it in her to go looking. When she didn't respond, Mary tapped Candice's leg, her frigid expression warming.

"It's time for bed, Candice."

The little girl stood up, but couldn't stop crushing her curls in her hand.

Mary selected a pair of cotton shorts and an old tee shirt for her to sleep in, both of which she found in one of the dresser drawers. She began yanking Candice's clothes off and getting her dressed for bed with the kind of lackluster authority you would expect from a hospice nurse.

Hannah felt a twinge of embarrassment during the brief moment that Candice stood naked but for her underwear. The girl was all skinny limbs and pale skin. But Candice was more or less oblivious and was soon dressed for bed.

"Sleep on your side or you'll wreck your curls," Mary told her, as she pulled the covers back for her sister to slide in. Hannah was quick to her feet to make room. Then Mary leaned in close to her ear and whispered something Hannah couldn't hear.

Keeping out of the way, Hannah walked into the hallway, as Mary pulled the blankets up to Candice's ear, arranged her curls on the pillow, and turned off the light.

As soon as Mary shut the door and joined her in the hallway, Hannah thought she caught the sound of Candice's feet pattering across the floor.

"Let's hang out in my room," she suggested.

Hannah followed her, but heard the distinct sound of metal scraping against metal inside the girl's bedroom, followed by more sounds of pattering feet.

Candice had climbed out of bed to lock herself in.

She had used the strange lock that Hannah had discovered, the one that was fastened to the upper edge of the door frame.

Why?

In Mary's bedroom, Mary wasted no time setting her desk chair in the center of her room. She rummaged through a plastic bin that was serving as a nightstand and produced a pair of hairdresser's scissors.

"Do you trust me?"

The answer came fast and hard, but only in her mind—*no*—and as an afterthought Hannah wondered why that was.

"Come on, I know what I'm doing. And you can have yourself a drink."

Awkwardly, she smiled at her younger half-sister. who was holding the scissors up in such a way that caught the light.

"She doesn't care, you know."

"Candice?"

"Yeah, she doesn't even notice if you drink around her."

The fact that Mary had intuited Hannah's craving for alcohol was unsettling. And in defense, she nearly pointed out that drinking around Candice wouldn't exactly set the best example, but she didn't think offending Mary would help matters.

"Well, you can drink in *here*," she offered.

"What makes you think I want to?"

Mary shot her a knowing grin. "Girl, your back pocket is bulging in the shape of a flask." As she braced the back of the chair she had pulled out for Hannah, welcoming Hannah to sit, she added, "Come on now, we've got the same blood running through our veins."

Hannah had to laugh, because deep down the sudden exposure made her feel strangely small.

"I like your top, by the way."

"Thanks," she said dryly.

As she lowered onto the wooden chair, pulling her flask free from her back pocket, she had to admit part of her felt good, like she was pleased to make Mary happy.

Mary leaned in close and studied Hannah's facial features, as she moved Hannah's hair, bringing it forward with her fingertips. Hannah hoped that Mary would be careful with those scissors.

"You handled Dale really well last night," she commented, as she twisted the top off her flask.

Mary stepped back to assess how she had framed Hannah's face, visualizing where to cut, as Hannah puffed out a short exhale to part her hair and fit her flask through to her mouth. She tipped the flask up without moving her head, drinking a long haul, then lowered the flask to her lap.

"Tell me about that guy, Cody. Why did Dale shoot at him?" Mary prodded, while carefully hooking the blades under Hannah's wall of hair. As she snipped and clipped and shaped bangs and fringe around her sister's face, Mary explained her strategy with Dale. "When it comes to Daddy, you don't think. You just do. But I've never seen him pull something like that. Shoot at a stranger like that.

So, why does Dale hate Cody? You said you would tell me."

"I used to be friends with Cody," she started.

"Friends? Have you ever slept with him?"

It was enough of an indication of where Mary was at with boys that Hannah needed another sip to feel comfortable with the direction this conversation was heading.

Mary paused while Hannah knocked her flask back and drank some more.

"Cody and I had a falling out, you could say, based on a bad night," she went on.

"So, that's a yes? You slept with him?"

"Christ, Mary. Yes. He took me to prom. Stupid as I was, I had built it up in my head."

"Prom or having sex?"

Reluctantly, she admitted, "Both, I suppose." Hannah mentally sorted out the best version of the nightmare so that Mary would never hear the worst of it. "I was crying when I finally got home. Dale did the math. He went after Cody."

Mary straightened up and it wasn't to evaluate her progress with the haircut.

Hannah met her gaze.

She sank into one hip, accentuating her many curves in a way that made Hannah realize men, all men, probably desired her sister regardless of her young age. Then her brow knit, which Hannah read as concern, but for Cody or herself, she couldn't be sure.

But what Mary said next surprised Hannah:

"Dale can be sweet. He probably meant to protect you."

Hannah said darkly under her breath, "Yeah, well, he went after the wrong boy…"

Mary hadn't caught what she had just said.

"Did Dale hurt Cody that night?"

Hannah drew in a breath and decided to come out with it. "I really don't know. I never wanted to see Cody again. I ignored him for the last two weeks of school then he graduated. I never crossed paths with him again until now."

"Why were you crying?"

"It was just a bad night."

Mary eyed her as though she might be able to pull the details out if she stared hard enough, but there was no way in hell Hannah would confide more than she already had.

After a moment of Hannah's silence, Mary got the message and eased the scissors to her forehead and began snipping along the other side of her face.

"Dale's drinking and all," she began, working up the nerve, "is that what those locks are about?"

Mary stopped snipping, her face instantly long and drawn. Her eyes went dead. She stared down at Hannah, incidentally causing the tip of the blades to point at Hannah's eye. Too close for comfort.

The question seemed to make Mary recede into a dark corner of her mind.

It reminded her of Candice.

From the front of the house, they heard the front door bang open, slam against the wall, bouncing off the frame, and slam shut again, Dale cursing and tripping and cursing louder, as he entered the shack.

In response, Mary barreled out of the bedroom and down the hallway after him.

Alert, Hannah listened hard, straining to hear over the rapid thuds of her pounding heart. Suddenly, she felt like she was eleven, twelve, and thirteen all over again, a frightened animal hoping the bear wouldn't find her. Terrified of what he might do if he did.

But Mary had it handled.

Dale raised his voice, she raised hers louder, and the crescendo of their argument gave way to murmuring.

Hannah heard the sound of a thud that conjured images in Hannah's mind of Dale dropping onto a chair at the kitchen table. Then a ceramic plate clanked down on the table in front of him, followed by the crack and faint hiss of a beer can opening.

Dale slurred, "Thanks, girl," and then Mary padded up the hallway.

Returning to the bedroom, she closed her door all but an inch, and grumbled an aggravated sigh.

"He drank too much," she softly told Hannah, as she grabbed her scissors from the dresser top. "I always keep a bowl of mashed potatoes for him in the fridge. It'll soak up the alcohol. He'll straighten out."

Hannah didn't want to point out that the beer Mary had just given him might work against that strategy, but the thought vanished from her mind when Mary started laughing and shaking her head to let off some steam.

When her laughter died out, Mary took to fluffing and shaking Hannah's hair to see where it naturally landed then lifted and snipped, lifted and snipped, again and again, as hairs fluttered all around Hannah and settled on the hardwood floor.

"Man, I am good," Mary said, admiring her work. She handed Hannah a mirror and smiled down at her. "You look damn foxy, I'd say."

Hannah almost didn't recognize the woman staring back at her in the mirror. She looked... *pretty*.

Not at all childish or blunt, her new bangs were feathered softly around her eyebrows and the sides hugged her cheekbones in a way that accentuated the lines of her face. The trim flattered her, but also made her feel strangely lost within the beauty that her facial features naturally implied.

The sounds of groaning came through the wall. The bizarre sound quickly surged into a scream—Candice!

Candice's high-pitched wails filled the house.

Mary ordered Hannah, "Stand in the hallway and make sure Dale doesn't try to go into Candice's room."

"Why?"

Hoisting her bedroom window open and swinging a leg out, Mary firmly repeated, "Don't let him down the hallway!"

Then she dropped into the cold night outside, as Candice screamed and thrashed, locked inside her bedroom.

Obeying, Hannah made her way down the hallway and peered at Dale just as he started yelling, "What's going on? Why is she screaming like that?"

Hannah stepped into the kitchen, but her presence didn't prevent Dale from muscling to his feet. How the hell was she supposed to stop him from walking down the hallway to find out what was wrong with Candice?

Suddenly, Mary called out, "Hannah!"

Hannah rounded into the hallway and found her sister standing in the open doorway of Candice's bedroom.

She rushed with Mary into the bedroom. Dale was at her heels. On the bed, Candice was flailing and yelling and gasping for air.

"Wake up, Candice!" Mary said, holding the little girl's arms down so they wouldn't hit the wall, but her feet were still kicking something fierce.

Stunned, Hannah felt immobilized, as Dale tore past her and caught Candice by her ankles.

"Sending her to a psychologist was too much for her!" He growled at Hannah over his shoulder. "She doesn't need to remember what happened to her mother! She needs to forget the whole thing!"

"Candice, baby, wake up. Come on." Mary gently slapped her cheeks to rouse her out of the night terror she was having.

Hannah had never felt more dangerous in all her life. Tears stung her eyes, as she watched them wrangle her youngest sister awake.

When Candice finally calmed and her eyes locked with Mary's, Mary said, "I'll stay in here with her tonight."

Mary settled on the bed beside her younger sister and indicated for Hannah to come over.

As she did, Dale lumbered out of the bedroom, shaking his head. He didn't even look at Hannah as he left, he was so disgusted with her.

Mary asked Hannah, "Want to grab me a tee and boxers? They're in my dresser. Maybe a beer?"

Her voice thin as a thread, Hannah breathed, "Sure."

When she returned with the items, Hannah eased the door so that it was partially closed then handed Mary her sleeping clothes, but Mary took the beer first.

"Has that happened before?" she asked Mary, referring to the night terror.

Mary looked just as furious as Dale had.

"No. It hasn't," she said, as she changed out of her jeans. She pulled her boxers on then changed her top quickly after removing her bra by pulling it through her shirt sleeve. "The good news is that now you can sleep in my room instead of on the sofa." She stared at Hannah then added, "You know where the lock is?"

"Yeah. Where's the key?"

HANNAH HAD NEVER felt so wrong. The conflict inside was pulling her apart at the seams. She had been certain that Judy had worked a miracle with Candice and that their time together had been a ray of hope since Kendra had disappeared. But if seeing Judy had caused Candice to have a night terror; if it had disturbed Candice so greatly that it caused the trauma of that night to emerge as nightmares, then what good was talking to a therapist?

Her crushing sense of shame at being so arrogant as to assume what was best for the investigation would be best for Candice made Hannah want to hide under a rock for the rest of her life.

But a greater sense of responsibility told her that she ought to spend a minute or two with her stepfather, as uneasy as talking with Dale would make her feel.

She rounded the corner at the end of the hallway and found Dale in the living room, monopolizing the sofa. He had one arm hooked around the back of the sofa, and he used his free hand to gulp canned beer, watching the TV that wasn't on.

Hannah dared to take a seat on the nearby wooden chair.

"There's more beer in the fridge," he offered without looking at her. He knocked back a long haul from his can next.

"No thanks." She leaned to the side, pulling her flask from her back pocket to show her bases were covered in that department.

"Just tell me Candice is fine now, please," he asked, and if Hannah wasn't mistaken, it looked as though Dale really cared.

"She is. She's sleeping now."

Hannah studied Dale for a moment while he stared off into space and cracked open a fresh beer that had been resting on the end table beside him. His dusty-blue eyes were dark under a jutting brow and thick hair. His mouth, weathered as it was, had a cowboy's snarl. He was attractive and it wasn't hard to see why Kendra had fallen in love with him, or fallen *in lust* with him, as the case had probably been all those years ago.

Hannah realized his attention was fixated on his own reflection that was staring back at him from the black TV screen.

"I know you don't agree with Candice seeing a psychologist," she ventured to level with him. "But I think it's important." She tried to gauge his reaction, but he didn't have one. "For her and for the investigation to find Kendra."

"Why do you call her Kendra? She's your mother." Beer to mouth, he knocked booze down his throat. Dale still couldn't look at her, or at least that was what his demeanor told her.

"I meant to say, Mom," she offered to show she was capable. "Candice talking with a psychologist is already helping the investigation." She hadn't really answered his question, so she added, "I call Mom *Kendra* because you know her as Kendra. I do that sometimes. Making dinner earlier tonight with Mary, I referred to you as 'Daddy'."

That got him grinning and he finally glanced at her.

"Daddy, huh?"

Her stomach clenched.

"I would rather have your blessing in terms of taking Candice to see a therapist, but make no mistake, I'm planning on continuing to take her just the same."

"I figured that." His grin vanished.

"It's good for her," she argued.

"She has never flipped out like that before," he countered, meeting her gaze in a way that shook her conviction. "Never happened before you came along, before you dragged her off to some shrink, who's probably itching to fill her head with all kinds of fiction. Those people have a perverted agenda."

They had a perverted agenda? That was rich coming from Dale.

"That's not what the therapist is doing," she assured him.

"Are you going to drink that, or is it just a prop?" he asked, referring to the flask she had been holding in her hands.

She had planned to, but the idea of drinking with Dale made her uneasy.

Then it occurred to her, being his drinking buddy could work to her advantage.

Maybe he knew what had happened to Kendra…

So, she showed a little good faith and posed as an ally so he would be inclined to open up about.

Hannah unscrewed the top off her flask and drank.

"I need to ask you," she began, "I found a couple things out about Mom. She had a few arrests for drug possession. You obviously knew about that…"

Dale snatched his beer, leaned forward, planted his elbows on his knees, and hung his head for a beat as though remaining comfortably reclined wouldn't do his answer justice.

"How did you hear about that?"

"I work at a police station."

He angled his eyes up at her, sighed, and leaned back on the couch again, as he scraped his teeth over his lower lip, thinking.

"Your mother decided to go down that road, Hannah."

"Why?"

"I don't know."

"When?" she demanded. "When did she start using drugs?"

"You think she called a family meeting to get our approval?"

"When did you first notice she was using, Dale?"

"I didn't." Again, he sighed, but this time he sounded like a man who knew he had failed his wife. "I found out at the time of her first arrest. I was shocked. Downright blew my mind." He managed a laugh. "You know what I always say?"

"If it can't be fixed with alcohol, then it can't be fixed," I supplied.

He brightened. "You remembered?"

Hannah glared at him. "I remember everything, Dale."

He knew what she was referring to, but he snorted a laugh, unintimidated.

She didn't have it in her to open up that particular can of worms, so she asked, "Why would she start smoking *meth*?"

"I don't know what she was thinking, but I know the result. That drug turned into her new God."

"Did something happen that caused her to believe her old God wouldn't be good enough?"

"I know what you're thinking. You think that she got involved with the wrong sorts and they dragged her off and killed her. Well, you're probably right. I'll be straight with you, girl, because it was really nice of you to take the time out of your fancy life to come on over to our corner of the lake. At first, I was torn up that Kendra disappeared. To this day, I miss her. But I don't give a rat's ass she's gone."

"What?" she breathed.

"The woman who disappeared that night wasn't the same woman I married. You don't understand what she turned into," he went on, perhaps needing her to side with him. "She had turned into a woman with cold eyes and an even colder heart."

A mile long stare came over Dale.

"The girls will get over it," he concluded. "You will, too, not that you have a damn thing to do with this family." He straightened up, gulped his beer, and chased it down with an optimistic statement, "The Lord, he doth work in mysterious ways." He looked bizarrely refreshed when he angled his eyes on her next. "You said you found out a couple things about Kendra, so what's the second?"

Her hand in a box came to mind, but Hannah decided not to tell him that. Instead, she went with, "Nothing," then got to her feet, visions of Mary's bedroom in the forefront of her mind.

She rose from the chair, told him goodnight, and headed for the bedroom.

Dale didn't let her get far.

"Hannah, I'm warning you. Don't tell the girls that there's any hope for their mother being found. There isn't."

CHAPTER TEN

MARY HADN'T SLEPT. Not one wink. She hadn't even properly laid down next to her sister but had leaned against the wall, watching the epic stillness ever since, shadows dripping off of even darker shadows, a sea of secrets all around her.

She had gotten Hannah back. First to Sanbornton and now into their house, it was something. It had been a little evil of her not to give Hannah the keys so she could lock herself in her room. She shouldn't have been such a bitch to her, but it was hard to resist, even harder quelling the resentment that seemed to influence her heart at times. She would do better, she told herself. She would have to.

Candice stirred, letting out a faint murmur, turning on her side, and releasing her in favor of laying her cheek on the cool end of her pillow. When she settled into deeper sleep, Mary grabbed her empty—a slick can that felt cool to the touch thanks to a steady draft that seeped through the windowpane, and climbed out of bed, certain not to shift her weight too abruptly and wake her sister.

She secured the can under the waistband of her boxers then eased the window open. A chilly breeze blew in, damp and carrying the marshy scent of the lake. Swinging her leg over the windowsill, she gradually wriggled out, bare foot pressing onto frost-encrusted grass, prickly until she crushed it flat, her foot meeting with the freezing, soggy earth.

Tugging the window down took three determined heaves, but she managed to shut it.

She started along the house for the other window. Overhead, the moon was waning, but it still offered a hint of light, which kissed the deteriorating wood siding, the window ledge, and the endless acreage at her back.

Goddamn, it was cold out. Her skin had turned to leather, it was so riddled with goose bumps, and her toes were already numb.

She pried the window up a few inches then crammed her palms under, pushed it upwards, tried to be quiet about it so she wouldn't scare the crap out of Hannah.

After hauling herself over the sill, wooden lip digging into her stomach, her hands met the floor and she crawled forward, scraping her length through. When her feet touched down, she steadied herself, placed the empty in a waste bin near her desk, and produced the set of keys she kept tucked under the band of her underpants.

Carrying her desk chair over to the door, Mary used her free hand to flip through her keys until she had the one she wanted. Then she stepped on the chair, slid the key into the lock, and twisted. The dead bolt grinded inside the door frame. She could hear Dale snoring in the living room. Of course, he hadn't put himself to bed. He would be her next stop.

She hadn't asked for this job, but couldn't deny no one was better suited.

When she stepped down, she returned the keys to her underpants then set the chair back where it belonged and glanced at her bed.

Hannah wasn't there.

It took the wind right out of her until she realized the bedding was gone as well and started investigating. Then she caught sight of her comforter poking out from the foot of the bed and her sudden panic subsided.

She eased across her naked mattress and spied Hannah, balled in a nest of blankets between the far side of the bed and the wall.

It amazed her how time changed a person—Hannah, Daddy, *her mother*. Mary had been seven years old when Hannah left, and at the time her older sister hadn't been nearly so bony, face like it'd been carved from marble, hair a wild mane she'd had the pleasure of taming earlier that night.

She didn't recall Hannah favoring sleeping on the floor like a mouse when they were growing up. Back then her sister had had a ray of innocence in her eyes. At eighteen, on the day she walked off and never came back, the innocent glint was gone, replaced by a grim sense of hopelessness she tried to mask with a plastic smile.

Mary had hated her for leaving and a greater part of her still did. It had taken their mother disappearing for her to come back. Dark circumstances. But now she had Hannah home like she always should have. She was pleased. And yet, she didn't trust her. Couldn't. The threat that she could walk out again never left Mary's mind.

A sick feeling came over her staring down at Hannah, love and hatred like a sandbag on her chest. Her stomach felt raw and empty or maybe that was her heart.

Angling over Hannah, Mary leaned in, set her cool cheek against Hannah's to feel her warmth, her softness, and remind herself her sister was just like her, alive and hollow. They needed each other. Didn't Hannah know that yet?

Cheek lightly brushing over cheek, skin on skin, she explored how Hannah felt. Angels' wings came to mind. That's what her sister felt like, feathery and as ethereal as air itself. She studied the arch of Hannah's dark lashes, the curvature of her nose and its fleshy divot below that pulled at her upper lip.

Then Mary whispered, "I'll never let you go."

When she drew back, straightening up, compulsion gripped her. She wouldn't be blindsided. Not again. Not for any reason.

Hannah's overnight bag was resting across from the foot of the bed. She went to it. It pained her to know her sister hadn't dragged her suitcase inside, but kept it in the trunk of her Taurus. She had seen it earlier, had popped the hood, and peeked in. It killed her to know Hannah hadn't embraced being home.

She only wanted an indication of where her sister's head was at, her heart, a little heads up so she could mitigate impending damages.

So, Mary started going through Hannah's belongings. A plastic case of toiletries was on top, which she set quietly on the floor. Next, she found clothes amounting to one outfit by her estimation.

She reminded herself that Hannah had bought a few things to experiment with the advice she had given her. It was encouraging, but not enough. Digging deeper, there were socks, a hairbrush, a toothbrush that should've been in the toiletries case, and then she felt cool metal on her fingertips, but it was knotted up in a bra—a handle, a barrel. She lifted it out and stared at the revolver.

For protection?

Mary would protect her.

She didn't like it one bit.

Then that awful question Hannah had asked her sprang to mind.

Ask Mary.

Her teeth clenched hard, causing her jaw to ache, tension rising with her heart rate, and a fresh wave of hatred rolled through her.

She fit the revolver down the front of her boxers, being sure to angle the barrel under the elastic band of her underpants so it would be sure to stay put, then returned all of Hannah's belongings to her bag.

She couldn't look at her sister as she crossed to the window, and it wasn't just because Hannah was tucked out of view. She eased out and when her feet hit the soggy grass she used the full weight of her body to draw the window down.

Jogging quickly, she rounded to the front of the house and padded across the porch, unlocked the front door, slipped inside where the air was stale and warm, and locked it back up good.

Dale was a heap on the sofa. Nearly two hundred pounds of pure trouble she would never be able to lift so she sat beside him, removed a beer can from his loose grip, and set it on the floor where neither of them would kick it on accident, then took to rousing him. An easy slap or two to his face, a jiggle to his shoulder that turned into a firm shake, pats to his leg.

He was a drunk mess.

Half asleep, he found her waist and groaned, "Come here, girl."

"Let's get you to bed," she suggested, countering his offer, which may or may not have been intended for Kendra. Who knew where he went in his drunk dreams. "Come on." She held his chin and shook firmly, rattling his brains, she hoped. It did the trick. He came to, gave a start when it registered it was Mary. "Don't make this hard on me."

He grinned, tugged on her hair, and asked her for that hug again, which she supplied now that she knew it was her that he needed. But his grip was too tight, like a bear smothering its rival. She wrapped her fingers in his salt-and-pepper hair and twisted so his scalp would burn and he released her, chuckling to himself.

Hooking his arm around her shoulder, she got him to his feet and he was good about not collapsing on her. He used her for balance, and together they slowly walked up the hallway—Dale, one heavy foot after the next, Mary's strides short and soundless, until they turned into his bedroom.

She let him fall to the bed.

She wrestled his boots off. Let them drop to the floor. His feet were dangling off the side of the bed and if he slept on his stomach like that, cheek to mattress, the angle would crook his neck something awful and she would have a whole new mess on her hands come tomorrow so she heaved him over onto his back, grabbed his feet and swung him sideways so he wasn't all cockeyed. His feet were still over the edge. If he woke, he could slide himself up.

As she stared down at him, Kendra surged to the forefront of her mind. Had she loved this man? Had she loved anyone?

Mary was pretty sure she'd known the first time her mother had come home high and twitching with excitement that couldn't be contained. It hadn't been long ago, though it felt like a past life. Mary had been nearing her fourteenth birthday. She had been sitting at the kitchen table, flipping through a party supply catalog and trying to remember how Hannah's fourteenth had gone. It had driven her nuts that she couldn't place it, which made her all the more mad her big sister wouldn't be at her party. Everyone knew Hannah had stolen off to Gilford, but no one made a damned effort to get her home, not really. Kendra should've begged. Dale should've set off, guns blazing for her. No one had the sense of urgency about it that had seemed to consume Mary on a moment-to-moment basis.

That day, Kendra had taken a seat next to her. Her eyes had looked wild, bloodshot and watery and white all around, pupils dilated like she had been living underground for ages. She couldn't stop picking at a hangnail, and she hadn't even noticed when her finger started bleeding. It was like she had been beyond her own body, hovering above it or maybe trapped inside.

With no preamble, she had started talking not to Mary, but *at* her, monologue fragments, which didn't make sense at first. The display had been jarring. The kitchen hadn't felt like her home during her mother's ramblings, hadn't felt like where she had grown up, but more like an eerie clone.

Mary had worked to grasp the thread of just what in the hell Kendra was talking about, but when she did, following the thin twine deep into her mother's mind, Kendra's twisted past came to light. And understanding it had forever changed Mary.

He used to keep me tied up, she had explained, *when I was pregnant with Hannah. I promised myself if I ever got out, I would take her and run far, far away. I didn't get far when I escaped, and baby it took me so long to realize why that was. It didn't matter that I had left the county, changed my name, and disappeared. I had to stare at his face every day once I had Hannah. She's got her father's face, spitting image of him and oh the shame I felt despising her because of it. I know you miss her, but it's for the best that she's gone. I don't know what I'd do if I had to keep looking at that face.*

When Kendra had finally run out of steam telling Mary about things her daughter could barely grasp, Mary had made the mistake of asking a question and the woman's eyes went dark. She had slapped Mary clean across the face.

The memory faded away and Mary realized a cold sweat had broken out across her skin. But she told herself it was because of her efforts getting Dale squared away and nothing more.

Leaving Dale's bedroom, she closed his door and took to fetching a kitchen chair so she could lock him in, safe and sound. She propped the chair under the doorknob. After spending a minute on that task, she listened to the sweet sound of silence.

Everyone was locked up good just how she liked.

Her family.

She reached the front door, slid her feet into her Converses and threw on her jacket before letting herself out. She was sure to lock up then started around the side of the house, thankful she had exercised a shred of self-care to keep her feet dry and shoulders warm. If she got sick everything would turn to hell.

Soon the lake came into view across the yard. Its black surface was glass, the dock motionless. Her sneakers squashed, making funny noises with each step, and because of it she almost hadn't heard a man's boots mashing the soggy earth, as he stalked towards her.

Mary froze.

Who was he?

He was little more than a dark silhouette, coming towards her from the edge of the lake.

He was tall and lean with wiry muscles under his layered clothing and jeans.

She recognized him.

Quickly drawing the gun from her shorts, she aimed the revolver at him, and held her ground.

Mary's racing mind went strangely calm.

Should she fire a warning shot?

No.

Should she order him off her property?

No.

Should she kill him?

He wasn't welcome, and he knew it.

He turned and walked off, hugging the lake, his boots slushing through marsh water.

Soon, he vanished beyond the tree line.

Anxious that he might return, she listened hard, but only heard the wind rustling the treetops.

Anxiety was quickly replaced by fury, and Mary began quaking as though the very core of her soul was erupting.

She aimed the revolver at her left thigh and pulled the trigger.

Before the blast tapered into silence, she threw the gun into the lake.

CHAPTER ELEVEN

TO HANNAH, Sanbornton Mercy had always sounded like a plea, like the whole town had rallied together to beg for mercy, praying to God so that life might get easier. But it never seemed to. For the Coles, life was only getting worse.

The family was at the hospital, gathered around Mary, who had been shot.

Mary looked as Hannah felt—destroyed.

In her hospital bed, Mary lain under woolen blankets. A crocheted Afghan that Candice had brought was draped over her, as well. A few pillows propped her up so that she wouldn't have to crane her neck, and her left leg rested on top of the covers.

White gauze was wrapped around Mary's upper thigh where she had been shot.

Someone had come to the house and shot her.

What Mary had been doing outside, no one knew.

Kendra had been the start of this, but she might not be the end.

Earlier that night, Hannah had heard the gunshot, and they had all run outside when they realized that Mary wasn't in the house.

Now, sitting beside Mary, Hannah was devoured by the likelihood that Kendra's kidnappers had come to the house and attacked Mary.

Black mascara and eyeliner were streaked down Mary's cheeks. Her eyes were puffy. And those surprised looking eyebrows were knit together with stress.

Mary hadn't let go of Hannah's hand since the nurses had invited them in. Dale sat with Candice on a nearby chair. He did what he could to comfort his littlest. He kept offering Candice reassuring smiles that didn't land quite right, while Candice stared wide-eyed at her sister.

"I feel like I'm totally out of it," Mary said groggily, as she squinted through the bright overhead lights.

"They drugged you up, good," said Dale. "I'll grab the nurse if you need more. Don't wait for the pain to come on too strong. We'll get you more painkillers before the sting comes back."

Kendra came to mind.

The door clicked open and a man in a white smock who could only be Mary's doctor stepped through. He poured over her chart without glancing at the family or his patient, as they waited anxiously.

Finally, the doctor addressed Dale, as he slipped Mary's chart into a plastic slot at the foot of her bed.

"Mary was very lucky. The bullet only grazed her leg. She will have a scar, but no significant damage was done. The wound is barely skin deep."

Dale asked, "How long will it take her to recover?"

"I would like to keep her for the night, but she should be able to go home tomorrow."

Hannah's heart started racing when she realized that the bullet shell casing could be somewhere in the backyard or in the nearby woods. Maybe Cody would be able to get a serial number from the shell casing and find out who had bought the bullets... Find out who had shot Mary and find their mother.

Hannah realized she had been spacing out.

"We're going to keep her on antibiotics," the doctor went on. "And I'll write a prescription for painkillers and more antibiotics that she can take at home."

Dale clenched his jaw at that, which told Hannah what was going on inside that head of his. He didn't know how he was going to pay for any of this.

"Thank you," said Hannah, because no one else was going to.

Dale winced, swallowed the bad taste that had formed in his mouth, and offered Mary a reassuring smile.

The doctor asked them if they had any questions, and when they didn't, he excused himself.

"It's going to be a long night," Dale told Candice. "I saw a snack machine up the way."

Candice watched him scoop quarters out of his pocket. He shook the coins in his hand, getting a sense of how much he had, but Hannah was already thumbing through her wallet. She passed a stack of bills over, which he didn't seem to entirely appreciate, but he accepted the cash.

"See if the cafeteria is open," she suggested. "The cafeteria food is better than vending machine Skittles and Ho-Ho's."

"She can have whatever she wants," he told her. "She eats healthy enough when things aren't turned to crap."

Hannah ushered Dale out of the room so her counter-argument wouldn't disturb Mary.

"You have to let Cody go over to the house and find that bullet and shell casing."

He grumbled, eyeing the cash instead of acknowledging her so she looked through the narrow window on the door. Candice was leaning over Mary and tracing her lips with her fingertip. Then the girl smiled and puckered her lips to kiss her. Mary grimaced, making a playful face. It was strange that her sister's trauma hadn't sent Candice into catatonic overwhelm. Quite the contrary. It had made her playful.

Dale agreed. "Fine, have Cody sweep the area if you think he'll find anything that will help the police find the bastard who shot Mary." He counted the cash again, after which he elbowed the door open, and called for Candice to come. She hopped over, using bouncy little skips until she reached the hallway.

"What do you want to eat?" he asked Hannah, surprising her.

"A sandwich if they have any," she told him. "And a cup of coffee would be great."

Candice was already barreling down the hallway, making a game of zigzagging so she could touch each wall as she avoided seams in the tiles. After Dale had started after her, he turned.

"For what it's worth, I'm glad Mary called you. I'm glad you're back."

"Thanks."

Returning to the hospital room, Hannah joined her sister and wrapped her hand around Mary's exposed foot. "You're cold."

She shrugged. "I didn't notice."

She pulled the blankets over her foot in such a way that kept her wounded leg free then sat down on the nearby chair.

"Mary, what happened?" she asked, hoping her sister would talk now that they had privacy. She hadn't said a thing before. "Come on, you've got to tell me while it's fresh in your mind."

Mary didn't answer right away. Finally, she said, "I don't know."

"Yes, you do. Come on, you can tell me."

More silence.

"Did you recognize the man?" When her sister didn't answer, Hannah asked, "What are you afraid of?"

"Are you going to stay?"

"I still have a handful of days off work," she replied.

"So, you're leaving after that?"

Hannah drew in a deep breath. She hadn't thought about how this complication—the fact that Mary had been shot—would affect her return date.

"I can see what I can do. I don't want to go until we find Mom."

"Never mind Mom," she snapped. "Why can't you just stay for good?"

Mary launched into sudden upset. Tears filled her eyes and her mouth quivered.

"You've got to trust me." She took Mary's hand between hers. "One thing at a time. We're all going through a lot right now. I'm here for you."

"But that's worthless if you're just planning on turning around and walking out."

She tried to wrap her head around where Mary was coming from, but was interrupted when she heard a gentle knock at the door.

Cody peered through the window so Hannah quickly opened the door.

"How is she?"

"Drugged up and emotional." Hannah slipped out into the hallway. "She hasn't said anything yet, but I haven't had much time with her."

"Ms. Cole?" The doctor was approaching them. "I wanted to speak with," he glanced at some kind of report, "Dale Cole. Mary's father."

"He's getting some food. You can talk to me."

The doctor eyed Cody with a distinct air of skepticism that appeared to be connected to the badge around his neck.

"He's fine," Hannah assured him. "He's a family friend."

The doctor stepped in and spoke low. "The weapon was fired at Mary at close range."

"How close?" Cody asked.

"The barrel could've been pressed against her skin at an angle," he explained. "We kept her boxer shorts in case the police needed them as evidence. There's a considerable amount of gunpowder on them."

"I'll get someone over here to take them," Cody told him.

"Even though she was shot at an extremely close range, her attacker didn't touch her otherwise, as far as I could tell. She had no defensive wounds, no skin under her fingernails, no signs of attack other than the gunshot wound."

Cody said, "Okay," poised for more information, but the doctor appeared to have said it all. He excused himself and continued down the hallway.

Cody's eyes were on Hannah but she didn't immediately return his gaze. It felt like he was studying her expression, drinking in the totality of her state, which seemed to pain him, worry and urgency and a touch of confusion causing him to grimace.

"How're you holding up?"

"I'm not," she admitted, regretting how strained her voice sounded.

He found her hand, held it, angled his face near hers, stepping in close, and the smell of him, the familiar comfort he provided, was her undoing. Closing her eyes so the tears wouldn't spill, she rested her cheek on his shoulder and let him hold her up. He was good at that. His arms wrapped around her, as he drew her to him.

"Mary had to have seen the shooter," she said, stepping back and wiping her eyes.

"Let's see if she'll tell us."

Cody opened the door for Hannah and they entered the hospital room.

Hannah noticed her sister's reaction to Cody, which was subtle. Mary lifted her head and seemed to glare at him.

"You remember Cody?" she asked Mary.

"How could I forget?" she replied.

"Can you tell him about what happened?" She explained, "He needs to know what you saw, and any details you can remember about the shooter."

As though her tune had changed or as if it would get him out of her room faster, Mary offered up all she could. "It was dark when I was coming around the house and saw a man on our property at the edge of the lake. I think he came from the tree line that curves around the right side of it."

"Good," Hannah whispered, encouragingly.

"He looked about six feet tall."

"Shorter than your dad?" Cody asked to get absolutely clear on the shooter's height.

"No, uh, about the same height, I guess. He's skinnier than Daddy, but not *skinny*. Lean I guess."

Cody was jotting this down, echoing the facts back. "Six foot two, thin build. White?"

"Yeah, he was a white guy."

"Could you guess his age?"

"Young," she said easily. "Not my age. Maybe twenty or younger than twenty-five."

"What did his face look like?"

"I didn't see him," she said quickly. "He never came more than eight yards from me."

Cody glanced at Hannah for what to make of that, but Hannah didn't know.

"Do you remember what he was wearing?" he went on so as not to tip her off that they knew she was lying.

"Boots of some kind I guess. Jeans. He had a jacket on."

In a delayed reaction, Hannah mentioned her sister was on some painkillers, hoping that would explain Mary's confusion.

"I can do this now," Mary insisted. "I don't want to have to deal with this stuff once we're home."

"Sure," he went on. "One last thing, here." Cody pulled a manila file folder from his satchel and extracted a thin stack of 8 x 10 prints. "Do you recognize any of these men as the one who shot you?"

She didn't take the stack of photographs, didn't even look at them.

"I told you, I didn't see his face," she said, impatiently.

Hannah ignored Mary's agitation and pushed, "Give them a look, okay?"

After taking the stack, Mary glanced at the first photograph then the next, flipping each photograph to the back of the stack. She continued in this manner, quickly flipping through the photos but she wasn't genuinely considering each suspect.

When she passed the stack back to Cody, she told him, "None of them look familiar, but like I said, I didn't see the guy's face."

Hannah looked to Cody for guidance then again made excuses for Mary. "She really didn't see his face. I wouldn't rule out any of those men."

He nodded, worked his jaw, and seemed reluctant about returning the photos to his bag as though doing so would admit defeat.

"I just want to forget the whole thing even happened," Mary groaned.

"A word?" Cody got to his feet, thanked Mary and wished her a speedy recovery, then started for the hallway.

"I'll be right back," Hannah told Mary with a smile. "That was good."

She joined Cody outside the hospital room.

"I know you think she's lying," Hannah said after she closed the door securely so Mary wouldn't hear.

"I know she is."

"It'll come back to her."

"Come back? It's already there, she's choosing not to tell me what really happened." It angered him, but he kept a stiff upper lip. "Does she understand that the man who shot her is most definitely the same man who has her mother? Does she get that he came for her or Dale or you and he'll come again?"

"I'll talk to her."

"Please do," he said, exasperated. Then Cody forced himself to breathe a little and shake it off, as he concentrated on what to do next. "I'm going to go down to the ICU," he informed her. "I'll come back up here before I leave."

"What's in the ICU?"

"Mr. Hand in a Box." When Hannah looked horrified, he said, "Sorry."

"That's what you guys are calling him?"

"Not to his face," Cody assured her.

"I'm coming with you."

"Hannah," he sighed. "Maybe you should stay with Mary."

"I'm not asking."

"The guy is..." Cody trailed off, wincing, "hard to look at."

"He probably knows who shot my sister. The shooter is still out there."

"I know that. You have to give me time to do my job."

Hannah held her ground. Cody told her this was a bad idea, but she didn't budge.

They made their way down the hallway just as Dale and Candice were returning. Candice beamed a toothy grin at how many sandwiches she was carrying, while Dale held a cardboard tray full of coffees. If Dale wasn't pleased to see Cody, he didn't show it.

Cody on the other hand couldn't hide the intimidation he felt.

"I'll be right back," Hannah told Dale, but the man didn't pay her any mind and handed her a coffee. "Thanks."

Next, Dale pointed his finger at Cody's chest. "You find the son of a bitch who did this."

"I'm planning on it," said Cody.

It wasn't until Dale and Candice had ventured past them and entered Mary's room that Hannah was struck by Dale's conviction, his passion for Mary's safety. But when it came to Kendra, he didn't show the same conviction.

It worried her.

The Intensive Care Unit on the ground floor was dismal and that was putting it mildly. The tiles, once white in their day, were badly scuffed, chipped, and cracked. The walls were no better, but it was the long row of tarnished windows that allowed anyone passing through to see the dire straits of the patients within the ICU rooms that truly set Hannah's teeth on edge.

She kept close to Cody and tried not to look at a man who was mummified in casts and gauze, leg braced and hanging from what appeared to be a small crane. As they passed, one of his machines beeped like a distress call announcing he was either dying or dead. A nurse rushed through, slamming the door open, and hustled to stabilize him.

"He's in there," Cody told her as they approached two police officers that appeared to be guarding a door up ahead.

Cody exchanged a few words with the cops, who seemed relieved that Cody's arrival meant they would get an impromptu break. Five minutes outside and they would get the second wind they had been craving. One of them laughed heartily at something Cody said and he smiled back.

It jarred her to see Cody in his element like this, being a cop, and sharing cop humor, or commiserating when the dynamic called for it.

He gave the other officer a friendly jab to his shoulder and the two of them set off, leaving Cody to get the door.

There was no mistaking the fact that he wanted to be the first one inside the room so that he could protect Hannah.

The man inside was nothing more than a kid, Hannah realized when she followed Cody into the ICU room.

He didn't have to be in his street clothes and throwing around an attitude for Hannah to see clearly that the guy was young. His left eye was swollen, there were lacerations and contusions on his chin, and he had a plague of bruises across his cheek.

For a kid who looked like he belonged on a basketball court, and not handcuffed to a hospital bed, Hannah had to wonder how the hell he had gotten wrapped up in this.

He pinched his mouth, consolidating his lips into a taut line as though doing so would center him, then assessed the detective with an air of familiarity. It was only after this that he glanced briefly at Hannah.

Perhaps because he had formed ideas about why they were here, the kid was suddenly on the brink of tears, but seemed to focus by squinting at Cody, manning up if such a thing were possible.

"It's time for you to communicate with me," Cody informed the kid, showing very little sympathy. Lifting a notepad out of his satchel and finding a pen, Cody set the pad and pen on the guy's lap. "We know there were three men who took Kendra Cole. What are the names of the other men?"

The kid stared at him. There was clear and present terror in his eyes.

"You'll have nothing to be afraid of if you tell me the names of everyone involved. I'll have them arrested within the hour."

He shuddered out a rocky exhale, shaking his head in refusal.

"You have to give me something," Cody pressed, his tone softening into the territory of pleading.

Maybe it was the late hour or the fact she had been exhausted for days or maybe it was that she was so near the frayed end of her rope that it felt like her entire body was screaming on a cellular level, but Hannah lost it.

Before she realized what she was doing, her hands wrapped around the kid's hospital gown and she started violently shaking him, pounding her fists against his chest.

His head slammed against the headboard of the bed, over and over, as she beat him and shouted, "Where are they? Tell me where they are! I'll kill you myself if you don't tell me, then you won't have a damn thing to be scared of because you'll be dead!"

She didn't care what she was doing or what line she had crossed or that she was peering into the black, bloody hole of his tongue-less mouth.

The only thing standing between her and finding her mother was a feeble little snot-nosed kid who was too stupid to come out with it. And she would be damned if she didn't try to beat him into spilling every last thing he knew.

Impulsively, she grabbed his nose and twisted, but Cody couldn't let her go there. He pulled her off him and stood in front of the kid as a barricade, telling her, "Enough."

He might've said more, but she was breathing too heavily to catch it.

She paced away so she wouldn't have to look at him, either of them, while Cody resumed his inquiry. He pulled the stack of photographs out of his satchel.

But the kid was writing something down.

Cody froze, stunned, which garnered Hannah's attention.

They both watched, as the kid scrawled a sentence on the notepad.

When the kid handed Cody the pad, Hannah rushed to him so that she could read what he had written:

My name is Dalton Gerrity. REMEMBER TO FORGET OR ELSE BE KILLED.

Dalton scrawled another sentence, which read:

Keep that psycho bitch away from me.

The name Dalton Gerrity was as good a place to start as any.

AS OFTEN AS Dale had off-handedly mentioned he had been keeping up with his church attendance, Hannah had not believed him for a second.

She, honest to God, thought Dale had been downright full of it…

Until the day he dragged the whole family there. The same day Mary had been released from Sanbornton Mercy.

"Got to get right with God, girls. We're going to need a damned miracle when that hospital bill comes," he told them, helping Candice into his pickup truck after Mary had slid into the middle seat.

Hannah mentioned her Taurus had airbags among other critical automotive precautions like seatbelts and brake pads that weren't worn thin, but Dale wasn't having it. He said he needed his girls close. He was going to watch them like a hawk from now on.

He climbed in behind the wheel and turned the key to get a jump on the three-to-five attempts it would take to get his truck started.

Hannah had to keep her boot pressed down on the gas, as she followed behind Dale's pickup, as his truck flew down the road in the direction of the Church of God, a place she had promised herself she would never return to.

She didn't have a damn clue what Dale was trying to prove when he sat them in the very first pew, but that's where they were, looking up at the pastor, who was so close Hannah could count the hairs sprouting out of his flared nostrils. She managed to tune him out well enough. She stole glances at Dale, Mary, and Candice whenever the congregation was expected to crack open their hymn books or say, 'Amen,' or one of the other cultish chants that made her stomach clench.

Dale's arm was wrapped around Mary's shoulder, which made the girl lean at an awkward angle into him. It was as though he needed her more than she did him. He clung to her, glancing down the length of her at times, which didn't come across as paternal concern for her comfort. Mary had her left leg crossed over the right, as a means to get away from him, Hannah thought. Or perhaps it was only to showcase her injury. As completely unnecessary as it was, Mary had wrapped an ace bandage over her jeans around her thigh where she had been shot to perhaps draw attention to her hardship.

The last time Hannah had been in this church was on prom night. After Cody had twisted their friendship into something more, they had stolen away into the desolate church and did what everyone was supposed to do on their prom night.

He should never have left her afterwards.

She forced the memory down, knowing it would be a hell of a lot easier to swallow if she had any hope of nipping at her flask. Maybe in the ladies' room after the blowhard behind the podium wrapped it up.

For some reason, her real dad came to mind. Rather than go down that rabbit hole, Hannah explored what might have caused her to think of him. It wasn't an easy leap to make, but she decided the theme between the two notions, being attacked in a dark church and wondering about a man she had never met, was *rescue*. She had needed to be rescued, and wasn't that a father's job, to protect and rescue and keep his daughter safe?

She wasn't sure she had ever met a man like that.

Dale snorted a laugh as though he appreciated the corny joke the pastor had made about sheep and shepherds.

No man was going to rescue Hannah, she decided. That's why Hannah had taken care of herself all these years. And why she would continue to do so.

Bearing that in mind, it would've been a nice touch had she remembered the revolver Cody had given her. Truth be told, she couldn't stand the smell of it, and wouldn't tolerate carrying it on her person.

In fact, she hadn't touched the gun since she had tossed her bag to the corner of Mary's room the other night. But Hannah knew she was going to have to get over herself and start keeping the weapon on her just to be safe. Mary had been shot. Who knew what could happen next?

Dalton Gerrity had been terrified in his ICU bed, and for some incomprehensible reason, Dalton felt as though *not* putting the bad guys behind bars would be his best bet in terms of staying alive. Which begged the question, how big was this thing? Dalton's reluctance to talk, or write as it were, gave Hannah the impression that perhaps there was a hierarchy in place, one so big that Dalton couldn't fathom who might be at the top of it. His refusal to cooperate meant that he would eventually be carted off to jail where he would await his trial should this case ever come to a head, and would undoubtedly get convicted. And yet, in Dalton's eyes, that scenario was the best one. Like he would be *safer* in prison.

It blew Hannah's mind every time she thought about it.

The most mind-boggling aspect, of course, was the fact that they had targeted her mother.

The hand must mean something. It had to be symbolic.

And Dalton's cryptic message, *remember to forget or else be killed* was practically a riddle. Even more puzzling was the fact that the attack on Mary was starting to make a shred of sense with respect to the message that had been dug into the dirt at the abduction scene.

Ask Mary.

What if Mary didn't realize that she actually did know something that these bad guys feared would get out? Maybe they couldn't risk that she would "remember to forget" because she didn't even know that she was playing their game? And maybe they went after her to kill her before she could blab.

As the pastor's hands floated up to the heavens, indicating this charade would soon be over, Hannah prayed Cody had gotten somewhere with the Dalton Gerrity piece.

Suddenly, Dale exclaimed, "Praise the Lord!" and Hannah jumped.

The Service was finally over, thank God!

Hannah stood and realized her butt was asleep.

Dale helped Mary to her feet and hoisted Candice up by her arm. Chuckling, he teased Hannah, "Are you surprised you didn't go up in flames?"

"Are you?" she hotly retorted, as they made their way up the aisle.

"Why don't we all make lunch at the house and eat outside by the lake?" he suggested. "The picnic table is off in the woods somewhere. I'll find the thing. Does that sound nice?"

"Sure." Hannah wracked her brain, trying to recall the food they had in the refrigerator. "You go on ahead then. I'll have to swing by the A&P grocery store."

Hannah stepped outside into the warm sunshine, following after them. Candice was helping Mary limp demonstratively towards a few teenage boys who were standing in a cluster. The girl certainly could milk her moments. As soon as Candice had served her purpose, Mary shoved her away and flirted with the boys, telling them her wild tale of fighting off a mad gunman. The boys looked impressed, but slightly more interested in her chest, as they nodded with astonishment and took turns giving her long, lingering hugs.

Dale worked some cash out of his wallet, which Hannah hadn't noticed until he attempted to give it to her.

"Oh, no really," she said, declining. "I'm staying at the house. I'm not spending nearly what I thought I would at the Super-8, Dale. Let me get the groceries, my treat."

"You sure?"

"Yes, please," she stammered, feeling odd that her heart was warming to him. "Thank you, but really, I've got this."

That was the thing about Dale. Any time he showed his softer side, or revealed that he was capable of being considerate, or showed his vulnerability, she latched on, desperate to believe he had changed and wasn't a monster. As if his hardness, his cold eyes, and flying fists were another person he was trapped inside.

Dale collected the girls and they crossed through the dying grass to the dirt parking lot where he had parked his clunker.

Hannah hung back, marveling at the radiant foliage and the wind rushing through the trees. It caused the sweetest sound.

The congregation thinned out. Most parishioners had found their cars, but some paced slowly, engrossed in spiritual conversations which were so deep, they couldn't look each other in the eye, their gazes instead resting lightly on their feet, the grass, or their watches.

Hannah wondered how many of these people were rapists.

From the dirt parking lot, Cody jogged towards her then slowed up when he caught her eye. Wind blew at him sideways. He wore a blue jacket, a gray sweater beneath, dark jeans and work boots, all of which gave him a more pulled-together appearance than he usually had.

"Are you running off?"

"I have to go to the A&P. Why?"

"Just thought I would catch you."

"About what?" She hoped this was urgent. That would mean that he knew something.

Distracted by the church, he smiled crookedly up at the steeple then met her gaze. "This is our place."

Her stomach clenched at his cluelessness. "I've worked hard to forget."

His smile faded and he searched her eyes. "I forget your parents used to drag you to church."

"And still do, evidently."

He got down to business. "We found the slug as well as the shell casing in the backyard. It was a .38 caliber, but forensics needs more time to trace the ammo, narrow the weapon, etcetera."

"That's great," she said eagerly.

Someone in the parking lot honked, but she ignored it, training her sights on Cody—the intensity behind his green eyes, his crisp jawline that was undeniably attractive, and the way he took care with every word.

"I got a jump on talking to Dalton Gerrity's parents this morning, who are down in Concord."

Another impatient honk bleated from the parking lot and when Hannah looked over, she saw a frustrating monkey-faced woman nudging her bumper towards the back of Hannah's Taurus.

"Oh shoot." She started after the woman. "I'm blocking you! I'm so sorry! I didn't realize."

Hannah shot Cody an apologetic look over her shoulder, then jumped into her car and bucked it forward so the woman could drive out. As she did, the woman leaned on the horn, undoing all that the good Lord had done for her during the Service.

"God bless!" Hannah shouted after her with more than enough sarcasm to compete with the woman's blaring horn.

"This might take longer than a minute," he said when he reached her, which prompted her to check the time on her cell phone.

"Come shopping with me. You can tell me there."

Cody was quick to climb in his truck and pull up behind her, as Hannah drove out of the dusty church parking lot and onto the road.

She knew it was bad, but she found her flask in her purse and drank on the drive over. She reasoned it was necessary, given the church sermon she had just suffered, as well as the dark memories that had formed.

Cody took the parking space next to her at the A&P grocery store, and made himself useful by snagging a stray shopping cart for them to use, which had been left awkwardly in the lane. Its front right wheel shimmied and barely met the asphalt, as he pushed it.

As they strolled through the produce section, Hannah realized that she had no idea what to buy. She needed Mary.

She tried not to panic, and kept an ear out for the good or bad news that Cody had promised to share.

The supermarket was crowded. Cody clipped more than a few heels maneuvering the cart, which garnered him some nasty glares from the other shoppers. But he kept up with Hannah, and only occasionally stared confusedly at her eclectic choices—strawberries, a can of plum tomatoes, microwavable popcorn, *jelly beans*, and a turkey large enough for Thanksgiving.

At times, she doubled back and removed an item in favor of another that made just as little sense. She tried to remember the word 'rhubarb,' but her mind kept offering *rutabaga*. The thing didn't look right, but she bought seven anyway, figuring there had to be a way to cook it.

Mary would know.

"Dalton Gerrity left home a few months back," Cody explained. "His folks couldn't reach him, but they considered that for the best. He had been in and out of rehab. No arrests though."

"Meth?" she whispered so the grumbling old man blocking the chips wouldn't hear.

Cody nodded. "The parents were able to tell me the names of Gerrity's closest friends. Granted, if Dalton had been getting involved with seriously bad people, I doubt he would bring them home to meet Mommy and Daddy, but I got some names that I'm looking into. Marjorie's son being one of them."

"Marjorie? *Gemma's Diner* Marjorie?" she asked, thrown by what a small world it was, or town.

"Yeah. I put in a call to her, but she didn't pick up. I bet she's on her shift so I'll swing by the diner later."

"Did you look into weapons? Did Gerrity have a gun?"

"If he did, it wasn't registered. He certainly doesn't have any medical training to do what was done… removing the hand surgically."

"Right."

"Another name on the list is Blake's cousin-"

"Blake?"

"Marjorie's kid," he clarified then went on. "Blake's cousin, Travis, was on the list. They're both long-time friends with Dalton, according to Dalton's parents, and get this, Travis' folks used to have a place over on Hermit Lake."

Hannah stopped, her blood running cold. "Where?"

"I'm looking into it."

"That's it. That has to be where they're keeping Kendra," she said, excitedly. "Mary saw the guy on foot! That means they're within walking distance!"

"I know, I know, it sounds promising, but it's more complicated than that."

"Did you look into it?"

"I'm in the process of looking into it. I'm going to check it out myself. According to the records that I was able to get my hands on, the house had a fire a good decade back. The family got the insurance money, but never rebuilt. They leveled the house instead. It's not there."

"But you haven't gone there yet," she stated.

"I sent a team over. And I'll take a look around myself."

Hannah exhaled, releasing some built-up tension. "Good. This is good. I have a good feeling about this."

"Good." He shot her an easy smile. "Better watch those hands, though."

"Huh?"

"Lethal weapons," he teased.

"He's lucky I didn't kill him," she said darkly. "You think I don't have it in me?"

He swallowed the lump that had formed in his throat. "I'm sure you do."

"Oh, shut up."

"I'm terrified of you," he teased.

She smiled and realized this was the first time she had laughed in days. "I'm going to take that as a compliment."

"You should." He eyed their cart. "I've got to tell you, I'm not seeing a meal here."

She cringed, knowing how right he was. "I'm supposed to make lunch. Can you fix it?"

"I'm not a miracle worker."

"You should come," she said, inviting him.

"I'm sure Dale would love that."

"Dale is coming around. Plus, we have to bring Candice to Judy's in a few hours anyway. Remember, Judy said she would squeeze Candice in today? And you should eat beforehand."

He ran his fingers through his hair, getting on board with the idea, then assessed the contents of her shopping cart. "I feel like we should just get a new cart and start over."

DALE BALKED when Cody arrived with Hannah, but Dale didn't really have a leg to stand on since Hannah had come bearing ingredients that only Cody knew how to turn into lunch.

Mary kept Dale occupied with beers. They were sitting together at an old picnic table that Dale had dragged out of the woods, while Candice wandered off to her usual spot and sat on the end of the dock.

Cody proved to be quite skilled in the kitchen. Under his directive, Hannah managed to put potato salad together, which didn't at all appear like a culinary disaster. Cody made grinders better than any deli she had ever set foot in. He also threw together Caesar salad and timed it all in the span of baking a blackberry pie.

In the kitchen, he found ways to stand near her and get her laughing, but he never seemed intrusive, and soon it was Hannah who intentionally brushed by him, indicating she was perhaps ready to admit what was in her heart.

By the time they carried lunch in all its splendor out to the picnic table, the tangerine sun was lighting the sky on fire. The lake looked beautiful, offering a breathtaking view despite the chilly temperature.

Mary handed out the grinders after placing them on paper plates, as Dale watched birds swoop over the lake, and drank his beer at intervals.

"Candice!" Mary called out when her sister hadn't come for her sandwich.

Hannah told Mary that she would bring Candice's sandwich over.

"Give me a minute," she said to Cody, giving his arm a little squeeze. She knew he wouldn't want to be alone with Dale for long, and curiously, Mary must have sensed it as well, because she rounded the table and took up where Hannah had left off, though Hannah hadn't gone two steps.

"Sit next to me," Mary smiled up at Cody, pressing her chest into his side and exaggerating her limp.

Dale glared at Cody.

"Why don't you all sit," Hannah suggested, as she walked off towards the dock with Candice's grinder.

She heard Cody let out a nervous laugh and Mary giggled like they were sharing an intimate moment, then Dale cleared his throat and everyone fell silent.

When Hannah looked over her shoulder at them, Mary had positioned herself up close to Dale, which relieved Hannah until she processed their body language. It was *familiar*, Dale's arm wrapped along her back, hand hooked around her hip, giving her pats, as he knocked back his beer.

Witnessing the intimacy of their exchange had Hannah's stomach knotted up good by the time she sat beside Candice.

"Here," she said, passing the plate to her youngest half-sister.

Candice took the plate, but seemed more interested in the water, slapping the sole of her boot a few taps against its surface and watching the thick ripples band outward.

"How are you doing?" she asked her. "If you're scared, that's understandable."

Candice looked up at her, her blue eyes reflecting the lake and trees with eerie clarity.

"That's why we're bringing you to see Judy again after lunch, so you can talk about it. Does that sound good?"

She stared, not vacantly but as if piercing through Hannah's pretense and peering into the most secret corners of her mind.

"What's wrong, Candice? You can tell me. You can tell me anything."

She held her gaze a moment longer then glanced out across the water just as Mary cackled a loud laugh from the picnic table.

Hannah looked over her shoulder at Mary who was tossing her head forward, bleached blond hair landing in potato salad, her arm draped around Dale, the presumed source of hilarity. Cody looked lost.

"We're going to find Mom, Candice. You have to believe that."

Then, thin as a thread, perhaps meant only for herself, Candice said, "Mary *is* Mom."

Hannah stared at her.

The child had to be confused. Or was she intuitive? Hannah glanced back at the picnic table, but Mary was getting to her feet, collecting paper plates, while Dale looked after her, those hungry eyes of his. He couldn't help himself. Maybe that's what the girl was picking up on.

"Mary's not Mom, honey," she said, then thought better of it. "Why do you think that?"

But Candice didn't respond. Mentally, she was somewhere out on the water.

Hannah gazed out as well, inspired to venture far away from this family if only in her mind, too.

Funny how a person could avoid revelations.

Soon Hannah started fantasizing about letting herself fall into the lake, submerging head to toe, feeling its icy water burn all over her skin, surging through the surface, reborn.

When she came back to her senses, Candice had eaten the better part of her grinder.

"Let's get you to Judy's. We don't want to be late."

❄

DRESSED LIKE A used car salesman and acting twice as pushy, Judy ushered Hannah and Cody into her office and closed the door.

Judy was bristling with energy.

When Hannah and Cody got situated on the sofa, Judy leaned on the edge of her desk and eyed Hannah.

"Has Candice been talking at home?" she asked eagerly.

"Not really."

Hannah glanced at the girl, who was stacking blocks as though she had regressed by at least eight years in Judy's care.

"Hmm," she pondered, eyes widening.

"Did she talk with you?" Hannah asked, hopeful.

"She did."

Hannah wondered why the woman wouldn't get on with it. "And?"

"I'm stumped that she hasn't opened up at home," she said, detouring from whatever discovery had had her chomping at the bit earlier. Judy shrugged and said, "Then again, if she's not nurtured at home..."

Hannah tried not to take offense to that, but it stung given that she had been home for days and was therefore partially responsible.

"What I'm about to tell you," she went on, "it's very important you don't push her on this or try to pull the details out of her. I've only scratched the surface with Candice and I need time."

When Hannah seemed in agreement, Judy got down to it.

"Candice told me that she has seen her mother's abductors in the house before."

"When? Who else was home? Did she say that Mary saw them, too?" Hannah started rattling off questions, Judy's instructions having flown from her head. "Did she say what they looked like?"

Judy narrowed her gaze on her and gave Hannah a moment to remove her foot from her mouth.

"I can work towards getting Candice to open up about that when I see her next," Judy offered.

"Great. Let's get her in tomorrow."

"I suggest a day off," she countered. "Give her time to process what occurred today. I can see her the day after next."

"Fine," said Hannah, urgently locking in the appointment. "How's she doing in terms of Mary?"

"I beg your pardon?"

"Mary, her sister. She got shot the other night."

Judy looked shocked. "Oh my God. Is she alright?"

"All things considered, yes," she replied. "It only grazed her." Hannah caught the peculiarity. "Candice didn't mention it at all?"

"No, Candice seemed in good spirits and felt relaxed and comfortable enough to share with me what she did."

Hannah and Cody touched eyes, and he seemed to find it equally puzzling.

"Is there anything else we should know?" he asked. "Did anything else come up?"

Judy frowned and shook her head. "Shall we set that appointment?"

Hannah made arrangements with her, while Cody hung back. Then she collected Candice from the blocks and escorted her through the door, overhearing Judy ask Cody about the billing. His reply was too quiet to hear.

Cody hadn't been paying the therapist bills, had he?

In the lobby, Hannah helped Candice get into her coat and zipped it up, and soon Cody came out from the office, rounded the receptionist's desk, and joined them.

"So, when should I expect a bill?" she asked Cody.

Like a deer in headlights, he froze.

"I've obviously got this," she said.

"It's fine. My department is paying for it." He motioned for the door, but she wouldn't let him brush over this so easily.

"No, they're not. That's not how it works. I know how it works, remember? I work at a police station for a living." She studied him. "Why are you paying for Candice's therapy?"

"Because it was my idea and I can afford it."

"I can swing it, Cody. I don't need you to step in like this."

"You're dealing with enough," he told her, keeping his tone low for Candice's benefit.

She considered it then shook her head. "No, I'm sorry. It makes me really uncomfortable."

He turned pink then beat red. "Then you're really not going to like the other thing I did."

"What did you do, Cody?"

"With Mary in the hospital-"

"You didn't-"

"And Dale hating my guts. I just wanted to help-"

"You did not pay that hospital bill!"

"I have savings and-"

"I can't believe you. That's insane. It had to have been thousands."

"Hannah." He swallowed hard, composing himself. "I hate it that we lost touch. I hate it that it was my fault. I can't stand all the crap you're going through right now. I know what it feels like not to be able to do a damn thing while things fall apart all around you. I paid the hospital. It's done. I'm paying Judy, so don't fight me, please."

And that's when the dam inside Hannah broke.

She kissed him, as the wall she had built to keep him out of her heart came crashing down.

His lips were warm and his breath was cool and the smell of him felt more like home than any place she had ever lived.

Later that night, when she collected her bag from Mary's bedroom and tucked herself into the bathroom at the shack, Hannah searched through her bag, trying to find the gun that Cody had given her.

But it wasn't there.

Her revolver was missing.

CHAPTER TWELVE

DALE HAD BEEN stewing for days. It was bad enough Hannah had let that sniveling son of a bitch into her life after he had reduced her to a ball of tears, but he thought he could just waltz in here, pay off Mary's medical bill like he was the second coming of Christ, and expect Dale to bow down, kiss his feet, and be grateful? Dale knocked back the warm dregs of his Coors, as scenarios of what he'd like to do to that man wormed their way through his mind.

Candice's TV show had him distracted, though, and the five beers he had consumed to take the edge off had made his ideas a tad slippery. Following the mental momentum of catchy comebacks and solid right hooks was more exertion than inspiration. A laugh track blared from the TV set underscoring Charlie Sheen's particular brand of degradation against his duck-face brother. Dale located the remote between the sofa cushions and hit the mute button, which sent the girls into an uproar.

"We're listening to that!" Mary balked, hot on the heels of Candice's complaining whines.

Defeated, he pressed unmute so they could listen to their show while they did whatever the hell they were doing over there in the kitchen. Giant oven mitts concealed Candice's hands and Mary had done the girl's hair up in a high bun so strands wouldn't fall into the—oatmeal? Oatmeal cookies? Smelled like oatmeal, but he couldn't come up with any other meal that called for oats.

The shower had been running for a good long while.

"Anyone tell your sister to make it quick in there? Hot water doesn't grow on trees!"

Mary wiped flour from her hands onto the apron she wore and started up the hall to address his gripe.

"Grab a fresh one for me on your way back?"

Candice hopped over, dainty puffs of flour billowing out as she clapped her mitts along the way. She sat and a cloud of it kicked up around her.

"Hey, girl." He shook his empty can at her and she tossed her mitts, took it, crushed it on the floor with her Keds so the thing would curve around her shoe then she took to hobbling around like an invalid. It wasn't even in the ballpark of what he had meant. "Why don't you limp into the kitchen and bring a beer back for Daddy?"

She worked her way over, rising and pattering down in a strange rhythm that resembled her sister's new gait. When she returned she had the remainder of his six-pack—two cold ones dangling from plastic rings. He tried to free one.

"Hold it firm, now."

She flexed her arm, trying hard, and he jerked a can loose.

As he cracked the can open, she plopped down and crossed her legs, beer droplets rattling around in that can on her foot. The sofa had another stain coming to it.

"What do you make of all this?"

She stared at her show, the humor in Sheen's sexual prowess lost on her.

Finally, the shower dried up and he momentarily wondered what the hell had taken so long. Maybe Mary had been spying on Hannah. Had she jumped in, joined her sister?

Then he glanced at Candice, telling her, "You need to loosen up, take a load off. Forget the past maybe." She didn't glance over, but didn't recoil, which he took as an invitation. "Ever sneak one of Daddy's sodas?"

"No," she said.

He shifted, inched in on her close enough to smell her hair through the dull scent of flour dusted across her cheek, and edged his beer towards her leg.

"A person has two choices in this world: to remember or to forget. You know how the pastor was going on about forgiveness? You hear him? I'm going to tell you a secret." He leaned in close, the cool tip of his nose meeting her fine blond hair. "You don't have to forgive if you can forget." He shoved his beer at her, pressed it firm to her flat chest which would one day blossom like her sister's. "Give it a try."

Candice took the beer, staring daggers at him, then turned it on its head and let it trickle like piss onto the wooden floor.

"Hey now!" He snatched it back. "Christ girl, don't waste it!"

"Damn, Candice!" Mary shrieked, charging down the hallway. "Can't you smell that?"

Dale eased off when Mary rounded the corner and yanked the oven door down, thin trails of smoke twisting out. She fought them fanning and cursing then announced the cookies would pull through.

"Smells good," he called out.

"Ha ha, very funny," She scraped cookies off the tray, checking their undersides, tossing the bad ones to the trash bin.

"Is that what's for dessert?"

"It was supposed to be."

"Where the hell's your sister?"

"She's not in the shower anymore." Mary had ways of dismissing him that so greatly reminded him of Kendra that at times he feared this wouldn't work. However, she redeemed herself by adding, "She's getting dolled up in my room."

"What the hell for?" Cody McAlister came to mind even before Mary said his name. Dale worked his jaw at that, drank his beer, and envied Charlie Sheen, who was reeling in an empty-headed model with a body not unlike Mary's. "He's not going to spend time here, is he?"

"You still have it in for him?" Mary approached with a plate of cookies and set it on a line of milk crates they were pretending was a coffee table.

Then Candice gazed up at him with her tight, blue eyes, and said, "Forget, right?"

Out of the mouths of babes.

"Are you saying I should take my own advice?" he asked Candice.

"Shut it, Candice," she snapped, forcing a cookie on her.

Candice crammed it in her mouth, while Dale rode the sudden wave of Mary's wrath.

"And don't worry," Mary went on, returning to his comment. "He's taking her out."

Good, he thought to himself. It had been harder and harder to slip away with Hannah here. Tonight would be the night.

Having let go of her piss-poor mood, Mary worked her wide hips between him and the arm of the sofa, breaking a cookie all the while and tossing chunks into her pretty little mouth.

"Pass it here," she ordered, her eyes on the last can.

He obeyed, but cracked it open for her first, and Mary washed her cookie down with it.

"I hate this jerk," she commented, nodding towards the TV. Then she softened up, leaned forward so she could eye her sister. "Hey." When she had Candice's attention, she said, "Sorry I snapped at you. It's good you're talking."

It didn't take much for Candice to beam that big, toothy grin of hers.

"I ran out of painkillers," she went on. "Guess I'm not very pleasant to be around."

"Sure you are." He pulled Mary's head over so he could plant a kiss on her temple and held his lips firm to her for a good long while, then thrust her back, mussing her hair so she'd get to jiggling, palm smoothing down the ratty tuft he had created.

"I'm going to have a scar," she bitched, giving up fussing over her hair to flick crumbs off her mountainous chest.

Dale watched every second of it.

At the risk of angering her, he commented, "It's not like you to leave the house without your derringer pistol."

Mary stiffened. She uncrossed then re-crossed her legs, hauled on her beer.

"I'm not trying to stir anything up," he went on since she hadn't wailed on him, which meant the part of her that wasn't freshly pissed off was listening. "But you can't be in the wrong place at the wrong time. Not now."

"Yeah," she grumbled.

Candice was watching them, more entertained than if they were Abbott and Costello, though he admitted the reference was so before her time it couldn't be accurate.

Hannah emerged from down the hall and stepped around their column of boxes. Christ, she was a bony thing, but her hair looked big and her loose sweater did a decent job of hiding her undesirable lack of curves.

Shooting her a crooked smile, Mary asked when they could expect her home, but before her sister could answer, she followed up with, "Maybe we shouldn't expect you?"

"I'll be back eventually," she stammered, her smile faltering. "Maybe midnight. That's not too late, is it?"

"Take your time." Mary flashed her a knowing grin, getting a bit dark about it. "It's always better when you take your time. Cody's good for that, right?"

Dale twitched under his jeans. He didn't mind when Mary talked like that, didn't mind at all. Hannah, on the other hand, seemed to. Her cheeks flushed to deflect and she hunted around for something important in her purse. Oh, it was her car keys.

When headlights cut through the room and he heard a horn bleat, Dale had to stifle his chuckle at the fact she wouldn't need her keys after all and the look on her face told him she knew he knew as much. Man, it was fun watching Hannah squirm.

"See you all later." She crossed on through and mumbled, "Excuse me," when she momentarily blocked the idiot box. "Don't forget to lock up."

"I never forget," said Mary. "Have a great night."

Enthusiastically, Candice shouted, "Bye, Hannah!" which gave her sister pause at the door.

"Thank you, Candice." Hannah's eyes were wide, her smile genuine. Then she left them, closing the door quietly.

"I can't get used to having her here," Dale said.

"Well, get used to it. She's staying."

"Indefinitely?" he asked, astonished he hadn't been consulted.

Mary clouded up as though he was prying. Abruptly, she rose and stalked off, calling for Candice to come on, as the next TV program started up, more laugh tracks. This time the show highlighted the humor of a poor family the network expected people like Dale to identify with. He didn't. Candice padded off and he hit the mute button, claiming a moment of peace and quiet.

Mary was getting out of hand.

It was one thing to replace Kendra. It was quite another to become her.

Problems like this wouldn't solve themselves.

When he heard his girls murmuring and giggling through the walls, he muscled off the sofa and gave his weapon a quick check, pulling it from the waistband at the small of his back and releasing the clip. Fully loaded, he confirmed, as he slapped it up inside his .45 caliber SIG, a semi-automatic pistol that had served him time and again.

He returned the gun to his pants, laced up his boots when he reached the door, and grabbed his coat, a weathered leather garment as rugged as he was. Damned if they didn't make them like they used to. Being mindful not to rouse the girls, he eased the door open and stepped out into the cold, dark night.

Wind whipped at him, burning his cheeks and knuckles as he locked the girls in.

The chilly air seeped down the back of his collar, and down his spine, giving him a bad feeling about the night, as he stalked across the porch then the yard, veering right so he could hook around the lake, its marshy lip, and disappear into the trees.

CHAPTER THIRTEEN

BLAKE HAD BEEN dreaming about the girl from the shack when he started to regain consciousness.

Mary.

During summers past, he had seen her run along her dock—long legs, toned and sturdy with each stride, water dripping down her pale skin, rolling along her chest, between her breasts, streaking translucently down her thighs, so much skin and so little bikini. The thing had barely covered her, two bunched up triangles over her breasts which bounced and swayed wildly like they were dying for his hands to contain them, squeeze them firm and press them together in a nice massage he knew she would like. There had been a puddle of lake water at her crotch, weighing that thin bikini bottom down, loose and trashy, but so damn perfect. When she had reached the end, she leapt off the dock, splaying her legs, raising her arms, and crying out. It had been crystal clear to him how he would fit inside her with her all spread like that, wet and free.

That's what his dream had been about, Mary frozen in time, mid-air, magical, him yanking her lake-drenched bottom down, thrusting in, holding her tight, and helping those long legs to wrap good around his waist. With his teeth, he had freed her breasts, peeling her top aside.

He had dreamt about the little noises she would make and the louder ones, breathy in his ear, moans, gasps, and sighs of sweet release like her body was begging for more and thanking him at the same time.

But when he came to, rubbing alcohol stinging his nostrils and the scent of mothballs irritating his throat, he knew his infatuation with the girl had gotten him killed.

He just wasn't dead yet.

He should've never gone over to her shack.

That's what this was about, wasn't it? The gunshot?

Blake lifted his chin, angling to see through the bottom edge of the blindfold that was wrapped around his eyes. His wrists burned, cable ties digging deep into the flesh. He realized his fingers were sticky. Blood. Yeah, those cable ties were braced tight enough.

Wherever he was, it was quiet. Too quiet.

He didn't recognize the chair beneath him, the particular brand of silence all around him, the smells. He couldn't be in the cellar. A sinking feeling came over him. This must have been where they had taken Dalton. People didn't wander off for no reason. His friend had disappeared.

Blake hated that they had gotten dirt on him. If they were a *they*. He didn't know, hadn't met them or him, or whoever the hell was at the top of this twisted pyramid.

He only knew two things—he would go to prison if he didn't do as he was told, and he wanted nothing more than to sexually bang Mary Cole's brains out. In a karmic way, he figured the two might have a prayer of being connected, suffering followed by salvation. That kind of thing.

But if he thought he'd been suffering before, now he understood he had been very, very wrong.

The real suffering was about to begin.

He heard a tap across the room, rubber soles meeting cement that set his heart pounding.

He wasn't alone.

Footsteps advanced on him and he whined in protest and tried to get his chair to hop backwards, but soon realized there was a wall behind him.

The next thing he knew cold steel was pressing across his throat. He let out a squeal then told himself not to move, not even swallow. He hadn't been cut yet and he would prefer to keep it that way.

The voice he heard was digital and reminded him of bad guys making ransom phone calls to politicians in poorly plotted movies.

"She wouldn't have shot herself if you hadn't gone there," said the voice.

"Shot herself? That's what that was? Is she dead?"

"No."

The man shifted and paced away, telling him, "But it weakens the message."

"It'll never happen again."

The man paused, his footsteps vanishing. "No, it won't."

Blake was anything but reassured.

When the man returned, he pulled Blake's blindfold down and at first Blake tried to fight this, knowing if he saw the man's face, it would mean he would surely be killed.

But the man was covered head to toe in black. A black mask covered his face, head, stretched down his neck and melted into the black shirt he wore. His hands were gloved, black leather stretched taut around each finger. There was some kind of box where his mouth should be, had to be the mechanism scrambling his voice.

The only part of him Blake could see were his eyes, but the room was too dim to reveal their color. They just looked black as the devil.

"Who are you?"

The black eyes stared down at him.

"How did you get those photos?"

Nothing. Not even a blink.

"Come on!" Blake yelled, releasing a stream of tears, because he could no longer deny where this was headed. "You blackmailed me into doing it and I did. Every step of the way, I did what you told me. Why am I here?"

"You're part of the message."

"Where's Dalton? What did you do to him?"

The man lifted his gloved hand to silence Blake, who collapsed, head hanging as he sobbed.

"Dalton served his purpose and I released him."

Blake calmed at that, faith washing over him, his chest growing warm. "You did?"

"I'm releasing you as well."

"You are?"

"You've done a very good job."

"What about Travis?" he demanded. "When are you going to let him go?"

"Soon."

"What is your message?" he asked. "Why did you make us do all this?"

An eerie digital laugh came through the box. The sounds were mixed with static and mechanical tones. Then the man walked away and rolled a steel tray over. On it, two human ears lain on a crisp, white cloth.

Blake retched at the sight. A thin trail of bile came up his throat, splattering to his jeans, until it turned into a string of saliva.

"God, why are you butchering her?"

"A mother's job is extremely important," he told him.

Blake thought there'd be more. There wasn't.

The guy was a maniac, out of his mind.

Gingerly, he set a cardboard box on the cement at Blake's feet. In it was a tangle of shredded packing paper. He then lifted the white cloth by its edges, holding it taut so the ears wouldn't fall in on each other, as he lowered them down into the box.

"What are you going to make me do?" Blake was terrified. "Frame me?"

"You're nothing more than a victim."

It scared the crap out of Blake.

Then the man grabbed his face, cool leather clamping his cheeks together. He lifted the knife and pressed the blade between Blake's lips, which he quickly bared back to avoid being sliced. The man tapped the point of the knife against Blake's tooth, used it to pry his teeth apart, as Blake whimpered, tears streaming down his cheeks.

"I want you to understand why you were chosen." The man had Blake's mouth open wide. He grazed the blade along the length of his tongue, as he recoiled. "You played a role in destroying her. And you, too, must be destroyed."

As the man began slicing through Blake's tongue, causing him to shriek, Blake thought of his mother and how he wished for nothing more than to be at home, stomping through her azaleas and driving her nuts.

The most precious things in this world weren't realized until the darkest despair claimed you.

"Remember to forget," the man told him, "or else I will find you, and you will be killed."

CHAPTER FOURTEEN

CODY KEPT HIS eye on Hannah, as she stepped carefully where his flashlight beam indicated.

"Are your shoes okay?"

"I could've used a heads up," she admitted, as she worked her high heel boot over a fallen log that was slick with marsh dew. "When you said *dinner,* I didn't think dessert would be a night stroll through the marsh."

"Yeah, sorry about that."

He trailed the beam ahead for her, tracing a straight path over a soggy mess of twigs and pinecones in order to help her to make her way through to where he stood between the trunk of an old maple and the edge of the marsh that spanned a good eight yards before it bottomed out into the depths of Hermit Lake.

Wind was whipping off the water, carrying the damp scent of the woods, as he studied her—her hair blowing back, gusts toying with her jacket, causing her to squint in concentration at balancing in her heels. He liked her jeans even though they looked too young for her, like a second skin like how the kids were wearing them these days. And her fingerless gloves were cooler than her usual fair. He figured Mary was rubbing off on her. He knew that was what her eyeliner was all about, some strange stab at bonding. Hannah was sweet like that.

He heard an owl overhead, two staccato hoots followed by a sustained one, which told him it was likely a Great Horned. It only added to the creepiness of the setting. Spindly clouds wisped across the moon beyond the dark canopy of leaves above them. Somewhere a bullfrog croaked. Coming here in daylight would've been a far smarter plan, but his team hadn't found anything. Cody knew he could do better after hours.

Hannah reached him, punctuating her accomplishment with a sharp sigh.

"Now that we're at the marsh we can head north," he explained, aiming his flashlight at her chest so he wouldn't blind her. The light bounced off her chin and cheeks, and gently illuminated her features. "Did you do something to your hair?"

She narrowed her eyes at him. "Ah, yeah, days ago and you've seen me many times since."

"You cut it?" he asked.

"Mary did. Trimmed my bangs."

"Yeah, that's it. It looks pretty." Cody locked eyes with her, hoping the compliment might warrant him another kiss, but she only grinned and shook her head. "Did you catch your breath?"

"Yeah."

She grasped hold of his arm and they started up the marsh. Cody was careful to keep her on dryer land, sacrificing his boots for hers. They had to hug the tree line running parallel to the lake, though, which put them at a disadvantage in terms of keeping completely dry.

As they made their way, Cody told her, "I spoke to Marjorie. Her son, Blake, who was on that list, remember?"

"Yes." Hannah was choosing her steps carefully.

"Her son, Blake hasn't been home in over a month. So, where things stand, everyone from Dalton's list was accounted for except the cousins, Blake and Travis."

"How do we track them down?"

"I'm working on it. Marjorie signed some papers giving me access to look into Blake's debit card history. They share a bank account, which could tell us something."

Hannah fell silent where she should've been demanding to know the logistics, the details of his plan, what else he was going to do. He wondered if she felt okay.

As if sensing he'd taken notice, she said, "I shouldn't have told my family we had a name."

"You told them?"

"It seemed promising. I don't know. I wanted to give them some hope. I don't know why I thought Dalton might spill his guts. I thought he would come around."

"Don't beat yourself up." Cody stole glances at her as they edged around the giant trunk of an oak tree. She looked downtrodden. When they cleared it, he offered, "We're getting close, Hannah."

"To the site, or finding my mother?"

He laughed a little. Something about her candor had a way of warming him. "Both."

They took the next few minutes in silence, all the while Cody was debating with himself. He didn't want to have to tell her the utterly bizarre news, but keeping secrets wasn't their way now.

"Look, in regards to Candice confiding in Judy that Kendra's abductors had been at the house..." He trailed off.

"What?" she asked.

"The slug and shell we found in the yard? It's a match to my .38 Special. The one I gave you."

Hannah stopped walking and stared at him.

"I should've told you."

"Tell me now," he said, eager and fearful.

"I hadn't touched it since you gave it to me. The other night I couldn't find it."

Cody's stomach churned, but he tried not to overreact. "Where were you keeping it?"

"In my bag."

"Where?"

"Near me always. Um, in Mary's room when I slept in there. In the living room when I was on the sofa."

"But you left it in the house unattended?" He hadn't meant to sound alarmed, but that's what he was, and then some.

"Don't be mad at me, please!" She hid her eyes with her hand then lowered it. "I'm just sick over this. Whoever is doing this is coming and going as they please? Into our home? They went through my bag? What if they're trying to pin the shooting on you? Or on me?"

"I'm not so worried about that," he said, urging her onward. "It's just up ahead."

They walked on then reached an area where the trees were cleared away. Thick overgrowth took its place, forming twenty square yards of bushes and fallen logs. Cody led her through it and stopped when they reached its center.

"This is where the house was," he said, pointing the flashlight along the brush and revealing the remnants of an old house's foundation.

"What are we looking for?" she asked, as she slowly stalked along the perimeter.

"Anything we can find." Cody worked his way in the opposite direction, but stopped when he saw Hannah holding her head in her hands.

"Look," he said, taking her hands. Clouds passed over the moon and her face fell into shadow then brightened. "I didn't want to have to say this before, but I'm looking at Dale."

"What?"

"I know you think he's nothing more than erratic and stupid and a drunk, but I think he's much smarter than that."

"There's no way, Cody-"

"Just hear me out. He had reasons to hate Kendra. He had reasons to hate the kids she was smoking drugs with-"

"And you think he roped them into harming her like that?"

"He's harming *them* too."

"You think he's that twisted?" Hannah looked ill. "He cut off her hand, is that what you think?"

Cody stared at her hard. "Candice isn't talking. Not really. Not to her family. She's dropped bits and pieces for Judy and Judy alone. Something's not right about that. Think about it."

He could see her mind was reeling.

"If she's living with the person who's behind this, how could she talk? She's probably scared to death."

"But-"

"Dale wasn't at home the night Kendra was taken. Candice ran home to Mary. You said it yourself, Mary needed you home because Dale was never around. What did Mary find out that caused him to shoot her?"

"He didn't shoot her."

"Do you know that or did he say that?" he challenged.

Hannah seemed to have to dip into her memory to find out.

"Ah, I woke up to the shot. I was in Mary's room. I went running through the house. The front door was open." As if she were realizing it then and there. "Dale was already in the backyard."

Decisively, he informed her, "You're not staying in that house."

Startled by his tone, Hannah stepped back, boot sinking into mud. "You think I'm going to leave the girls there with him?"

He eased back, rethinking things.

Hannah started shaking her head. "We know Mary lied about how close the shooter was, but if it had been Dale, you think she wouldn't tell me? Cody, she was clinging onto me for dear life in that hospital. All she wants is for me to stay."

"I'm not trying to undermine your perspective, but you've got to understand how domestic violence works. You don't know what happened to those girls the second you left when you were eighteen. You just don't. Victims can feel worthless. They start to believe everything their abuser says. Mary and Candice, a seven-year old? A four-year old? They only knew what their parents taught them. If their dad raises them to think he could kill them at any time, and they can't leave, then they're going to start to live by those rules. They accept them. That's how they survive. Think about it. Kendra turned to drugs. She started going off on her own. Dale picked up on it. She was breaking the sick, abusive world he created. Maybe she could influence the girls to stray. So, he gets rid of her."

Hannah drew in a deep breath, processing his point.

"I'm going to be sick."

Cody did her the courtesy of keeping his flashlight off her when Hannah started heaving into a bush. His hand was on her back, rubbing until she had gotten it all out, wiped her mouth on her sleeve and straightened up.

"We have to get them out of the house."

Cody nodded.

"He's got custody," she added, tallying the roadblocks they faced. "He's not going to let me take them. I doubt he'll let them out of the house."

"We'll figure something out."

They spent the next hour searching every inch of the foundation, and found nothing but crushed beer cans and a pile of cigarette butts, which Cody collected into a plastic bag.

Then Hannah's heel clanked against something metal. The contact sent a hollow echo through the earth. In an instant, Cody was on his feet, walking towards her, as she stomped on it.

"Angle the light right there."

When he did, the beam showed a metal surface beneath the brush then he flashed it over a bulky padlock.

"Oh my God," she said under her breath, then looked at him, eyes white all around. "Some kind of cellar?"

"I'll get the team over here."

✳

HANNAH WAS ON the brink of collapse by the time Cody had gotten her to his house on the other side of the lake. She hadn't needed much convincing. She didn't want to go back to the shack and when Cody had offered to keep a cop outside the Cole house, she felt satisfied the girls would be safe for the night. There wasn't much left of it anyway, an hour at best.

It had taken far too long for the team to arrive and when they did it was hardly a team—one cop who was half asleep, one paid intern from the forensic department, and a locksmith. No one had been pleased to be there.

By the time the locksmith had broken the padlock off and they lifted the trap door, the moon was sinking into the horizon.

Cody had told Hannah not to come down and she had listened for a few minutes then clamored down the steps anyway.

The cellar had been empty.

No one had been more heartbroken than Hannah.

She had sat in a comatose state on his passenger seat. She had drank. He had been most worried she didn't cry.

They had found blood in the back room and a sleeping bag. In the front room, there had been more sleeping bags, a milk crate, methamphetamine paraphernalia, and canned food so thick with dust he doubted the perpetrators had brought them.

Grim quarters.

When Hannah had taken in the reality of it all, grasping that her mother had lived down there for nearly a month, he could've sworn he saw another piece of her die.

"There's a lot this place can tell us," he had assured her, meaning to soothe and comfort her, keep her spirits high. But his hopes had plummeted, as well.

Stepping into the warm glow under the portico, Cody fit his key into the lock of his modest Colonial house, Hannah swaying inebriated beside him. He helped her through the door once he had swung it inward, flipped on the hallway light, and guided her into the living room.

She perked up, seeing his home, freed herself from his arm which had cradled her waist, and with heavy steps paced slowly around the room, eyeing the bookshelves, their many novels and inspirational books, then took her time analyzing the framed family photos.

"So, this is what your life looks like now?" She seemed to scowl at his sofa. Maybe it was the plaid upholstery or the overall woodsman feel to the place, he couldn't decide.

"I guess."

"It's nice," she commented, sitting on the coffee table, perhaps having overlooked the magazines fanned across it. Resting her elbows on her knees, she untwisted her flask. "Do you ever feel like the world is working against you?"

"Yeah. All the time."

She nodded at that and drank.

"Maybe you've had enough?"

She was somewhere else entirely.

"I don't sleep in beds." She scanned the room like its contents no longer interested her. "I don't like them. It feels like they're trying to swallow me, like they want to suffocate me, like they want me dead."

He wasn't sure what to make of that, but tried his best to fit it into context. "I was going to offer you my bedroom, but you can sleep out here on the sofa if you prefer."

"I like the floor. It's solid. Supportive. You can trust it."

"Okay."

"Has anything bad ever happened to you?"

She narrowed her eyes on him, turning the question into an accusation.

"I think so."

"If you *think,* then you don't know," she said, definitively. "Do you know why I stopped talking to you?"

"Because I shouldn't have left that night."

She took a moment to consider his answer.

"Do you know what happened to me?"

He stared at her. She looked like a wreck, and all he wanted to do was hold her. "I left and I guess you had to walk home. Dale socked me good for it if it's any consolation."

"It's not." She locked eyes with him, but he could see it pained her to look at him. "I didn't just walk home." It seemed to take a lot for her to communicate the next fragment. "Some kids came into the church where you left me. And they attacked me." She took a deep breath. "I've never said that out loud before." Another deep breath. "I blamed you."

He was stunned. Words wouldn't come. Offering an apology seemed too small.

"I also loved you," she added as though it somehow made things worse. "Did you love me?"

"Yes."

"Do you still love me?"

His breath hitched in his throat. "Yeah." He had the impulse to ask the same, but wasn't sure he could handle the answer. He didn't trust it would be what he hoped.

Hannah got to her feet and gradually closed in on him. When she did, she gazed up into his eyes, taking his hand.

"I don't know why, but I still love you."

"I'm so sorry, Hannah."

She waved off his apology and led him out of the living room.

When they reached the landing at the top of the stairs, it wasn't a mystery where his bedroom was located. His house wasn't that big. Once inside, Hannah let go of him and left him in the dark. She started stripping the comforter and sheets off the bed and kicking them into shape on the floor. Then she returned to him, took his hand, and slowly walked backwards, bringing him there.

He felt like a wild animal was inviting him into its den as they lowered to the blankets. He was cautious, yet fascinated, and made no sudden movements.

Hannah laid down and he did the same, lying beside her.

Softly, she said, "Mary doesn't want me to leave."

"I don't want you to leave."

"I don't either."

Then she curled into him, fitting herself perfectly against his body, her head in the crook of his neck, her hand on his chest, and one leg draped over one of his. When he was sure she was settled, he wrapped his arms around her and drifted into sleep.

❄

CODY WOKE TO the warm sunshine on his face. Hannah was curled around him like she had been, but the comforter now cocooned them.

Strange night magic.

He kissed the top of her head, breathing in the scent of her hair. It felt so good having her here like this. She loved him. Something good was coming out of the Coles' nightmare. Was that wrong to think? He hoped not.

Hannah stirred. Her hand smoothed down the length of his chest and she glanced up at him, kissing his neck and his cheek, venturing over, light pecks here and there, until she found his mouth and kissed him.

"Did you hear something?" she asked.

"No," he groaned, returning his lips to hers.

She kissed him back. "That?" she said. "Did you hear that?"

Cody listened for a moment and heard the distinct sound of someone pounding at the front door. Then nothing.

"Wait," she whispered, listening out.

Another single knock at the door.

It couldn't have been seven in the morning.

"I'll check it out."

"Are you expecting someone?"

"No."

Cody started down the stairs. As he approached the door he heard a miserable-sounding groan that set his teeth on edge.

He cocked his GLOCK, as he shouted, "Who's there?"

Other than groaning, there was no formal response.

In an instant, he threw the door open and aimed his gun at a bloody-looking kid who was standing outside.

The sight of the kid was so jarring that it took a second for Cody's brain to make sense of him.

Dried, crusted blood streamed down the kid's chin.

His eyes were terror-stricken.

He was holding a cardboard box in his bloody hands, just like Dalton had the evening he had stumbled into the Sanbornton police station.

Hannah padded down the stairs.

"Stop, Hannah!" Cody ordered her, "Go back upstairs!"

Confused, she froze and asked, "Why? Who's at the door?"

"Go upstairs, Hannah!" he barked.

When she retreated up the stairs, Cody ushered the kid inside, motioning with his gun for the kid to follow him into the living room.

There was no mistaking. The kid's tongue had been cut out just like Dalton's had been.

The darkest blood oozed down his chin.

Cody used his gun to indicate that the kid should set the box on the dining room table.

"Why did you come here?" he demanded, speaking in hushed tones. "Why not the station?"

The kid groaned.

"You need medical attention. I'll call an ambulance."

Suddenly, the kid screamed, shaking his head and slicing his arms as if to say, *no way*. Then he stumbled through the room in search of something to write with..

Keeping his gun aimed at the kid, Cody grabbed a pen and a pad of paper out of the nearby end table, and handed both to the kid.

With pen and paper in hand, he collapsed into the sofa and began scrawling. When blood dripped on the page, he smeared it away and kept going.

Cody hadn't heard Hannah come back downstairs. He didn't know she was in the living room, looking on with horror. It wasn't until she peeked inside the box that was resting on the table and gasped that he realized she had disregarded his orders.

"Hannah," he breathed, but he had to ask, "What is it?"

Her voice trembled as she said, "Ears."

The kid offered Cody what he had written, but Hannah was the one who took it and scurried back a safe distance from the kid.

As she began reading, he was already writing more.

"It says…" She swallowed hard to steady her voice. "My name is Blake Abbott. He still has my cousin, Travis Danbury. Kendra Cole is alive. He took her."

"Who?" Cody demanded. "Who is *he*?"

Hannah retrieved the second page, which she first skimmed to see if he had revealed the name of the man.

"Was it Dale Cole?" Cody demanded.

The kid stopped writing and looked up at Cody, then he finished writing big blocky letters across the page, which he held up:

I DON'T KNOW WHO HE IS.

"Damnit," Cody said, spitting through his teeth.

Hannah turned back to the next page and read it out loud for Cody.

"He dresses in black. He uses some kind of a voice distortion device. It looks like a box that's positioned over the mouth of the mask he wears. He didn't see me take it."

She froze, staring at the kid with wide eyes.

Cody asked, "He didn't see you take *what?*"

The kid shoved his bloody hand into the front pocket of his jeans and extracted a key chain that didn't have any keys attached. There was a flat, plastic square hanging down from the key ring. Hannah took it, and Cody realized it was a little photo frame. Hannah turned the frame over in her hands, as though she couldn't believe her eyes. Then she referenced the page and read more.

"He says," she began, "the man had it on his work table. It seemed important to him. It was the only human thing he seemed to have."

She stared at it again.

Encased in the plastic frame was a black and white photo—a photo booth photo.

It was a photo of Mary.

She was pursing her lips for the camera.

Lastly, the kid wrote one more note. This time Cody grabbed it.

His blood ran cold as he read:

Ask Mary.

"Kendra didn't write that in the dirt," he surmised. "The kids had written it. They had wanted out from the start."

CHAPTER FIFTEEN

MARY EXAMINED HER reflection in the cracked bathroom mirror, though it was fogged up with shower steam. She looked like an apparition, floating in purgatory between life and death. Ghostlike—her blond hair slick to her scalp, her pale skin washed out from lack of makeup. She looked as though she didn't fully exist. Or maybe that was how she felt. She was only fully alive when she was taking care of everyone else around her.

She wiped the glass with her palm. In the back of her mind, she wondered if her plan to get Hannah to return home for good was working.

It didn't feel like it was.

A towel was resting on the toilet lid, but she didn't reach for it. She breathed in the steamy air from her shower, and then pulled the bathroom window open wide.

The outside air felt freezing on her wet skin, as hot mist escaped into the crisp afternoon, dissipating into the stark orange light that cut through the trees.

Hannah hadn't come home at all last night. Nor had she returned today, which pleased Dale, but made Mary furious.

Dale had been getting antsy with Hannah here. He was getting harder to control.

Flipping her head upside down to shake off the excess water, Mary grabbed her comb on the counter and began straightening the tangles. When she stood up again, her spiky hair pointed at strange angles so she lathered a dollop of gel between her palms and massaged the hair product in. Never mind using a blow dryer. This would do.

She didn't dawdle about the rest. She dragged eyeliner across her upper lashes then the lower ones and followed up with a few strokes of black shadow. Then she brushed rose blush onto her cheeks in circles and dabbed some gloss on her lips.

No sense in getting too dolled up.

She fastened her bra around her waist and slid it up, getting it situated just right. Then she threw on her jeans and a thin tee shirt, which was too thin and hugged her too tightly to leave much to the imagination.

By now, the brownies were probably done.

On her way to the kitchen, she peered in at Candice. The girl was splayed out on her bed, flipping the glossy pages of a magazine that Mary had provided.

Being the smartest person in the house was often a lonely position to hold, but she kept everyone safe and happy so it was worth it.

"Keep your door locked for the next hour or so," she told her younger sister.

Candice looked up from where she was lying on her bed, and nodded. She was a good girl and would obey.

When she rounded the kitchen, she grabbed the paper towel roll and a plastic container, and set both on the counter. Then she opened the oven. Her timing was impeccable.

It didn't take more than a minute to cut up the brownie squares and stack them neatly in the container. She kept the lid off so they wouldn't sweat and spoil the texture.

"You're not going far are you?" she heard Dale call from his bedroom.

"No, Daddy. I'm coming right back."

"I had a hell of a night and a worse day," he went on.

"That's your own damn fault!"

Christ, he was weak.

In the foyer, she balanced the brownie container on her hip and slid her feet into a pair of sneakers.

Then she was out the door. She crossed the porch and started down the driveway.

The cops were so damned conspicuous, it was embarrassing.

Did Cody really expect her to buy that the police were here to keep her safe? They were obviously here to keep an eye on her family, because Cody was suspicious of Mary and of Dale and of all of them.

Poor bastards, she thought. They didn't even know what they were looking for.

She swayed her hips as she walked up to the police cruiser, holding the container full of brownies under her boobs so that the cops would have to think twice about which goodies she was really offering.

Seated in the driver's seat, the cop was quick to roll down his window and greet Mary.

She leaned over. She smiled. He smiled, too, and so did his partner in the passenger seat. They looked giddy, but nervous.

"Hi, fellas," she said, making eye contact with each of them. She glimpsed their surnames above their badges—Calhoon and Sanders. "I thought you might like a snack."

The nearest one chuckled anxiously, as she put the brownies in his lap and slowly withdrew her hands.

"They're brownies," she added, as though it wasn't obvious. "I made them just for you. We *really* appreciate you guys being out here. Your job seems so interesting."

She offered them another big smile.

Of course, they lit up like fireworks.

"On a good day," they agreed. "Today is certainly shaping up."

"I bet," she cooed, laying it on a little thick, as the officers tasted the brownies.

"This is delicious."

"Made with love," she told them. She made slow work of taking a brownie for herself. She took a bite and sucked the taste off her fingers. After she swallowed, she winked and said, "You guys have a great night."

As she walked across the dirt road and rounded a tree, heading up the driveway, she thought to herself, *men were so stupid*.

Inside the house, she found Dale in his bedroom, seated on his bed with the bible, of all things, in his lap. There were canned beers on the nightstand beside him.

"Are those assholes still out there?" he asked.

"Yeah," she sighed. "But they're about to get some serious diarrhea now that they're eating the brownies, so I'm sure they'll leave soon."

Mary grabbed one of the beer cans and cracked it open.

"Have a seat," Dale said, inviting her to his bed.

She remained on her feet, gulping beer down, and tried to figure out how to get the hell out of there.

She didn't want to upset her father. She didn't have the energy to manage one of his rages.

But then again, it had been awhile since he had flown into a *real* rage…

Damn if getting Hannah back in the house hadn't been the best thing that Mary had ever accomplished.

"Come here, Mary," he said, losing patience.

"I have to start putting dinner together," she said.

"It's the afternoon."

"We've got an extra mouth to feed," she pointed out.

"No, we don't, because your mother is gone. It's the same amount of mouths."

"I must get my high IQ from you, huh?" she tcascd. "You're a regular mathematics genius.

Dale asked her, "Are you torn up about your mother's disappearance?"

Kendra had never *listened* to Mary. The woman's ears had done her no good. She had been deaf to Mary, deaf to her daughter's pleas that Dale had turned on her. He had been angling in on Mary and trapping her like a mouse, coming to her in the night. But Kendra had refused to hear it.

All Kendra had cared about was her own salvation and when she couldn't find it in the church, she sought it out in the trailer parks, in the woods, with strangers who smoked drugs and were willing to share with her.

Mary looked him dead in the eye and said, "I don't miss her at all."

Suddenly, Hannah filled the open doorway, surprising Dale and Mary.

"Don't you know how to knock?" Dale barked.

"The door was open."

"You're back now?" he asked.

"I am," she told him. "I should've called to say I wasn't coming home last night. Sorry about that."

Dale told her, "We did just fine without you."

Hannah noticed the beer cans and the dim lighting. She asked her sister:

"Is everything okay?"

Dale answered on Mary's behalf, "Everything is great. Or it was, until *you* showed up."

"Really?" Hannah said, skeptical.

Dale said, "We were just passing the time."

Mary joined Hannah at the door and said, "I'll close this for you, Daddy, so you can nap."

As Mary closed the door, he grumbled something neither of them understood.

Hannah looked weird, or spooked maybe, like she had seen a ghost.

"What?" Mary asked her.

She stared at Mary for a long moment, then said, "You shouldn't be around him when he drinks like that. He's dangerous."

As if Mary wasn't aware…

They walked into the living room and Mary tried to initiate a casual conversation.

"So, how did it go last night with the hunk?"

"Fine." Hannah looked out of sorts, which Mary found a tad annoying.

"Care to tell me about it?" she pushed.

Hannah turned white. She narrowed her gaze on Mary, unnerving the younger girl.

Then Hannah asked:

"Why did you ask me to come here? Tell me the truth."

CHAPTER SIXTEEN

SINCE DALE AND Candice were in the house, Hannah convinced Mary to speak with her outside where their conversation would be private.

"What do you need to talk to me about that's so private?" she questioned.

"Mom's case," Hannah told her.

Suddenly eager to be Hannah's confidant, Mary agreed.

"I'm right behind you," she told her younger sister. "I just have to use the toilet."

"I'll be on the dock," Mary whispered before she bundled up in the foyer and headed outside.

Hannah didn't need to go to the bathroom. She needed to hunt around Mary's bedroom without the girl barging in.

The moment that Mary had shut the front door behind her, Hannah rushed up the hallway and quietly entered Mary's bedroom.

Her heart was in her throat and her mind was reeling.

She shut the door quietly behind her, and remembered that she had no way to lock herself in.

She leaned against the door, taking a moment to steady her breathing.

The sight of Dale and Mary alone in his bedroom was already giving Hannah flashbacks.

The image of them burned into the forefront of her mind.

The dark, sexual energy that Hannah had sensed in the air…

Hannah feared that Dale was abusing Mary.

Her stomach lurched at the thought.

She mentally screamed at herself not to think about it for the time being.

Instead, Hannah began rummaging through Mary's bedroom for clues. Hannah wasn't clear on what *specifically* she was looking for. But she was *convinced* that somehow Mary was at the center of this thing.

Hannah would find *something* so long as she kept looking.

She had to.

As she moved from the desk drawers, a sense of anguish crawled through her.

Dale had always been scheming, suggestive, and manipulative. He had crossed more than a few lines with Hannah when she had grown up here.

For one, introducing Hannah to alcohol had been far from appropriate. But when Hannah had been living in the house, Dale had constantly offered her lingering hugs. His roaming hands had often touched her in inappropriate places, and he had meant to. Dale was always trying to see what he could get away with. He used to "accidentally" walk in on Hannah when she had been in the bathroom or changing in her bedroom. At times, Dale had given her inappropriate, sexual gifts which had made no sense, like a skimpy bathing suit, and a *bra*. He had been such a cliche, it was pathetic, but Hannah had never been able to laugh it off. She had spent her upbringing terrified of him.

And worst of all, Kendra had turned a blind eye to Dale's perverted advances.

Hannah knew she was lucky to have left home for good before Dale had ever gotten the chance to molest her outright, but that didn't mean Hannah hadn't felt violated every day of her life growing up with Dale as her step-father.

Her gut was telling her that Dale had crossed the same line with Mary... And he might have been doing worse to Mary now than he had to Hannah all those years ago...

But Mary handled Dale so well, how could this have happened?

Hannah searched through Mary's nightstand, opening the top drawer, but she couldn't focus on what she was doing.

Her eyes welled up with tears. She never would have left if she had ever thought, even for one flashing moment, that Dale would be capable of making sexual advances on his own flesh and blood.

She prayed to God that she was jumping to conclusions, but she feared she wasn't.

All of a sudden, Cody's theory added up. If Dale was sick enough to manipulate Mary, he would be sick enough to want to get Kendra out of the picture. He would be sick enough to mutilate his own wife.

In the bottom drawer, under a disorganized heap of old make-up, Hannah found a strip of black and white photo booth photos, and gasped.

They looked similar to the black and white photo of Mary that had been in the little plastic frame, the one that Blake had given to Cody.

As Hannah stared at the small, square photos in her hand, she felt suddenly queasy. She had hoped some pervert had been stalking Mary or something, and had stolen the strip of photos before Mary had gotten out of the booth.

But the strip of photos was in her hand—Mary looking up at the camera, smiling. In the next photo, Mary was grinning wide with her tongue out, silly.

The last photo was missing.

The bottom edge where the photo should have been was frayed, as though the final photo had been torn off. Perhaps *given* to whoever was behind this?

It had to be Dale.

A moment of clarity washed over her when she spotted a set of keys in the drawer.

Thinking fast, she took them.

Hannah was on her feet in an instant. She tucked the strip of photos into her jeans pocket and tore through the house.

She had her wits about her enough to shut the front door on her way out, then she crossed the backyard, heading out to the dock.

The sun had fallen beneath the tree line across the lake, as dusk gathered across the sky.

Standing at the edge of the dock and looking out at the sunset was Mary. She held a beer in her hand, the others were at her feet.

As soon as Hannah set foot on the dock, Mary glanced over her shoulder. Mary's facial expression was flat, her eyes dark and discerning.

It gave Hannah pause and caused her heart to race all over again.

Though her legs felt suddenly rubbery, she ventured across the dock and joined Mary at the edge.

"Sorry, my stomach has been acting up," Hannah lied to explain what had taken her so long.

"So, what's going on with the case?"

Hannah needed a moment to get her bearings in terms of how best to get her sister talking.

Studying Mary's young face, she saw worry and wonder in her eyes. The admiration she held for Hannah. Mary *needed* Hannah to stay.

Hannah reminded herself that Mary was just a kid.

"First of all, let me just say that you and your sister have to start going to school again."

She took it like a slap in the face.

"Don't look at me like that. Staying home all the time isn't healthy."

"I was just shot. You remember how I was shot, right?"

"Yeah, I haven't forgotten." She didn't look away and neither did Mary. Water lapped at the edge of the dock, as Hannah searched her sister's face and saw defiance. "I know you were shot," she went on, digging deep to get to the bottom of this. "And I know you lied about it."

Mary's demeanor went cold. "What do you think I lied about?"

"You said that the man who shot you had been standing a good eight yards away. Your doctor told me that the gun barrel had been against your leg when the trigger was pulled."

Hannah let that hang so she could read her sister's reaction, but all Mary did was turn to stone.

"I'm going to ask you something, Mary, and don't you dare lie to me or I swear to God, I'll go back to Gilford before the sky is dark tonight."

Mary's eyes went white all around. Good, the threat meant something to her.

"Did you take my revolver and shoot yourself in the leg?"

Mary stopped breathing. She tensed up, right down to her very core.

"There was a man out here that night," she insisted. "And I really didn't get a good look at his face. He really was yards and yards away."

"So, you shot yourself?"

Mary couldn't look at her big half-sister, she felt so ashamed.

"You could've done serious damage, Mary, my God! What if you clipped an artery? You would be dead."

Mary locked eyes with her. "So what?"

"Don't talk like that."

"You don't know what it's like here."

"You're right," she said, her voice pure compassion.

"All I know is that since you've come back, everything is better," said Mary. "All I know is, you have to stay."

Hannah suddenly realized that her sister was deranged. Mary might have even been as sick as Dale, but in very different ways, if she had shot herself in the leg to get Hannah to pity her and stay.

"You told me you were going to head back to Gilford," Mary went on, sobbing. "I only wanted you to stay."

Hannah had never encountered someone so messed up, but who could stay sane living with a father like Dale?

She held Mary by her shoulders, and promised, "I will *not* abandon you. I won't."

Laughing and crying with relief, Mary threw her arms around Hannah. "Thank you!"

"I'm going to get you and your sister out of the house."

"Now? Tonight?" She seemed worried. "He's probably passed out by now. I'll just lock him in his bedroom like I always do."

"You guys can't stay here," she affirmed.

"But it's late anyway."

It wasn't late. It was five o'clock.

Hannah almost asked her why in the hell Mary would want to stay, but she decided to keep her mouth shut for the time being.

"If not tonight, then when should I get you and Candice out of the house?"

"Things are good when you're here," she said, implying no one had to leave.

Mary's change in attitude gave her an uneasy feeling. Her sister wasn't making a lick of sense. She had shot herself as some kind of convoluted cry for help, and yet she didn't actually want to be rescued? She didn't want to merely be with Hannah or to merely have Hannah in her life. She wanted Hannah *here. At the shack*? She wanted her in her house and in her world, as twisted as it had become. "Let's talk about the case then."

She had Mary's full attention.

"Did you give anyone a photo of yourself recently?" asked Hannah.

Innocently, she cocked her head. "I'm not sure."

Hannah produced the strip of photos and grazed her finger across the torn bottom edge.

"Who did you give the missing photo to?" She needed her to say 'Dale.' This needed to come to a head. Now.

"You went through my things?"

Hannah reminded her, "You went through my bag and stole my gun."

"I didn't give the photo to anyone. The photo strip fell out of my back pocket in the Belknap Mall and when I found it again, the last photo was gone," she snapped, her teenage attitude rearing its ugly head. "What does this have to do with Mom's case?"

"Are you lying to me right now?"

"No!" She crossed her arms, then realized drinking would be a better idea and got to it.

"Do you know Dalton Gerrity?"

"No, never heard of him."

"He never came to the house?"

"No," she snapped again, screwing her face up.

Hannah had to seriously watch herself. Mary was slippery, too clever for her own good.

"What about Blake Abbott and Travis Danbury?"

"This has to do with Mom?"

"Just answer my questions."

"If I knew you were planning on interrogating me, I wouldn't have come out here!"

"Do you want to find Mom or not?"

When Mary didn't respond, it occurred to Hannah that her younger sister might not want to find their mother.

"Mary," she sighed.

"Fine," Mary snapped. "Blake is some pervert who I know from around town. I mean, I don't *know* him. I just know he's obsessed with me, but lots of boys are. He's a creep. What does he have to do with Mom?"

"Could he have taken that photo of you?"

"Who knows."

"Did he ever speak to you? Or approach you at any time?"

"Yeah," said Mary as though she had already implied as much. "I told you, he's obsessed with me."

"Why would that be?'

She shrugged. "Guys just are."

Blake wasn't behind any of this. His only role was as a pawn. Hannah knew that, but she sensed that Mary knew even more.

"Mary, I'm warning you, you have got to tell me what you know."

"Why do you think I know anything?" she challenged.

"Because I talked to Blake."

Mary froze. "Meaning?"

"There's a running theme here, Mary. People are pointing their fingers at *you*."

"What are you talking about?"

"I'm talking about this whole *Ask Mary* business. Remember I told you someone carved 'Ask Mary' in the dirt where Mom was taken? Well, Blake told Cody to do the same. To ask you. So, I'm asking you."

Mary smiled and said, "Tell me what you know. Everything. And I'll do the same."

Hannah was taken aback. "You think this is a game?"

"No. But you haven't told me anything. I'm a genius, in case you've forgotten. I can help."

Hannah stared at her in disbelief. "You're not as smart as you think you are, Mary. Trust me. And you definitely lack wisdom, which counts for a hell of a lot more."

Mary gulped her beer and didn't look at her.

Hannah went on, "Cody thinks that Dale took Kendra."

Mary mulled that over. Drank. "Does he have proof?"

"No."

"Then why does he think that?" Mary challenged.

Darkness had fallen all around them and the moon shone high in the sky. A strong gust of wind blew off the water and Hannah folded her arms against it.

"Mom was on drugs," she added, surprising Hannah.

"You knew about that?"

Mary nodded. "Those kids, those names you said. They were her dealers."

"How do you know?"

"I'm not an idiot."

"Why didn't you try to get Mom the help she needed for her drug addiction?" said Hannah, which was the wrong thing to say.

"Are you blaming me?" Mary yelled, offended. She flew off the handle and blurted out, "Mom knew about what Daddy was doing to me! She knew! I told her, but she didn't care!"

"She knew about...?" Hannah could read her sister's mind, and yet Hannah's brain refused to accept it.

"She did!" Mary exclaimed. "I told her. She wouldn't listen. Then she started turning a blind eye. Her drugs helped." She forced some beer down her throat to take the edge off. "I confided in a few people at school. Maybe word got around. Maybe that's what the whole *Ask Mary* thing is about, I don't know! Maybe Blake felt sorry for me. Maybe he hated Kendra, too. Maybe Daddy *did* do it! Maybe he killed her before she could get him locked up in prison for what he's been doing to me! I don't know anything! I just want you to stay with us forever!"

"Why won't you let me take you and Candice out of the house?" she asked, trying to get Mary to calm down. "Why won't you let me save you?"

Mary picked up the six-pack by its plastic rings, motioning to go. "You want to save us?" she said. "Have you even saved yourself?"

Then Mary started off for the house.

Hannah watched her younger half-sister until the girl went into the house.

Fog rolled in.

The air was freezing, but Hannah couldn't feel it. She couldn't sense the dock beneath her feet.

Panicking, dreadful thoughts had seized her, yanking her from her surroundings, out of her body, into a frenzy of incomprehension, horror, and sudden sickness.

Her stomach clenched and her mind wouldn't stop racing—the photo, the abuse, her mother's hand in a box, the eerie foundation and cellar door poking up through weeds and bushes.

Ask Mary, but Mary wouldn't tell.

Ask her, but she refused to leave the house.

Ask her, but Kendra hadn't listened and hadn't stopped the abuse.

Kendra hadn't listened to Hannah either all those years ago…

The onslaught of horrifying pieces surged through Hannah's mind, tearing her psyche open, and scrambling her from the inside out—Mary leaning into Dale's embrace at the picnic table, at the church, where else? Candice declaring that Mary *was* Mom. Dale and Mary drinking in his dark bedroom just like Dale and Mom used to do… Just like Dale and *Hannah* used to do when he had taught her how to drink.

Intercut with images that haunted her, Hannah remembered the church, how she had sat in the pews only days ago for the sermon, and how she had scraped herself off the floor years ago after she had been gang raped the night of her prom, in the very same church.

She wanted to scream and cry and throw herself out of her body and float away to some better place.

The vision of her mother's hand in a box and her ears in another box surged to the forefront of Hannah's racing mind. Blood oozing from Blake's mouth filled her mind next, and the disturbing memories refused to leave her alone.

She tried to make it stop. She screamed but no sound escaped her. *Remember to forget, remember to forget, remember to forget, or else be killed.*

She couldn't take it! Her vision tunneled inward. She grew dizzy.

What was happening?

The next thing she knew, she fell into the lake.

She went down, down, down deeper and deeper as though the lake had no bottom.

Icy water cut across her skin, stinging her eardrums, shooting up her nose, and freezing her heart, as blackness closed in all around her.

The darkness pressed in, threatening to crush her skull and freeze the blood in her veins.

Finally, her boot struck the bottom of the lake, stirring up muck and sand and debris that made her skin crawl, like creepy fingers, like Dale's drunken advances.

No, no, no!

She pushed off, surging upwards, desperate for air.

The war Kendra had survived came to mind.

Who had waged that war against her?

Hannah broke through the surface of the lake, emerging, bobbing, and gasping for air.

She knew the answer.

She knew who had trapped Kendra in a war that she had barely survived.

Hannah's father.

Her real father had waged the war.

Hannah floated like a corpse, as ice water lapped her cheeks, her coat fanning out all around her.

Kendra had left him. She had never looked back, and had never spoken a word about him to anyone.

Had he come after her?

"CODY?" HANNAH stood shivering at his front door.

He cursed under his breath the moment he saw her.

"What the hell happened to you?" he asked, as he pulled her inside his house.

He scanned the darkness beyond the door, but no one had chased her here.

Again, he asked, "What happened? Why are you soaking wet?"

Hannah was frozen stiff. Her knees barely bent. Her clothes were completely waterlogged from the lake she had fallen into.

He walked her deeper inside the house, into the living room, until she couldn't take another step. Looking her up and down, assessing her state, he guessed, "The lake?"

She nodded, her teeth chattering.

He left her for a moment in favor of fetching towels from the bathroom.

Quickly, he began getting her out of her wet clothes. He pushed her water soaked coat off her shoulders, though it clung with wet suction to her sweater, then pulled her sweater over her head, stripping her down.

He handed her one of the towels so that she could cover herself as he worked to free her from her waterlogged clothes.

She had trouble holding the towel. Hannah saw that her hands were shaking from hypothermia. Her fingers were white and blue.

"Step out of your boots," he instructed.

She hadn't even realized he had unbuttoned her pants.

She did as she was told, placing the claw of her frozen hand on his shoulder for balance, and shook the right boot off with his help, the left one next. He ripped her socks off too then yanked her pants down.

When he had gotten her out of all of her clothes, Cody ushered her into the downstairs bathroom. She sat on the toilet lid while he ran a bath.

Steam billowed up from the faucet as hot water filled the tub.

Cody left her again, this time for longer, and returned with two space heaters, which he immediately plugged in. He turned the dials to maximum heat. They clicked on, fan blaring, and soon the little bathroom was warm. All the while, Hannah watched him, but she felt very far away.

He rolled up his sleeves, placed his wrist under the faucet, and adjusted the temperature accordingly. He stroked his hand through the bathwater. The tub was nearly full. He looked up at her from where he knelt on the tiles, his green eyes framed in anguish at the miserable sight of her.

"What happened?" he asked for the third time. "Was it Dale?"

She thought to herself, *in a manner of speaking, it was...*

Her teeth were chattering, but she clenched her jaw, stealing a moment's relief, then answered, "I fell into the lake. I lost my balance."

"Had you been drinking?" he asked, concerned.

"Not enough, if you ask me."

"If you're able to crack jokes, I think you'll live," he told her, shooting her a smile. A thought crossed his mind, and he said, "I think I have bubbles somewhere."

He tore through the cabinet beneath the sink. Half-empty shampoo bottles toppled over and loose toilet paper rolls bounced out. When he located the container, Cody popped the top and squirted it under the faucet. Bubbles filled the bath.

"You should be all set," he told her. "I'll be in the kitchen making tea."

She watched him go, but decided to call out, "Bring it in here?"

He turned, locked eyes with her through the crack in the door, and said, "Okay," before he closed the door.

Her muscles screamed as though every cell in her body couldn't handle the excruciating contrast from ice to heat, as she submerged, gradually lowering into the tub and discarding her towel, until she was sitting, knees to chin, in the bubble bath.

The sting of the hot water softened and soon its warmth soothed her. She slid down and rested her head on the ledge, embracing the sensations. As good as the hot water felt, it did little to conquer the dread in her heart.

If only she had an idea of what she wanted her life to look like, she could cling to that. It would be the hope that would carry her through.

But her life didn't have meaningful direction.

Over the years, she had loosened her grip from her dreams. Hannah had thought that that was what becoming an adult was all about.

She realized that she had always wanted to attend the Police Academy and become a cop. In a lot of ways Cody was living the life she had hoped to live, herself, not that she was envious. She wouldn't mind living in a nice house like his, too, quaint and quiet. She had always imagined Mary and Candice in her life. She wasn't proud to admit that, deep down, she had been waiting for Dale to drop out of the picture, or maybe drop dead, before she reconnected with her half sisters. Facing that fact now shined a spotlight on her cowardice and she cringed.

As the years had passed, she had never stopped thinking about Cody. She had never stopped wondering about him. Often, he was on her mind when she laid down at night and he was the flicker that woke her in the mornings.

In so many ways, she was destined to return here, she realized.

There came a knock at the door. Hannah checked that the bubbles were hiding her nudity, then told Cody he could enter.

Cody pushed the door open. He was carrying two steaming mugs of tea and set hers on the edge of the tub.

"You're getting some color back," he noted as he sat on the toilet lid with his tea in hand. "You look better."

He seemed careful about where he rested his gaze.

"Do you feel better?"

"Yeah. I can't believe I fell in."

"I can't believe you drove here."

She could.

"What do you want out of life?" she wondered out loud.

Cody searched for the answer in his mug of tea. "To run the homicide department, maybe. "Start a family, I think. Otherwise, what's the point in anything?"

Cody's parents were good people and they had raised him well, providing a stable home for him as he had grown up. People like Cody could fathom having families of their own.

People like Hannah, who had been raised with threats all around them, couldn't.

"Any prospects?" she teased.

"For a wife? Just one," he told her and winked.

"You're in for a world of trouble, my friend."

He turned a bit serious and told her, "I don't think I am."

His conviction scared her, and yet, more than anything Hannah hoped he really *was* serious.

"Bad things happen all the time," he explained. "Bad things happen to good people, as well as bad people. You get to a point where you accept it and focus your efforts on making things whole again, and helping the people around you become whole, too. I'm not sure how far the justice system can carry that goal. There should be more safe places that survivors can turn to, more support centers, and more therapy programs. I would like to get involved in that type of project. Maybe open a shelter or a center."

"How do you help people who don't want to be helped?" she asked, as Mary came to mind.

Cody held her gaze for a long moment and answered honestly, "I don't know."

"I'm drowning in guilt, Cody. I'm all alone."

"You're not alone."

"I wish that was true… I wish I lived in your world."

"We live in the same world, Hannah. Your corner of it just happens to have a few more shadows, but they'll clear away and things will brighten."

Cody brought his mug to his lips and drank.

"Tea's cooled off," he said.

She drank hers, but couldn't take her eyes off him. He was beautiful, a good man with a pure heart.

Who would she have been if she had never left Sanbornton?

Would Cody have saved her?

Would he have made her so strong that Hannah could've saved Mary and Candice, Kendra, maybe even Dale from himself if such a thing were possible?

Hannah set her mug on the tiles next to the tub and rose to her feet, water cascading off her every curve.

At first, Cody appeared dumbstruck. He stared at her with wide eyes.

She didn't feel embarrassed or exposed or self-conscious about her figure, even though she had always thought she was skinny and unattractive. She wanted him to see her, even if it meant seeing all of her flaws. She wanted Cody to look at her, because the way he did often made her feel not only remarkably beautiful, but appreciated, cared for, and cherished.

On his feet, he asked, "Towel?"

"No," she said softly. "Just you."

He neared her, pulled her in, and kissed her.

She whispered, "Take me to your bed."

"What if it swallows you?"

"It won't."

HANNAH WOKE before dawn. Cody's room was dark, but its shadows didn't scare her. She glanced at him sleeping. His cheek was smooshed against the pillow, his brown hair a mess of cowlicks, his shoulder rising and falling with each breath.

She slipped from the bed, threw on one of his old sweatshirts and a pair of pajama bottoms, and quietly padded through the hallway and down the stairs.

She felt comfortable here, as though she was intimate with his home simply because she knew him so well. She helped herself to his coffee, popping the lid off the canister and setting a fresh filter in the coffeemaker.

Once it started gurgling and dripping, she stalked through to the sliding glass door, which opened out onto the rear deck.

The crisp, chilly air brought her to life, and she observed the sunrise warming the sky. Morning dusk.

Holding the banister, she gazed out at the lake, its surface as smooth as glass, and took in the hardy scenery. A pair of loons paddled along the shore, nuzzling each other at times, having mated for life.

Off in the distance, on the other side of the lake, was the rickety dock she had grown up with. The shack sat behind it.

She stared at it. That house wasn't to be trusted.

Decisively, she entered the house, crossed the living room, and exited the house again through the front door.

She found her purse on the passenger seat of her Taurus and brought it inside.

The coffeemaker hissed on the counter and steam puffed out of its top, indicating the coffee had brewed and she could pour herself a mug, so she did. She splashed some cream into her coffee then grabbed her cell phone and brought both outside onto the deck.

When she rested her coffee on the ledge of the deck, she was already dialing. As she listened for the line to open up, she scanned the shore of the lake, wondering where those loons paddled off to.

"Hello?" A groggy voice came through.

"Cranston?"

"Christ, is this Hannah?" She heard rustling like he was checking the number on his cell. "Hannah?"

"Yeah, I need a favor."

"Is everything alright, Hannah? It's extremely early."

"I'm so sorry about the early call," she apologized. "I need you to look into something for me."

"Of course, what do you need?"

"Can you look into my biological father? I don't know anything about him. I need his name, his address, and, well, everything that you can find out about him. He was married to Kendra Cole if that helps."

"I can do that, yes, but it won't be until I get into the station in a few hours. I'll call you when I have something."

"Thanks," she said, breathing a sigh of relief.

She waited for him to hang up then she sipped her coffee.

As she drank, she studied the shack across the water.

She didn't know how her real father tied into this mess, but Hannah was determined to find out.

CHAPTER SEVENTEEN

KENDRA HAD PRIED the nail out of the brick wall before the man came and moved her to this new location.

It was a nine-inch nail.

The kind that had nailed Jesus to the cross.

She had hid the nail in her boot. The metal had dug into her ankle, scraping her skin, but it had been worth it, and still was.

The nail was her only weapon.

She would have to be very smart about when she used it.

Maybe she should have used the nail and fought the man when he had moved her to this new location. But she hadn't. The right moment hadn't presented itself, and now she was locked away in a brand-new hellhole.

The man had tied her down, drugged her up something nasty, and had surgically removed her ears, just like he had her hand weeks ago. All the while the Lord's nine-inch nail had stayed with her, tucked in her boot.

The right moment to fight would come, she told herself.

But first, she needed to recover from the trauma and from the drug haze.

She just had to hold tight and keep the faith.

She wondered where all her body parts were going, and for some reason the thought made her laugh. Maybe they were being used as the centerpiece of a satanic ritual. Or maybe they had been nailed to the gazebo in the town square as a reminder to Sanbornton's residents that there was no place you could hide where the devil wouldn't find you. That's who was doing this, right? Satan himself?

Peering out the bottom edge of her blindfold, Kendra spied shadows and not much else, but the smell of rubbing alcohol and mothballs, bleach and formaldehyde told her she was in a sterile environment, probably not a hospital, though.

Maybe she had been abducted by mad scientists, that made her chuckle a bit, too.

She was lying across a steel table, tied down, but her arms weren't bound together, nor were her feet. She tested how much leeway she had. Arching her back indicated less than a few inches. Lifting her legs yielded the same give. Exerting that much effort had her heart rate up so she stopped experimenting and caught her breath.

Hannah's face came to mind.

The girl had looked so much like her father that Kendra could barely stand the sight of her.

The day Hannah had left, Kendra didn't fight her. She hadn't told Mary and Candice, either. Hannah had packed her bags in the morning, and the girls hadn't been aware that their big half-sister would be leaving for good right after her graduation. Kendra had kept the girls occupied, while Hannah had made trip after trip, carrying her belongings to the beat-up Volvo she had scrimped and saved up for by working at the DQ and the bowling alley after school just so she would be able to afford it.

As one big happy family, they had gone to Hannah's high school graduation, sat in those miserable folding chairs, and tried not to squirm, as Kendra's eldest daughter walked across the stage, accepted her diploma with her left hand and shook the principal's hand with her right. All the while, Kendra had counted the minutes, knowing Hannah would soon be out of her life for good.

No, Kendra hadn't fought her daughter one bit to keep her at the house. She had lied to the girls that Hannah would meet them back at home after the graduation ceremony. She hadn't stayed to watch Hannah say goodbye to her friends, which was a farce in the first place since she didn't have any.

The last moment she had ever seen her daughter, the girl was screaming at Dale, getting in his face aggressively. Then Hannah had pointed her finger so close to Dale's eyeball that Kendra was worried he would break it off her hand. Hannah had warned him to stay away from Mary and baby Candice, which was preposterous. Dale was their father.

Kendra had thought that with Hannah gone, she would get some relief. But apparently, Hannah had poisoned Mary's mind before she had left home, because it was only a matter of years before Mary had started telling Kendra about the same kind of crap that Hannah had… as if Dale was some kind of monster.

Truth be told, Dale probably was a monster. But Kendra had been through too much in her life to tolerate hearing about it.

If Kendra had to face the possibility that she had married the same man all over again—if Dale was only a different version of Hannah's monstrous father—the reality would have broken Kendra.

And yet…

… there she was…

… broken just the same.

She refused to break.

She was filled with a fighting spirit just thinking about it.

She began wriggling her shoulders. She arched her back, getting the nylon straps to loosen as much as they would. She had to press the back of her skull against the table, but she managed to hold her hips up.

She lifted her shoulders to where her ears used to be, and pulled her right arm up as far as it would go, shifting and bucking and working her arm out from under the strap. But when her elbow reached nylon, she realized the result wouldn't free her.

Grunting, she began trying to free her legs.

She had tucked the nine-inch nail down her left boot, so she bent that leg first, sliding her foot up until her boot got caught on the strap.

She paused and made herself breathe, getting focused, and lifted her head off the table, craning to see what the trouble was.

From the bottom of her blindfold, she could see enough to understand that the big floppy tongue of her boot was t-boned against the nylon strap.

Damn.

Her mind started racing for how to get the nine inch nail in hand, as a sudden swell of urgency came over her.

She was lucky to have been left alone for this long.

There was something about this place…

She feared that when the man returned, his goal would be to finish Kendra off.

She straightened out her leg again and hung her heel off the edge of the table. The idea was to get her boot off so that she would be able to grab the nail with her hand. But the only way to remove her boot, since she couldn't reach down with her hand, was to use the edge of the table to pull it off.

Gently, she bent her knee more, moving ever so slowly to ensure the heel of her boot would stay clipped against the table's edge.

Finally, her boot slid, but didn't come off her foot.

Before trying again, she shook her foot to see if the boot would loosen more and drop on its own. But she only felt the nail inside loosen.

All she had to do was get the nail to drop out of the boot and onto the table. Then she could try to reach it with her fingers.

She didn't want the nail to drop to the floor, though.

Her skin broke out in a cold sweat as she kept trying to get the nine inch nail to roll out of her boot and onto the table.

Suddenly, the nail clanked against the table.

"Thank you, Lord!" she said under her breath.

She began reaching for the nail.

Arguing voices startled her. The voices coming through the walls.

"I have no control over what he does!"

That was Travis. She recognized his voice.

Then she heard the man respond. His digital-sounding voice petrified her.

"Your time has come."

"No, no, wait." Travis sounded panicked. "I'm not my cousin. Just because Blake ratted… Hell, we don't even know who you are! How could he possibly rat you out?"

"You betrayed me."

"What? No, I didn't!" Travis insisted.

"You all betrayed me."

"Look, man, I don't know what you're talking about."

Kendra had worked to get the nail beneath her thigh, hiding it just in case. But when it seemed as though Travis and the man weren't going to enter the room, she did everything within her power to get the nail into her hand.

She lifted her hips, swiping her fingertips carefully over the table, straining, praying, and keeping faith alive.

She felt the nail's head with her middle finger and breathed a sigh of relief. Sweat beaded across her hairline.

She reached even farther and she grasped the nail!

She held it tightly in her fist just as the door opened.

Travis stumbled inside, though she could only get a sense of him through the crack beneath her blindfold.

Then the door closed, and Kendra heard the man's digital voice:

"We're going to take her eyes."

"You're a psycho, man," Travis exclaimed, his tone trembling. He weakened, then he cried, "You're out of your mind."

"Hold her down."

Kendra felt strong hands pressing her shoulders.

"Just kill me, man," Travis whimpered. "I don't want to do this."

Without making any sudden movements, she slowly lifted her chin, spying the kid who was holding her down. She sensed more than saw that the other man was to her right, so she kept the nail hidden under her rear end, keeping her hand at her side, ready.

Then the man crossed through to the far end of the room and she realized there was another table there. He lifted some kind of ghastly instrument up, inspecting the blade with his back to her.

It was clear Travis wanted out. This would be the way.

Kendra willed the kid to look at her.

He was cowering over her.

She grasped hold of the nail, prayed to the Lord, and tapped it once on the table.

Travis perked up, lifting his head.

She eyed the man, but he hadn't heard, so she grazed the nail slowly, faintly, over the table then stopped.

Travis was all eyes, staring at her. Then he glanced over his shoulder. The man was considering another surgical tool—a curved knife.

Travis released her shoulders and took the nine-inch nail.

All of a sudden, the nylon straps that were holding her down went slack, Travis having popped the fasteners open.

What happened next was a blur—stomping boots, yelling voices, Kendra spilling off the table, tearing the blindfold off her face.

Travis plunged the nail into the base of the man's neck, as the man stabbed a knife into Travis' leg.

She fought terror as she slammed against the exit door. She scrambled and thrust the door open, and bolted into another room.

She managed to glance over her shoulder. Travis was on the floor. The man was chasing after Kendra.

She sprinted through the basement.

As she ran, her gaze darted left and right, desperately scanning for a way out.

Another door!

She threw it open.

Stairs!

She raced up them, all the while she could hear the man's boots stomping after her, his strides long, but she reached the landing.

Christ, it was a house. Nice things. The man had money. A leather sofa, oak end tables, alabaster light fixtures, and large windows—finally, she understood she was running through a living room.

Where was the front door?

Frantic, she ran faster, rounded into the kitchen, sprinted to the other side.

The man was at her heels when she finally found the front door.

She threw it open and charged out of the house, sprinting with all her might into the blinding sunlight.

But she stumbled and tripped. Her palms smacked the ground, as she landed hard.

She scrambled to her feet, trying to sprint off, but her legs felt wobbly.

That's when she saw a lake.

Her lake?

Hermit Lake?

There was a road ahead. As she ran for it, she screamed for help at the top of her lungs, praying that someone, somewhere would hear her.

Suddenly, the man grabbed her from behind, and they fell together.

Kendra's head smacked against the ground, and once again Kendra's world went dark.

CHAPTER EIGHTEEN

"YOU'RE NOT TAKING my girls!"

Dale charged towards Hannah, but she stood her ground, filling the open doorway of Candice's bedroom.

"Yes, I am!" she asserted.

Behind her, Candice was in an absolute frenzy, plucking tchotchkes off her shelves and throwing everything she owned into her backpack, a suitcase, and duffel bag. She grabbed a sock, two sweaters, another sock, all her underwear, a pair of jeans, flip-flops? Who cared, she tossed them in, as well. She squeaked and squealed, turning this way and that on her heel, yanking at her hair as though she hadn't already come undone.

"Get out of my way." Dale seethed, towering over Hannah and breathing like a raging bull.

"I'm not moving," she told him. "Candice, hurry up!"

"You think I'm going to let you take them?"

"What are you going to do?" Hannah challenged. "Call the police?"

She could smell sour beer rolling off him, as he laughed at her. "If you want to stop me, you'll have to kill me," she warned.

He stared dead at her and said, "I know."

"I know what you've been doing to Mary."

His gaze hardened, but he was rattled.

Hannah told him, "If you come after us, you'll be sorry."

Dale's jaw clenched and his face turned all kinds of colors she had never seen on another human being.

"I got news for you," he said through gritted teeth. "Mary doesn't want to go."

"Get out of my way." She shoved him into the hallway and slammed the door in his face.

"Keep packing. Don't let him frighten you," she told Candice.

The girl was getting the shakes, so Hannah took over, packing her things quickly.

"That's everything," she said. "Let's get you into my car."

Candice held her backpack tightly against her chest, as they made their way out of the bedroom.

Hannah kept her eye on Dale, who was seething in the hallway with his hands on his fists, as Candice cautiously padded out of her room then down the hallway with Hannah.

Sounding miserable, Dale called after his daughter, "Are you going to leave your Daddy?" Candice paused. "You're going to leave me all alone, Candice?"

"Ignore him," Hannah told the girl, as she opened the front door.

She waited until her half-sister went outside before starting up the hallway for Mary's room.

Dale advanced on her, as she entered Mary's room.

She knew he would try to manipulate Mary, since he was so damn good at it, so Hannah positioned herself in-between them.

"Hurry up, Mary. You don't need to pack everything. Just enough for a day or two, and I'll come back here for the rest," said Hannah, as Dale pleaded with Mary from the sidelines.

"What's going to happen to me, Mary? What am I going to do without you?"

Mary looked ill, paler than she should, and she was slow to gather her things.

"What do you need?" Hannah asked her, starting for her dresser. "I'll help you."

Dale yelled, "Don't you leave me, Mary! Don't you dare leave me like your mother!"

Hannah barked, "Kendra didn't leave you! She was kidnapped! God!"

"Please, Mary," he pleaded, his voice raw with desperation. "You know I live for you, girl."

"Enough!" Hannah shouted at him. She urged Dale out into the hallway then doubled back and grabbed Mary's empty bag. She ripped a dresser drawer open, grabbed clothes by the fistful, and began stuffing them inside the bag, working her way around the room as quickly as she could.

When she glanced over, Dale was embracing Mary. The girl wasn't reciprocating, but she also wasn't resisting him.

Hannah tore up the hallway, ducked into the bathroom, and collected everything that looked relevant to her sisters, packing each item inside the bag.

"Let go of her!" she ordered when she returned. "Get off her."

Pushing Dale away, she grabbed Mary by the upper arm and led her through the house and out the door.

"What you don't have, we'll buy," Hannah promised.

Outside, Candice was sitting in the backseat of Hannah's car with her nose pressed to the glass.

Hannah ushered Mary into the passenger seat and shut the car door, but didn't leave.

Not yet.

She charged back into the house, locked eyes with Dale, and warned him:

"If I ever see you with one of them, I will not think twice, I will not hesitate. I will kill you."

MARY WASN'T HER usual, confident self in Cody's kitchen, which was apparent as soon as she had entered the lofty room. But she insisted on whipping dinner up for everyone just the same.

From the dining room table, Hannah watched her sister wander between the counters and islet like she was a stranger in a strange land. Mary explored every inch of the kitchen—the marble countertops, the pots and pans that hung above the islet, the glass cupboards and the porcelain dinnerware stacked inside. She even turned the burners on and off, holding her palm above the glass coils, as though she wasn't quite sure what to make of it, the absence of flames and all. Then she submerged herself in the refrigerator, exploring each shelf, every drawer, taking mental inventory of the groceries.

"Does she need help?" Cody asked. He was sitting at the table with his laptop computer and some files.

"She's just getting settled. I'm sure she's fine."

Hannah turned her attention to Candice, who was seated beside her at the table, trying to do her homework. She poured over her textbook and its many math problems. She was a week behind in her schoolwork, but Hannah had assured her teachers that Candice would catch up. Hannah had even promised the principal that both girls would be in attendance from here on out without incident.

"Do you need help?" Hannah asked as she reached for the girl's calculator.

Candice smiled and told her that she could figure it out. She continued with a sense of eagerness to do her best, using her calculator and scribbling answers in her binder, her pencil scratching hard against paper.

In the kitchen, Mary finally got her bearings. Butter sizzled in a pan. Mary whisked eggs in a bowl. She had found one of Cody's cookbooks on a shelf beneath the islet.

When it seemed the girls would be occupied, she asked Cody if he would have a word with her.

"Sure, outside?"

"Be right back," she told the girls, but both were so engrossed in what they were doing, they barely lifted their heads.

On their way out, Cody flipped on the floodlight and the rear deck brightened. He followed after her, being sure to slide the glass door closed behind him so the girls wouldn't hear their conversation.

"I've got to thank you for letting us stay here," she started, folding her arms and hunching her shoulders against the cold breeze. It was downright freezing, and the temperature would only continue to drop.

Cody grinned, letting her know she was welcome. She tried to return the sentiment and smile, but she was full of apprehension, and it showed.

"I need to ask you about something."

"Okay."

Hannah hesitated. She didn't want to reveal how truly messed up her family was, but she wasn't sure how to ask for Cody's help without disclosing the truth.

"I want to get Mary and Candice out of the shack permanently."

"You mean get custody from Dale?"

"How do I do that?"

He scraped his teeth over his bottom lip, thinking. "Custody stuff really isn't my area of expertise."

"What about assault?"

His brows knit together. "Did Dale assault the girls?"

This was the last conversation she wanted to have.

"Hannah?"

"I think he's been abusing Mary."

"Sexually?"

She grimaced.

The information didn't slam into Cody like Hannah had thought it would.

He asked, "Did Mary confide in you?"

Hannah nodded. "This isn't purely my suspicion. She told me it was happening."

Cody scanned the dark lake that sat at the edge of his property as though doing so would help him wrap his head around this.

"We would have to get her into the police station. She would have to give a statement, which could be a drawn out process, depending on how long the abuse has been going on. Dale wouldn't necessarily lose custody on the spot, Hannah. The law is designed to protect the rights of the accused, but it's likely he would be arrested. There could be a trial later down the road if Dale denies the allegations."

Hannah frowned. It had been brutal getting Mary out of the house. Hannah wasn't sure Mary would be willing to turn her father in to the police for abusing her. Mary's head was so messed up that she had actually thought the solution was to remain at the house, but with Hannah there.

Cody offered, "If you want him arrested immediately, I can get him locked up for having fired his rifle at me. But the judge will release him the second Dale argues that I was trespassing. This is still New Hampshire, after all."

Hannah ran her hand down her face, thinking.

"I still think Dale is our most likely suspect for Kendra's disappearance," Cody told her.

She wished she thought the same… but now, she wasn't so sure.

"Hey, look," he said, taking her shoulders. "All of you can stay here at my house as long as you like. If Dale comes here and tries to take the kids back, I'll do what I have to. The entire police department will be on my side."

"Would you lend me another handgun?" she asked.

He smiled and shot her a sideways glance. "I thought you ruled out all of my firearms."

"Yeah, well, beggars can't be choosers and that revolver you gave me isn't coming out of the lake anytime soon."

Two seconds after she had said it, she realized her error.

"What did you just say?" Cody asked.

"Crap."

"How do you know it's in the lake?"

Hannah preemptively said, "Don't blame her, alright?"

He narrowed his eyes. "Blame who?"

"With the abuse and her fearing I would leave, Mary's head isn't right," she explained

"She shot herself in the leg?" Cody blurted out.

"You don't know what it's like living with Dale," she reminded him.

His eyebrows shot up to his hairline.

"Honest to God, I'm grateful she didn't shoot herself in the head with all the garbage she's been dealing with at home."

"Right." He glanced out at the lake again, holding the ledge of the deck in a white-knuckle grip. "Did you ask her about the photo?"

"She told me that the strip of photos fell out of her pocket at the mall. When she found it again, the bottom photo had been torn off."

"And you believe her?"

"Yes. I don't know," she wavered, unable to decide. "Did Blake tell you anything else?"

"A lot. I have him with Dalton now." He snorted a mystified laugh as though he wasn't sure whether to be touched or disturbed. "Their reunion was memorable to say the least. You would think they had survived Pearl Harbor the way they were laughing and crying and clinging onto each other like they couldn't believe the other had lived. One thing is for sure. They're not interested in protecting the guy anymore."

"When were you going to tell me?"

"I *was* going to tell you. How about after dinner?"

She nodded in agreement, as Cody evaluated her shivering, hunched posture, and suggested they go inside.

Nothing brought Mary back to her senses like cooking.

When Hannah and Cody returned, they found Mary bossing Candice around, as the girl carried a stack of plates to the table and began arranging each place setting.

"Bring this to the table, too," Mary summoned, calling Candice back so she could give her a giant bowl of salad.

Certain not to get in Mary's way, Hannah scooped forks and knives out of a drawer and set those around the table, as well.

"Smells good," Cody told her,

Mary grinned at him in a way that made Hannah nervous. She shook it off and asked Mary what smelled so good.

"It's Quiche," she said, beaming a huge smile, as she walked the hot dish to the table. "Candice, the pot holder."

It might as well have been a foreign word the way the girl's face screwed up.

"The quilted square thing on the islet," her big sister told her.

Again, no comprehension. She was stuck on the word, *islet,* so Hannah grabbed the pot holder and placed it on the table, while Candice breathed, "Oh."

Candice tapped her mouth with her index finger before bolting into the kitchen where she collected four glasses. She set those out and assessed what else might be needed.

"Sit down, girl," Mary ordered her sister.

When everyone settled in around the table, Mary began serving with Kendra-caliber precision.

"You don't have any beer," she mentioned, shoveling a heap of Quiche into her mouth.

"I don't," said Cody. "But I'm sure the adults don't mind."

"This adult does," she countered.

Cody touched eyes with Hannah before he asked Mary, "How old are you, again?"

"Forty."

Cody laughed, but Mary was dead serious.

"Maybe pick up a case the next time you're out," she suggested.

He deferred to Hannah.

Hannah told her sister, "There's no drinking in this house."

"Yeah, right."

Hannah wondered if she would be able to live up to the rule, herself, then confirmed:

"This is a sober house."

Mary didn't appear to like the sound of that, or believe Hannah, but she decided not to argue. Instead, she asked, "What do you guys feel like doing tonight?"

Cody offered, "I have a ton of DVDs."

Candice smiled at that, her eyes widening.

257

Mary asked, "Do you have Beauty and the Beast? That's one of Candice's favorites."

"I might," he said. "I have a whole library, so you can take a look after dinner."

As they ate dinner, Hannah realized that this was the closest thing to normal she had experienced in ages.

A little slice of heaven, Hannah thought, smiling to herself.

This was nice.

Though brash as ever, Mary seemed relatively content, considering she wasn't getting drunk on beer. And Candice seemed relaxed. She had been talking a little more freely.

As dinner unfolded, Mary shared her plans to fix up the shack and build an extension for when she would have kids. Hannah and Cody exchanged deeply worried glances. But they silently agreed that now wasn't the time or place to explain to Mary that the world was much larger than Dale's tyranny. Candice participated in the conversation, which spawned sibling spats and brief flares of bickering, but those soon resolved naturally.

When everyone was finished eating, Candice began clearing the table, but Hannah told the girls they could hang out in the den.

Candice went gaga over Cody's entertainment system, which had a giant screen TV, and his large assortment of DVDs. The girls got comfortable on the pull-out sofa, which was also where they would sleep tonight.

Cody helped Hannah with the dishes, and after they had cleaned up, Cody invited her to his office upstairs. She told him to go ahead. She wanted to check on the girls.

In the den, Candice was sprawled across the couch, her head propped on pillows, her arm dangling off the edge. Mary sat cross-legged in a nearby beanbag. A teen movie about an urban dance troupe played softly, which had Candice patting her leg in rhythm to the song and humming off key. It also had Hannah wondering why in the hell Cody owned a teen movie about an urban dance troupe.

When Mary realized that Hannah was hovering in the doorway, she got to her feet and wrapped her arms around Hannah, surprising her with a hug.

"I like it here," she said softly.

Hannah stroked her hair and rubbed her back.

"Do you think Daddy's okay?" Mary asked and glanced up, fearing her big sister's response.

Hannah told her as kindly as she could, "Dale needs help. Serious help. And he'll get it. It will be okay."

Mary looked confused and Hannah figured that the girl probably thought she *had* been helping him.

Mary breathed, "Maybe all this will be over soon and we can start our new life together. Put everything else behind us."

Hannah wondered what would constitute this 'being over,' but gave Mary a reassuring smile, as she urged her back.

"You're a very smart girl, Mary. I want you to think about what you would like to do with your life. It's time for you to really embrace your potential. You have more to offer this world than fixing up an old shack."

"Yeah, okay."

"I'll be upstairs if you need me."

She pulled Mary in for another hug, then said, "Have fun."

In the upstairs office, Cody had laid his firearms across a wooden table.

Hannah joined him. The office was like the rest of his home—cozy and organized and woodsy. An oak desk spanned the far wall under the windows and there was another plaid sofa, though smaller than the one downstairs.

"Take your pick," he said, referring to the handguns.

She scanned the row and a GLOCK 27 jumped out. Taking it, she asked, "Is this new?"

"No, I just didn't bring it before."

"It'll do." She glanced down its left flank then the right, feeling its weight in her hand. "Nine rounds?"

"Plus one extra in the floor plate." Cody walked to the far side of his desk where a closet was ajar. "I have a number of holsters. Shoulder or hip?"

"A hip holster? I can't walk around town like it's the Wild West." She tucked the weapon down the back of her jeans. "I'll do just fine keeping it like this."

"Suit yourself," he said with an easy smile, as he opened his laptop on the desk and offered her the chair.

As she eased into her seat, already tense with anticipation, he sat on the edge of his desk.

"According to Blake, the entire operation to abduct Kendra consisted of Dalton, Travis, and Blake. There were no others involved in the woods that night. Blake told me about the van they had used during the abduction. Since the abduction, the van has been sitting at a mechanic's lot in Tilton. A forensic team is currently investigating the van for DNA, and we're talking to the autobody shop owner, too. I'm not sure what DNA will do for us, since we already know who the three abductors were, but you never know."

"That sounds good," she said.

"Both Dalton and Blake were blackmailed into participating."

"Blackmailed?"

"It's fair to assume they were targeted because of their pre-existing relationship with Kendra, selling her meth and what-not. But we learned that both Dalton and Blake were straightforwardly blackmailed with incriminating photos."

"Incriminating photos of what?"

"Whoever is behind this is careful and smart," he said, changing the subject.

"I can handle it, Cody, just tell me," she said, impatiently. The anticipation had to be worse than the information. "What incriminating photos?"

"Let me just preface this by saying, we both know that Candice is downstairs right now. She's safe and fine."

Hannah's eyes went white all around. "What are you telling me?"

"This is the whole story. One day, Blake received a letter in the mail, which told him to come to the house-"

"Dale's house? The shack?"

"Yes. The letter mentioned the date and time that Blake was to show up. The letter itself was signed by Mary."

"What?"

"Bear in mind, Blake *said* it was signed by Mary, but he had never seen her handwriting before. Anyone could have written it."

"Okay?"

"The letter implied that Mary wanted to have sex with him. That she was kinky and he would have to be game for that. It also said he would have to burn the letter, and like a Goddamned idiot, he did."

Sickness roiled through her.

"When he got to the shack," Cody went on, "no one was home, according to Blake. Then he heard a girl calling his name from the woods at the edge of the lake. He figured it was Mary. It wasn't. It was Candice."

He paused as though he already regretted telling her the next piece of information.

"Blake found Candice naked near the lake. He said she looked scared."

"What?" Hannah breathed, barely wrapping her mind around the twisted facts.

Cody gave her a minute to process that much.

"So how was it blackmail?" she asked, sickened.

"Someone took photos of Blake standing near naked Candice, and as you can imagine, the photos told a story."

He took a breath as though he needed to recover as badly as she did.

"Blake received the blackmail letter about a week after that. They had instructions, and included a threat that Blake would go to prison if he didn't comply. Unlike the first letter, however, the blackmail letter promised a large payout to Blake if he did what he was told. Like the first letter, Blake burned the blackmail letter."

"Was the blackmail letter from Mary?" asked Hannah. "Or, I should say, forged as though Mary sent it?"

"No," he said. "It came anonymously. Now, by this point, Blake didn't think Mary had anything to do with this. If you ask me, that's up for debate. But I'm focusing on one thing at a time. Blake roped his cousin Travis in, because he wanted someone to have his back. Blake kept him high. Apparently, Travis was the worst addict of the three."

"I hate to ask this, but was Dalton blackmailed with the same thing? Did Candice have to...?"

Holding her gaze was enough of an answer. Hannah sprang up, desperate to distance herself from this as if such a thing were possible. As soon as she did, she saw a shadow in the hallway beyond the doorway and rushed out.

Her heart skipped a beat when she found Mary eavesdropping.

They locked eyes.

Mary spoke in a tone so devoid of emotion that it made Hannah's blood run cold, asking:

"What are you guys talking about?"

THE NEXT MORNING, Hannah functioned like a soldier—stoic, steadfast, and on high alert.

Her sleep had been plagued with nightmares and she had woken with a dark sense of foreboding that rattled her bones.

Despite her unease, she got the kids up, handling Mary with extra caution, keeping her distance and limiting eye contact.

When they were fed and dressed, their teeth brushed and textbooks collected, she ushered them to her car and drove them across town to school.

All the while, Hannah remained reserved in her interactions and direct with her responses. When Candice had a question, Hannah answered the girl succinctly. When Mary complained about having to go to school, Hannah sympathetically commiserated, but chose her words carefully.

Hannah wanted to believe that Mary was a victim in all this, but the pangs in Hannah's gut told her the girl was warped.

At the school, she pulled up along the curb and shifted her Taurus into Park.

"I'll be here at three-thirty," she told them.

"Three *fifteen*," Candice corrected her.

From the passenger seat, Mary told her, "My building is around the back."

"How about walking? You can get some fresh air?" Hannah suggested.

Mary rolled her eyes, popped her door open, and climbed out.

"Have a great day, girls!" Hannah called out.

"Bye Hannah!" Candice was sure to meet her gaze before she shut the back door. Then she took off running and joined a herd of students who were filtering through the entrance doors.

Hannah pulled out from the curb and kept her eye on Mary as she rounded the side of the school building.

Hannah eased through the parking lot. Something told her to follow Mary, or at least tail her long enough to make sure she went into the high school building.

When Hannah reached the corner and couldn't drive any further, she squeezed the brakes and watched Mary walk along a cement path that flanked the schoolhouse.

Wind blew her blond hair sideways, exposing the delicate nape of her neck, as a torrent of red leaves fluttered across her path.

Were men obsessed with her? Was infatuation with Mary an infectious disease? Was the mere thought of being with Mary so seductive that men far and wide would do anything for the chance?

Hannah found it impossible to comprehend, but the fact of the matter was that Blake had been lured into a trap because of Mary's signature.

Was the girl really that mesmerizing that her *signature* could get men to do the unthinkable?

Was she oblivious to this? Or was it a skill she exercised?

Hannah told herself that Mary was innocent. Some maniac had used Blake's infatuation with Mary against him, knowing that by signing Mary's name to a note, he would be able to trap Blake.

Up ahead, a rusted-out Jeep honked at Mary. The Jeep came to a stop. She waved at whoever was behind the wheel. A boy jumped out, approached her with swagger, and gave her a hug.

Mary pointed to her school building with an apologetic shrug, but the kid tried to convince her to get in.

Hannah breathed, "Don't do it."

Mary gave the boy a playful shove and he walked backwards, grabbing his heart as if she had broken it. Then he climbed back in and the Jeep tore off down the road.

"Good girl," Hannah whispered to herself.

But Mary didn't enter the schoolhouse.

Instead, she walked to the road and looked up the street, tapping her foot. At times, she glanced towards her building like she needed to get out of there before one of the school administrators caught her.

A moment passed and Hannah wracked her brain to recall whether or not the girl had a cell phone. She had never seen her with one. If she was waiting for someone, then who? And how had she contacted them? Had she used Cody's landline?

Then a black luxury car rolled up. The vehicle—an Audi—was sleek and classy with tinted windows.

Hannah couldn't believe what she was seeing.

Mary bounded over to the black car, opened the passenger side door, and hopped inside.

As soon as the car drove off, Hannah hit the gas, following the Audi at a distance.

The straight road soon became windy with bends and curves and dips and hills, as the woods—grand plumes of bright foliage—thickened on either side. The Audi came in and out of view, until the woods gave way.

There was a playground up ahead, which the Audi pulled into, its tires kicking up dust as the vehicle rolled to a stop.

The playground was a wasteland of rusty swings, tattered rope climbs, and dingy seesaws. This wasn't a place for kids. It was a place for junkies.

The dying grass was littered with syringe-needles. On one of the benches, a man oozed sideways, high on drugs. Near the swingset, a cluster of kids stood in a huddle and passed a bowl around. Every time one of them exhaled, billows of gritty smoke rose up into the air.

Hannah didn't drive into the parking area, but instead pulled over onto the shoulder of the road just shy of the playground, keeping the Audi in sight.

A minute passed before Mary climbed out. She had discarded her coat and sweater, and wore nothing but a skimpy undershirt as a top, which she had tied into a knot to expose her stomach.

Swaying her hips, she approached the cluster of kids, who were smoking. They were boys. None of them were girls, Hannah noted.

The tallest kid, who also appeared to be the oldest, took the initiative with Mary. He smiled crookedly, leering at her. He put his whole head into it as he looked her up and down.

She offered him her hand, but he hugged her instead, lingering, the guys behind him whistling and hollering.

When he released her, Mary felt his muscle under his sweatshirt, flirting, then she pressed up against him, whispering something in his ear.

The kid's eyebrows shot straight up to his hairline in response to whatever she was telling him.

He eyed the Audi in the parking lot. Then he eyed Mary and offered her the bowl. Declining, she shot her thumb over her shoulder, again indicating the Audi.

Next, Mary took the bowl and passed it to the other kids to smoke.

She said something else, and the kid was sold.

He followed Mary over to the Audi and climbed into the backseat with her.

As soon as the back door closed, the Audi reversed out of its parking spot, crawled through the dusty parking lot, and drove off.

Hannah ducked behind the wheel as the Audi drove past her car. She checked her rearview mirror, watching the black car disappear around a curve.

She threw her car into Drive, but hadn't gotten her foot on the gas when her cell phone rang inside her purse.

"Crap," she muttered, searching through her bag for her phone, her gaze locked on her rearview, hoping not to lose the Audi. "Yeah?"

"It's Cranston. Is now a good time?"

"Yesterday would've been a good time."

The Audi was long gone, so Hannah reached for her flask, twisting off the top one-handedly, and took a slug.

"I have information," he said and she was all ears. "When are you coming back, by the way?"

Christ, she hadn't been keeping track of the days. Quickly, she thumbed into the calendar on her cell phone and told him, "Three days from now."

"Well, we can't wait. Homicide has turned into a Goddamn circus without you."

"Cranston?"

"Yeah?"

"That's the best news I've had all week."

"I'm not trying to flatter you," he teased. "Anyway, are you ready to write this down?"

"Hang on." She clamped her cell phone between her ear and shoulder, and dumped the contents of her purse onto the passenger seat. When she found a pen and paper, she said, "Go ahead."

"Looks like your dad lives in Sanbornton-"

"Really?"

"I said, *looks like*," he corrected her.

"Okay," she calmly responded, understanding that she shouldn't get her hopes up.

"His name is Walter Warfield-"

"Warfield?" The irony was palpable. "No kidding?"

Cranston sighed into the receiver and she expected a sarcastic remark, but apparently he could do without. "Walter Warfield. Date of birth-"

"Don't need it. What's his address?"

"74 Circle Point Road."

Gradually, her brain grasped hold. "That's on Hermit Lake."

"If you say so."

"Did you get anything else?" she asked eagerly. "Do you know where he works? Does he have any arrests?"

"He might be retired. His employment history went cold after 2005, but when he was working, he was a veterinarian. And no arrests, no history of drug abuse or alcohol, and no record of domestic violence. He's clean on paper."

"Married?"

"Nope."

"Kids?"

"Other than you?"

"Point taken." She eased back in her chair and tucked the address into the breast pocket of her coat.

Cranston took on a gentle tone and asked, "How are you doing over there?"

"Two sheets to the wind, if I'm being honest with myself."

"God, Hannah. I thought you were done digging yourself out of that hole."

"Maybe I'm exaggerating. It's probably just one sheet at this point, a small one, like the white flag of surrender," she sighed. "I don't know."

"What about the Police Academy? You can do it. It can be more than just something you talk about at the water cooler."

"Yeah, I've been thinking about it."

When she trailed off, growing silent, he told her, "We're all praying for you."

"There's been a lot of that going around. I'm not seeing the effects yet."

He held the silence with her.

"Thanks for the address, Cranston. I'll see you soon."

She let him hang up before doing the same then sunk into her seat, resting her head back and pondering how in the hell her father had managed to exist in Sanbornton, right under her nose all her life, without her ever finding out.

Her cell phone rang, but she couldn't deal with talking to anyone.

The trees were too pretty.

She watched the leafy treetops sway in the breeze like they were waving at her—hello or goodbye or hang in there. It was anyone's guess.

Her phone quieted and a beep followed, indicating she had a new voicemail message.

She needed to drive over to Circle Point, face her father, and ask him about Kendra.

She hoped like hell that whatever he told her would help shed light on what had happened to her mother.

Emotionally, Hannah dug deep, mustering what little gumption she had left, and got on the road, driving towards Sanbornton and Hermit Lake.

As she drove, the voicemail message nagged her. She fought, but eventually gave in when she came to an intersection that would take her towards the lake.

After making the turn, Hannah punched her voicemail code into her cell phone, and listened.

Dale had left her a drunken, blubbering, pathetic-sounding message, she soon realized. But soon, his nonsense turned her world upside down:

"Hannaaaaaaah! This is your step-Daddy! It's Kendra! I found her in the lake!" Wailing cries came next, followed by snotty-sounding, gurgling gasps. "On the shore! She's dead, Hannah! I, I, I can't even speak of what they did to her!!!" A pause, then Dale exploded. "I need my girls! Bring me back my girls! Hannah!"

As the voicemail message continued to play, there was more crying and gasping and begging from Dale.

But all Hannah could think was…

Her mother had been found…

Dead.

CHAPTER NINETEEN

THE KENDRA COLE case was now officially a homicide.

Two officers, Sanders and Calhoon managed to quarantine Dale and his abominable hysterics inside the house, giving Cody the peace and quiet he needed to investigate the scene undisturbed until forensics arrived. The officers seemed leery of the shack, haunted by flashbacks of diarrhea-brownies, but Cody reminded them no one had put a gun to their heads. "Don't eat anything," he said, as though the solution to their problem was obvious.

Sanders seemed skeptical of the advice. "Mary isn't going to be here, is she?" he asked, implying he was powerless in the face of a voluptuous blonde.

"Christ," Cody muttered, pointing to Sander's skull. "Your brain is up *there*."

All the while, Dale sat on the sofa and wailed for his girls as though they were the air he breathed and without them he would surely die.

Cody stalked out the door and crossed the yard.

Convenient timing, Cody thought, as he stared down at what was left of Kendra and mentally worked through the timeline.

Hannah had taken the girls from Dale, after which Kendra had turned up dead. Dale was now using the murder as a way to get the girls back. The man's twisted logic set Cody's teeth on edge.

Cody stood over the body.

Kendra was lying face up on the shore. Her head was in the mud. Her legs were bobbing in the water.

Cody formed an overall impression, as he studied Kendra. Her clothes were dirty and torn. Her boots were loose on her feet. There were a few bruises on her face—on her chin and left eye, specifically.

There was gauze wrapped around her left wrist where her hand used to be. Whoever had dressed her wound knew what they were doing, medically speaking.

Then he kneeled down, getting a closer look at her. She had a fair amount of color to her pallor. She couldn't have been dead that long. He would like to think that she looked peaceful since her eyes were closed, but he saw matted hair at the sides of her head where her ears used to be, and decided against it.

Cody told himself that Kendra was in a better place now.

Mud had seeped through his jeans at the knees so he stood up and found a pair of latex gloves in his inner pocket.

As he worked them onto his hands, he scanned the mud and soil, looking for footprints, but the entire expanse of the shore had been thoroughly trampled by all the police officers who had arrived on the scene.

Dale had told the responding officers he had been at his church, after which he had gone straight home and straight inside the shack. It hadn't been until he had come out for a little late afternoon target practice that he rounded the house and caught sight of the body floating in the water.

The sum total of Dale's drunken proclamations was that he didn't have an alibi after leaving the church.

He had gone on to promise he hadn't touched the body. When he had found Kendra dead, he ran back inside to call Hannah. Then he had called 911.

The pastor over at the Church of God had yet to get back to Cody, but Cody had a feeling that that portion of Dale's timeline wouldn't hold water.

Gingerly, Cody inched his fingertips along Kendra's hairline towards the back of her skull and continued exploring in a circular fashion to investigate if she had received any blows to the head.

At first blush, her cause of death wasn't obvious. He felt no gashes or lacerations, so he ventured to lift her shirt from the bottom.

Cody discovered stitches along her lower abdomen, suturing what appeared to be stab wounds, which called Candice's account to mind. The wounds appeared to be healed, and merely looked like streaks of pink scar tissue. Again, the same medical precision had been employed.

Upon further examination, he confirmed she had received no lethal blows to her chest.

What the hell had killed her?

Cody heard tires crunching over gravel and glanced over his shoulder to discover the Chief pulling in along with the medical examiner and coroner, which meant forensics couldn't be far off.

When he returned his gaze to Kendra, her eyes were open.

Cody's heart skipped a beat, and pounded hard against his chest cavity, as he stared down at Kendra.

Suddenly, she gasped for air, and began flailing her arms and trying to dig her heels into solid earth that wasn't there. Lake water splashed all around.

"Medics!" Cody yelled over his shoulder without taking his eyes off her. "Kendra, Kendra, I'm Detective McAlister. Can you hear me?"

She kept flailing, her eyes wild with terror, as she jerked this way and that, panicking.

Gently, he held her and again asked if she could hear and comprehend him. "I need you to stay calm. We're going to get you to the hospital."

She was whimpering and gasping in a fitful display of terror and utter confusion.

"You were abducted-"

She frantically nodded and grasped hold of his forearm just as the medical examiner breathed his astonishment, setting a gurney down into the mud with a clank.

"Holy hell, it's a Goddamn miracle," Chief Marley blurted out as soon as he saw Kendra alive. Everyone worked to hoist Kendra onto the gurney.

'Miracle' was too small a word.

As they rolled Kendra towards the driveway, Cody shifted his gaze from Kendra, whose hand he was tightly holding, to the house.

If Dale was behind this, the last thing Cody wanted was for him to know the unlikely turn of events.

He asked the Chief, "Let's keep this quiet?" Marley cocked a brow at him. "Keep it between ourselves until we catch the son of a bitch."

Agreeing with the strategy, Chief Marley suggested, "Admit her under Jane Doe at the hospital."

Marley stared at Kendra with wide eyes, as though he still couldn't believe it, as the medics angled the gurney into the back of the ambulance.

"Get her to Sanbornton Mercy fast," Cody told the ambulance driver. "She's alive. But don't use the siren."

The driver responded with, "Copy that."

Cody joined the Chief, as the ambulance swung around and started off for the hospital.

"We need at least two officers outside the ICU to guard her," Cody told his Chief.

"I'm with you, but we're spread thin. Already got two officers on Gerrity and Abbott."

"Kendra was supposed to be dead. We don't know who this guy is. We won't have any way to see him coming if he does, and he *will* come if he catches wind that Kendra survived."

Marley drew in a deep breath, clenched his jaw, and said, "I'll make it happen."

A vehicle crawled towards them, and Cody realized it was Hannah.

Cody thanked the Chief and Marley took off for Sanbornton Mercy, as Cody met Hannah at her car.

She looked devastated. Her eyes were pink and puffy and filled with despair. As she climbed out, she looked as frail as a paper doll. He could almost hear the tormenting thoughts bouncing around her head.

She was already fixated on the lake.

"Hey," he said.

It didn't draw her attention.

"Where is she?"

"The ambulance took her." He squeezed her shoulders and she looked at him. "I'll tell you what's going on, but you can't breathe a word of it to anyone."

She didn't even blink.

"There are a couple police officers in the house with Dale. The girls are at school?"

"Yes," she responded. "Mary cut classes, but I'm sure she'll be back in time for me to pick them up."

Mary cutting school was the least of his worries. "Dale said he found Kendra's body on the shore."

Hearing that, Hannah burst out sobbing.

He cradled her and said, "Dale thought she was dead. So did I. But she's alive."

He urged her back and looked at her.

A moment passed before the information took hold. Hannah brightened, though confusion lingered on her face.

"She's alive?" she whispered. "Alive?"

"Hannah, listen to me. This is extremely important."

In an instant, every part of her was alert, listening.

"No one can know she's alive. Not Mary, not Candice, not Dale. I don't care if you're alone in the forest and get the urge to tell a tree. No one."

"But the girls-"

"No one, Hannah. She's in critical condition and even though there will be police officers stationed at her ICU room, she's vulnerable. We can't risk word getting out that she's alive."

"Okay." She looked as though she was wrapping her mind around how she was going to conduct herself around the girls. "What do I do?"

Sensing someone might be coming, Cody glanced over his shoulder at the house, but they were alone.

"Dale thinks she's dead. You're going to proceed as though she is."

"Christ, Cody." She closed her eyes, wincing. "You want me to tell Mary and Candice their mother turned up dead?"

"Yes, I want you to proceed with a memorial. I want an obituary in tomorrow's paper. The whole nine yards. Hey, hey," he said, catching her by the shoulders as she folded in on herself, crying. "It's only until I catch him."

When she returned her gaze, she asked, "How am I supposed to pull off a memorial without a body?"

"Even if she was dead, the body wouldn't be released from evidence that quickly," he supplied. "Simple as that. Make arrangements with the church Dale likes so much."

"Okay." She seemed to ride a swell of apprehension, but she asked him, "Is Dale behind this?"

"Once I talk to Kendra, I'll confirm."

CHAPTER TWENTY

CODY PLANNED TO stay with Kendra in the hospital, watch over her throughout the night to ensure she wouldn't be attacked, and God willing, pull as much information out of her as possible the moment she became stable, which left Hannah to deliver the harrowing lie to her half-sisters.

She knew her strategy would be like a BandAid on a bullet wound, but she picked up a case of Coors beer and two gallons of ice cream for the girls, and a jug of whiskey for herself. It was going to be a long night.

As she drove to the school to pick them up, she reminded herself that it was only a matter of time before the girls would know the truth and be reunited with their mother. They would understand why Hannah had no choice but to lie. They would forgive her.

She kept her eye on Mary the entire drive home, thoughts of the black luxury vehicle and Mary's strange dealings in the park causing Hannah's brain to burn.

When they reached Cody's house, she sat the girls down at the dining room table, handed Mary a cold can of beer, which surprised the girl, and passed Candice a gallon of Rocky Road with a spoon.

Then Hannah struggled to convey the lie that she knew would break their hearts.

Mary broke down. Tears erupted from her eyes, though her demeanor quickly turned to steel after that. Candice was shocked and horrified, but she went vacant after that. Soon she was tucked so deep in her own mind that Hannah feared she would never again come out.

"I'm going to make some calls," Hannah softly explained. "Reserve the church for tomorrow. You might want to write down some nice words about Mom to read at the memorial."

She so badly wanted to tell them it would be okay and show some hint that things weren't as they seemed, but she would only come off looking callous and detached if she did.

They sat in silence, the air thick with despair, invisible walls rising between them, isolating each to her grief.

Hannah felt herself slipping away, as well, consumed by thoughts of the lake. Just days ago, she had lost herself to its icy waters. She had floated like a corpse on its surface as though she were a living premonition of her mom. Yet, she had lived and so had Kendra. The watery grave had claimed neither. Mother and daughter undergoing fates so similar, she wondered why God had seen it fit to create two people instead of one.

Mary took a long haul from her beer, lifting her chin and letting the cold liquid fill her mouth. She was so much like Dale that Hannah couldn't help but stare—parents and children, one in the same, everywhere she turned.

She was interrupted from her reverie when Candice, suddenly sour, tried to attack Mary. The little girl lunged across the table at Mary and grabbed the beer can out of her hand. Beer splashed and sloshed, as Mary jerked away yelling, "Get off!"

Screaming, Candice hurled the can against the wall. On impact, it exploded, mirroring the rage she couldn't contain.

In a delayed reaction, Hannah rushed to Candice and held her, but the little girl slapped her, wildly fighting to be freed.

Resigned, Mary said, "Leave her alone." Her voice sounded hollow, as she crossed to the kitchen. "I'll just get another one."

Hearing her say that sent Candice into another screaming fit. "It's killing us!"

Hannah held Candice back from attacking Mary again.

Mary glared at her younger sister as she passed through to the sliding glass door to let herself out.

"Candice, honey, it'll be okay." Hannah was kneeling and looking up at the girl, whose blue eyes were raw and fiery.

Her face scrunched into a snarl and she seethed, "You shouldn't have come home." Then she tore through the living room, heading for the den, where she plopped onto the sofa.

Hannah glimpsed the can of beer on the floor from the corner of her eye, its contents still gurgling out and pooling across the shiny wooden floor, but she couldn't deal with it.

Rounding the kitchen islet, she found the jug of whiskey resting on the marble counter. She grabbed a glass from the cabinets, and poured generously.

When she joined Mary on the rear deck with her drink, the girl was staring out at the lake, as dusk gathered across the sky. She was tempted to ask about the black Audi, and the junkie Mary had courted so easily, and the driver, whose face Hannah hadn't seen. She wanted to ask about the luring letters, Mary's signature, how it could've possibly come to pass that her name had been woven throughout this nightmare.

But Mary said, "I followed you."

"What are you talking about?" She met her at the ledge of the deck, but Mary didn't acknowledge her.

"It was so long ago, but nothing's changed." She drank and Hannah studied her, trying to pinpoint where in her mind this memory stemmed from. "You looked so pretty."

"When?"

"The night of your prom."

Hannah's stomach dropped.

"Your dress was yellow. Sleeveless. It was too short." She smiled faintly. "When you were showering, getting ready for Cody, I put it on. It was swimming on me." She glanced at Hannah then returned her gaze to the lake. "I wanted to be just like you. I had all these fantasies in my head about what you would do that night, and what the prom would be like. I went there. I walked to the high school building in the dark."

"You were only seven."

"I knew where it was. I climbed a dumpster outside, and watched you through the window. I never took my eyes off you." Mary paused to drink then set the can on the ledge of the deck so she could cross her arms to ward off the cold wind. "I heard Cody suggest the church. I knew where it was."

Hannah breathed, "God."

"It took me so long to get there. I didn't even have a flashlight. It was drizzling."

Hannah prayed as hard as she could that her sister hadn't seen the worst of it.

"When I stepped through the door…" Mary cringed as though the memory was overcoming her. "Those horrible sounds. What they did to you…" She trailed off. "I was petrified. I barely understood what I was seeing. I didn't know what to do, but I knew they were attacking you. I felt so small and helpless. My mind kept screaming at me to *kill them*."

Mary locked eyes with her, as shadows fell all around them.

"I hid in the bushes outside," she went on, and Hannah could barely stomach it. "I watched those boys take off. Waited for you to come out. I followed you home, walking yards behind you. I felt a sense of duty, like I could protect you on your journey home."

She swallowed the lump that had formed in her throat.

"I just want to keep you safe, Hannah."

Hannah fought deep, internal trembling. She wasn't sure her legs would hold. Tears stung her eyes.

"I don't know if he knew or he sensed it or if Daddy had been waiting for his moment to pull me into darkness, but later that night was the first time he handed me a beer. And it worked, Hannah. I drank and felt funky and tried not to look at his bloody knuckles. He had gone after Cody that night, after he had seen you come into the house looking disheveled, hadn't he?"

Her voice was a thread, "Yes."

"Drinking did the trick. The alcohol helped bury my rage, the hatred I felt. And beer has helped ever since. Candice doesn't understand." Again, Mary met her gaze. "But you understand. Don't you?"

Her response was a breath. Had it been more, she would've shattered.

"It doesn't make you forget, though, "Hannah said. "That's where he lied."

Now Hannah knew why Mary was warped. She had witnessed the horrible attack that had occurred at the church and had watched her older half-sister crumble apart as a result.

Had it filled Mary with delusions of grandeur? Had Mary staged all these horrors that had befallen Kendra in order to get Hannah back home just like she had staged her own shooting?

"When you finally left us, I knew that was the reason. Sure, Dale contributed and Kendra contributed, living in a shack in the woods played its part. But it was that night, what you suffered, that drove you away. And I know if I could've stopped it, if I could've saved you, or gotten there earlier and made Cody stay, you would've never walked out on us."

It broke Hannah's heart, because it was true.

Hannah mustered a response. "You can't blame yourself."

"Yeah," said Mary without agreement. She knocked back her beer. "I got you here. No matter what happens, I'm not letting you go."

Trepidation twisted through Hannah. Mary had been guarding so many secrets. Suddenly, her heart sank. Had Mary orchestrated this entire tragedy as a means to get Hannah back?

"I'm going to write up a little something for Mom," she said, pulling the sliding glass door open. "Maybe you can read it over and make sure it sounds good?"

"Sure."

Before disappearing inside, Mary told her, "I don't give a crap she's dead so long as I have you."

As soon as Hannah was alone, she realized she was stunned.

THE MEMORIAL was bizarre.

Residents of Sanbornton had crawled out of the woodwork and piled into the church. Everyone in attendance was eager to pay their respects to a woman whose body wasn't there. They had crammed in the pews and stood along the walls. Children sat in the aisle. There were even people looking in through the windows, straining to hear the pastor who had far too much to say about heaven, Kendra's final resting place.

Hannah was seated in the front row between Candice and Mary, who clutched Hannah's hand as if doing so would give both of them strength. For what, Hannah feared to imagine. Not to get through this, that was for sure. Mary had made herself clear that Kendra's murder had no effect on her.

Candice was staring through her eyebrows at a giant blown-up photograph of Kendra that was propped on an easel stand. In the photo, brown curly hair framed Kendra's pretty face. Her eyes were huge, and her mouth looked frozen in an awkward smile as though she hadn't expected the click. The photo was surrounded by bouquets of flowers.

Across the aisle from Hannah and the girls sat Dale. He was surrounded by his buddies—men dressed in duck hunting gear. Dale's face was stained with tears, and he kept shifting his horrified attention from his girls to the pastor and to his girls again. He had already interrupted the proceedings several times to shout, "Make us whole, Jesus Christ!" In response, his buddies had gripped his shoulders and pulled him back to his seat where he let out his emotions loudly.

Hannah couldn't look at him.

Mary's warm hand, her tight grip on Hannah's hand, made Hannah uneasy.

And the way Candice didn't blink, as she glared through her eyebrows like a rabid animal, staring at her mother's photo, set Hannah's teeth on edge.

When it was the girls' turn to say a few words, they approached the podium using soft, solemn steps. Candice tripped before she reached the lectern, which the congregation found adorable. Mary kept her arm around her younger sister as they spoke. The fact that Kendra was recovering across town made their speeches all the more gut wrenching.

Candice spoke about one day joining her mother in heaven and Mary followed up with warm sentiments, all of which Hannah had written days prior right after she had crossed out everything the girl had written about their mother.

When they stepped down, Dale ran up and captured them in a big fat blubbering hug. It turned Hannah's stomach, but she pried him off, ordering him through her gritted teeth to sit down.

He did, and then he realized it was his turn.

After getting up again, he pulled his speech from his pocket, and as he unfolded the papers, Hannah realized he had written quite a bit about Kendra. There were seven pages in Dale's hands, and he had written on the front *and the back* of each sheet of paper.

Dale couldn't get through one paragraph, though. He collapsed into a miserable knot of sobs. His buddies peeled him off the lectern, and ushered him to his seat.

Dale shook his fist at the heavens next, crying out for Jesus Christ while calling him a son of a bitch at the same time. He followed up with threats against God that he hadn't a prayer in hell of executing.

Appalled, Hannah stared at Dale, and she wasn't the only one.

But then Hannah caught sight of Candice. The girl was smirking strangely.

It was unsettling and struck Hannah as highly abnormal.

As Dale took all the time in the world to fall silent, the pastor was gracious enough, exercising patience before making excuses for Dale. He offered words of hope and unity to the congregation. Then he invited everyone to the potluck outside, noting that Marjorie Abbott's homemade coconut cookies were sinfully delicious.

Outside, people gathered around the picnic tables. Hannah and the girls exited the church, avoiding the pastor as much as Dale, who were standing in the church vestibule.

When they reached the food, Mary and Candice wedged themselves in and began making plates, as Hannah kept an eye on them and accepted condolences from a number of family friends.

Soon Dale emerged from the church. Hannah excused herself from the people she was talking to, and met Dale just shy of the church steps.

"I need to bring the girls to the shack right after they eat. They need to pick up more of their things," she asserted. "You stay here."

He angled in on her, all signs of grief gone from his face, and threatened, "This isn't over, Hannah. This is just getting started."

"Do not come to the house," she warned, cutting him off. She kept her strides quick as she walked over to the girls. "Come on. We're going to get your things now."

"We just started eating," Mary complained.

"You can eat in the car and we can come right back," she said, negotiating, not that they were interested in compromising. "Come on. Let's go. We need to do this before your dad goes home."

Candice shoved two coconut cookies into her mouth and tossed her paper plate into a trash bin.

As they walked to the car, Mary said, "The memorial was weird."

WHEN THEY REACHED the shack, Hannah let the girls go ahead so she could check that the GLOCK 27 Cody had lent her was in proper working order. It was. She tucked it down the back of her pants then made sure that the gun would remain hidden under her coat.

She unzipped the inner compartment of her purse, found the set of keys she had stolen from Mary, and shoved them into the front pocket of her jeans with the intention to return them to Mary's bin where they belonged. No one would need them anymore.

She thought about Kendra as she popped the trunk of her car and grabbed the empty suitcase she had brought. Cody hadn't called or texted, which she was taking as a good sign. Her mother was still alive and the longer Kendra held on, the more certain it would be she would pull through and fully recover, and hopefully tell Cody every last detail she could recall. Hannah's heart raced at the thought.

Inside, the girls seemed bewildered. Candice was standing in the hallway and peering into her bedroom as though it frightened her, and Mary was wasting time by tending to the dirty dishes in the sink.

"Grab more essentials," Hannah instructed, "and put them in the suitcase." She set the suitcase in the hallway between the girls' bedrooms. Then she doubled back for Mary. "Dale can clean his own dishes."

"He won't. He'll live in filth and try to drink his way out of it."

"We don't have much time, Mary."

Mary kept on, so Hannah stepped in, taking over.

Reluctant as she was, Mary finally started up the hallway, leaving Hannah to scrub pots and ponder why in the hell that girl had a soft spot in her heart for a brute like Dale. She gritted her teeth at the thought that crossed her mind—Dale and Mary could be in cahoots, and behind the entire abduction. Hannah told herself not to think about it. The truth would come out soon enough. It was only a matter of time.

After doing the dishes, Hannah cut up the hallway to check on the girls' progress. The suitcase wasn't even half full, she discovered when she pressed their clothes down flat inside.

"Pack more jeans and sweaters," she suggested. "We can buy toiletries, socks, and underwear."

The girls went to task.

Dale's bedroom stole Hannah's attention.

At first, she only peered into his room from the hallway, thinking that would cure her curiosity. The bed's comforter and sheets were a mess on the bed. Beer cans littered the floor. His nightstand lamp was flickering. Everything about his room reflected his dysfunction. But glimpsing it didn't satisfy her curiosity, so Hannah milled through, observing the nooks and crannies as though they might tell her his secrets.

She was so engrossed in snooping that she didn't hear the front door unlock and creak open. She didn't hear Dale's heavy footsteps cross the living room. She had no idea that Dale had come home until his mountainous shape filled the doorway of his bedroom.

Instinctively, Hannah withdrew her weapon and aimed her GLOCK at Dale's chest.

He wasn't fazed.

The house sounded too quiet. She realized she couldn't hear the girls. "Where are they?" she demanded as she trained her aim on him.

"They're staying here with me."

"Where are they?" she yelled, as she kept the handgun aimed at Dale.

"Safe and sound in Candice's room." He slowly raised his hands, but Hannah didn't trust he was surrendering.

"Don't you see what you've done to them?" she asked. "They lock themselves in their rooms to get away from you." As she spoke, Hannah grew acutely aware of the fact she was trapped.

"You're not taking them." He crept towards her with confident steps. "It doesn't have to be like this, Hannah."

"Stay where you are," she warned. "I'll shoot."

"You'll shoot? I'm sure the crows you hit will be very sorry when you pull the trigger." He laughed and kept stalking towards her. "I know you're not going to fire at me with the girls in the house."

"You killed her."

The statement fazed him as much as her weapon.

She grimaced at the thought that Dale had orchestrated all of this, that he had manipulated Mary, forced Candice to stand naked in the woods, and perhaps recruited his sick buddies to move Kendra's body. Hannah wanted to throw in Dale's face that he had failed, because Kendra was alive. "I don't know how you did it, but I know it was you."

"You're a stupid woman," he spat through his teeth. "You don't have half the brains your sisters do."

"I said, don't move!"

He lunged at her.

Hannah leapt onto the bed and stumbled across the mess of sheets to get away from him. Her boot became tangled in the blankets and she tripped and slammed into the wall, no longer able to keep her gun aimed on him.

Dale charged towards her, but she sprinted past him and darted into the hallway.

He fired his gun and a bullet zinged past her head.

"Girls!" she screamed, as she panicked to ascertain whether or not she had been hit.

She hadn't.

Scrambling, she turned up the hallway.

Her gaze locked with Mary's. The girl was standing in the hallway with a chair, and the sight of her scrambled Hannah's brain. Why was she in the hallway? Why did she have a chair?

"Lock him in!" Mary ordered.

Thinking fast, Hannah turned and slammed the bedroom door in Dale's face, just as Dale tried to grab her.

He shoved the door, but Hannah and Mary braced their full weight against it to prevent him from getting out.

Dale pushed hard from inside.

The door bounced in and out of its frame, banging and cracking, as Hannah shouted, "Get the keys in my pocket! The right pocket!"

Mary shoved her fingers down her sister's jeans and yanked the keys out then quickly clambered onto the chair, her hands shaking, as she frantically searched for the right key.

Dale yelled threats, as he pounded harder and harder on the door, but Hannah fought to keep the door closed, as Mary fit the key into the lock overhead.

Straining to hold the door shut, her every muscle trembling, Hannah glanced up at Mary, who finally managed to turn the key.

Once Dale was locked in, Hannah yelled:

"Come on!"

She grabbed the suitcase, kicked the chair aside, and shoved Mary forward down the hallway just as Dale started firing his gun at the door frame, aiming to bust the lock off. "Where's your sister? Candice!"

As the sounds of gunshots pierced her eardrums, Hannah pushed Mary onward, while she dragged the suitcase, tearing through the living room and out the door.

Candice was outside, leaning against her Taurus, casually eyeing the fall foliage as though it was any other lazy afternoon.

"Get in the car!" she ordered, hauling the suitcase towards the trunk. "He'll kill us all!"

"He didn't kill Mom," Candice told Hannah with a strange glint in her eye.

"What?" Out of breath, she hoisted the suitcase inside the trunk, slammed the trunk shut, and started for Candice. "How do you know?" Hannah grabbed Candice by the shoulders and shook her. "Do you know who did that to Mom?" She shook her again. "Do you?"

Candice looked smug, which made no sense to Hannah, so she threw the girl into the backseat of the car and shut the car door.

Mary tugged Hannah by the arm. "We have to get out of here!"

Shots kept firing from inside the house, but they sounded a hell of a lot closer than Dale's bedroom by the time Hannah and Mary jumped into the car.

Hannah turned the engine, but it wouldn't start.

"No! Don't do this to me now!" She tried again and again, all the while Mary screamed at her to hurry up and get them out of there. "I'm trying!"

All of a sudden, Dale barged out of the shack and spilled across the porch.

"Go!" Mary yelled.

"I can't!"

Dale lifted his gun, taking aim at their car.

The engine turned and Hannah stomped the gas pedal down.

Dale fired his weapon, but they were already tearing down the driveway, the car kicking up dirt and dust under squealing tires. His aim had been off and they weren't hit.

Candice went flying in the backseat and slammed against the inner door when Hannah turned onto the road, cutting a hard left at the end of the driveway.

Soon, the trees shielded them. Dale fired and fired, but he didn't have a prayer of hitting them.

Once they had driven a safe distance, Hannah's gaze snapped to the rearview mirror to check that Candice was alive and well back there.

The little girl looked like she was sneering.

"If you know something, Candice, you have to tell me," she demanded, as she fought to catch her breath, but the girl ignored her.

Then Candice started belting out that low, creepy tone.

Hannah looked over at Mary.

The teenage girl was smiling when their eyes met, and she said:

"I saved you."

CHAPTER TWENTY-ONE

THE MAJORITY OF Sanbornton's residents lived below the poverty line, though it wasn't a fixed given. Hermit Lake, located on the northern edge of town, attracted rich and poor alike. Some had shacks as depressed as the Coles', while others lived in modest homes like Cody's pre-war Colonial.

On the western side of the lake lived Sanbornton's wealthiest residents. They had bought land and built three-story estates that clashed with the landscape as if wealth and nature didn't get along.

The richest of the rich dominated this stretch of land, and Hannah felt like a trespasser because of it.

She had asked Mary to look after Candice, who had been acting more and more bizarrely—smug one minute and defensive the next. Earlier that day, Hannah had found Candice with a dead mouse. The girl had been grinning from ear to ear as she had pressed its soft body between her palms. Hannah's intuition told her that Candice had killed it, but the very concept disturbed Hannah so greatly that she decided she must be incorrect. Instead of questioning Candice about how the mouse had died, Hannah had pinched the thing by its tail and thrown it into the outside trash bins in front of the garage.

The girls would be fine for an hour or two, or so that was what she had told herself. If she hadn't, she wouldn't have been able to make the drive to 74 Center Point Road, which was the address Cranston had given Hannah—the address of her biological father's house.

As she pulled up the driveway, the headlights of her car illuminated the architecture, a Colonial Revival design with white columns, a large portico, and four chimneys jutting from its shingled roof.

She couldn't help but wonder who she would have become if her father had stayed in her life. Would she be just as screwed up, but spoiled rich? Or would she have turned into a decent person who didn't abuse alcohol?

Unlike most lakeshore homes which had been built with the lake in back, Walter Warfield's ran parallel to the water, the lake to its left, a light dusting of trees straight ahead, which Hannah had driven around, following his winding driveway.

She noted that most of the windows were aglow with interior lights.

Walter was home.

She killed the headlights, next the engine, and climbed out of her car.

Cold wind whipped at her sideways.

It was freezing, but that didn't embolden her to reach the portico quickly. Nothing about Hannah in this moment felt bold.

For a man who she had envisioned to be her hero countless times, it had only recently occurred to her that her real father might be anything but, and a biting mix of hope and dread filled her chest because of it.

What had happened between her mother and him all those years ago? Why had Kendra regarded her marriage to him as unspeakable? Had their divorce foreshadowed Kendra's attack, and would knocking on her father's door lead Hannah to the answers she was desperate for?

There was only one way to find out.

She pounded on the lofty front door so that she wouldn't have to knock twice then stepped back and hoped her racing heart would calm.

The passing moment felt like an eternity then the door swung inward, revealing a man whose face looked so much like Hannah's that her heart skipped a beat.

His every facial feature—the dark eyebrows, the delicate nose, the wide mouth, the strong jawline, and high cheekbones—appeared to be the same as Hannah's.

"Can I help you?" he asked.

"Hello," she stammered. Her voice cracked so she cleared her throat and tried again. "I'm sorry to show up unannounced. I'm..." She trailed off, sensing his impatience. "I'm Hannah Cole. I'm your daughter."

Walter appeared devoid of emotion and unmoved that his long, lost daughter was standing before him. He was probably in shock.

She suddenly noticed that white surgical gauze was poking up from his shirt collar. Two strips of surgical tape held it in place where the left side of his neck extended from his collarbone.

Had someone attacked him?

"I know this is terribly rude of me to stop by unannounced," she blathered on when he hadn't said anything. "I wanted to tell you in person that my mother, Kendra Cole, has passed away."

"Yes, I heard." His response came without emotion, even though he said, "I'm so sorry for your loss. Would you like to come in?"

Hannah smiled nervously and accepted the invitation.

She followed Walter into a grand foyer with marble floors and arched ceilings. She waited awkwardly, while he closed the door.

"Hannah Cole…" he said to himself.

"I had no idea you lived in Sanbornton, or in New Hampshire for that matter," she mentioned.

"You would have if your mother hadn't been…" He didn't finish the thought.

Hannah nodded. "Yeah, I know how she was."

They left it at that, which was a relief to Hannah, and he led her into his living room.

As Hannah took in the decorum—a leather sofa, expensive-looking end tables, fancy alabaster lamps, the walls lined with handsome bookshelves—she noticed medical journals were fanned out across the coffee table.

"Please, have a seat," he said. "Can I offer you something to drink? A water perhaps? I also have coffee and espresso."

"Actually, a drink would be nice. I've been on edge," she admitted. "Do you have whiskey?"

Smiling in a way that struck her as condescending, he said, "I don't believe in drinking alcohol. I think it's evil."

She didn't quite know what to make of that so she simply said, "Water would be fine."

"Wonderful," he said before leaving her momentarily.

Her mind went suddenly blank as soon as she was alone. She felt overwhelmed. How was she supposed to talk to him? What would be the best way to initiate a conversation about what had happened between Kendra and Walter all those years ago?

Hannah realized that she wasn't afraid she would blow her chances of learning the truth. She was terrified to hear about Kendra's lifelong secret. The prospect of discovering the truth scared her.

When Walter returned, he set her water on the coffee table in front of her, and she thanked him. He sat on an adjacent leather chair. It squeaked as he crossed his legs. He studied her for a moment, making her slightly uncomfortable.

"As I mentioned," she began, feeling overwhelmed, "Kendra passed away."

"She was murdered," he coldly corrected her.

"Right." She took a quick sip of water and asked, "Were you part of the search party for her?"

"I wanted to be." His brow furrowed with emotion, but to Hannah, he didn't seem genuine. He looked as though he were *pretending* he had regrets. "Kendra and I had a short and difficult relationship. I had to assume I would be the last person she would want to help rescue her."

He fell silent and Hannah sensed tension rising between them. She soon realized that he was suspicious of her. But she couldn't turn back now. He had opened up about his long-ago relationship with Kendra. Hannah needed to seize the moment, and ask him about what had occurred in their home before Kendra had gotten pregnant with Hannah.

"I hear you work in the homicide department of the Gilford police station," he said, changing topics.

How did he know that? Maybe he cared. Maybe he had missed her and had wished he was in her life and had learned all about her on Facebook.

"Well, I'm only a receptionist."

"But you're interested in going into the Police Academy." It wasn't a question and Hannah wondered how he knew that.

"Well, yes, I've thought about it." After a pause, she added, "I'm sorry, how did you know that?"

"Gilford is not so far away." He feigned an easy smile. "The girls must be devastated."

"They are," she allowed. She inhaled a deep, fortifying breath and asked, "Why didn't it work out between you and Kendra?"

"That's not an easy question to answer," he said, honestly. "Have you been looking into things? Have you been following the investigation?"

"Of course."

"Cody McAlister, leading the charge," he teased, and again, Hannah was surprised at how much Walter knew.

"You could say that."

"He's a good guy. He acts like he has a lot to prove at times. He doesn't know he's already earned his keep." Walter mused, getting a bit lost in a memory, but he didn't share his ruminations with Hannah. "Did you hear about some of Kendra's recent problems?"

It was clear he was alluding to Kendra's drug use. "Yes, unfortunately."

"Hannah," he began explaining in a weird tone. "Back when I was with your mother, I saw her vulnerability, and I did what I could to make her strong."

Chills skirted up her spine and she suddenly felt cold. "What does that mean?"

"It means that when we were together, I could see the demons behind her eyes. They clawed at her. I feared to imagine what they would make her do. And when she got pregnant, I chose to protect you."

Hannah realized she was shaking her head. "Kendra has always been God-fearing. She spent her life in a church. What demons are you talking about?"

"I'm talking about my intuition." He offered her a smile, but it looked brittle. "You can't blame people like Kendra, you know. There are only two things you can do with them. Steer clear of the person, or cast the demons out. Unfortunately, if you're like me and you fall in love with someone like Kendra, then you have no hope of walking away. You have to expel the demons from them." He became severe, as his advice got more intense. "You starve the devil out of them if you have to. There's no other way."

"What was she doing?"

"Nothing. I prevented it."

A cold sweat broke out across her chest. She felt like she was fighting to keep her head above water, the freezing lake hungry to devour her all over again. "How did you prevent it?"

"Do you know what her parents were like?" he countered.

"What does that have to do with anything?"

"A lot. Maybe everything. My parents were doctors. They were loving. They nurtured me.

Provided for me. They took interest in my friends, and they supported me, not only financially, but emotionally." He smiled in remembrance of his mother and father, then went slack, his eyes sharpening with disdain. "Kendra's parents weren't parents." Again, he paused to give weight to his next statement. "No one is *born* with the devil in them. They let the devil in. And sure, he's clever. He'll fight to get into your heart and control you. But you must expel him. If you can't, then humanity must expel you from the world." He let that hang, as he studied her. "She was treated like an animal growing up, and she wanted to escape the bad memories, so she turned to the devil for help. Hannah, I had to keep her locked in our cellar to cast out her demons."

"But she wasn't actually acting on her demons?"

"Eventually she did," he said smugly. "She turned into a drug addict, didn't she?"

"And you saw it coming decades in advance," Hannah challenged, though it terrified her to do so.

"And the world ultimately rejected her because of it."

"You don't seem to mind that she's dead."

"Being a mother is a very important job."

Hannah knew she would risk coming off as his adversary, but the thought of agreeing with him made her sick.

"Mary and Candice are holding up okay." She gauged his reaction, scanning his face for any flicker of interest he might have in them, Mary especially.

"I imagine they'll be doing much better now."

"Have you ever met Dale?" she asked. If Walter had a righteous bone in his body, he would come undone learning what Dale was capable of.

"I know of him. I've seen him around."

She raised her eyebrows as if to ask, *and?*

"He's a questionable man."

Intentionally provoking him, she said, "Dale is not so bad once you get to know him."

Walter glared at her with horror. "It seems he has a very special *relationship* with one of his daughters."

In an instant, Hannah felt like the room was spinning. She focused all her attention on not toppling over. She didn't want to give in to the nausea that was coming over her. Bile stung the back of her throat. How did Walter know about the abuse?

He went on, "Wouldn't you agree that some devils must be expelled?"

Holding on by a thread, she said, "What are you telling me, Walter?"

He smirked. "I thought we were speaking figuratively."

She dared to ask, "What happened to your neck?"

His demeanor suddenly shifted, making her blood run cold.

"I'm afraid I have a prior commitment," he said flatly, as he stood from his chair. "It was thoughtful of you to stop by, unexpected but thoughtful."

She didn't wait for him to lead her to the door. She remembered the way. When she reached it, however, he did the honors of opening the door for her, and smiled as though their time together had pleased him.

"Thanks for speaking with me," she managed to say.

As she started down the walkway, he commented, "The fact that she was butchered like that..."

Hannah turned and found Walter shaking his head as though the mutilation Kendra had endured was a shame.

She couldn't believe this man was her father.

It wasn't until Hannah was safely tucked behind the wheel of her Taurus that she felt an emotional avalanche crash down over her.

Walter had made his demented sense of morals all too clear. He had all but confessed orchestrating Kendra's abduction, and the subsequent attempted murder that had followed..

But Hannah needed to prove that Walter had done this.

Her gut told her that the injury he had suffered to his neck would be her only chance at linking Walter Warfield to Kendra's abduction, torture, and attempted murder.

As she drove off through the dark night, Hannah hoped like hell that her mother had been the one to deliver that blow to Walter's neck, and that Kendra would be able to explain the ordeal in detail to the Sanbornton Police.

CHAPTER TWENTY-TWO

"I NEED MORE days, Jenny." Hannah couldn't leave the girls. Not now. Not when they thought their mother had been brutally murdered. Not when Kendra had yet to recover. Their lives had yet to be put back together. Her biological father had yet to be arrested. "Do I have any sick days left?"

"You already used them." Jenny was apologetic, yet firm.

"How about future holidays?"

Jenny sighed and asked her to hang on while her fingers clicked across her keyboard, sounding faint and tinny coming through the line.

Hannah tried to center herself feeling the warm sunshine on her face, as she paced back and forth on the rear deck of Cody's house, taking in the scenery and at times glimpsing Candice through the sliding glass door. The girl was making herself a straightforward breakfast of Cheerios.

Hannah had gotten virtually no sleep last night. Mary hadn't come home, and Hannah hadn't let herself doze off. She had waited up on the sofa.

Cody hadn't come home, either, but at least she had known where he was.

"Best I can do- Hannah?"

"Yeah, I'm here."

"The best I can do is give you today," said Jenny, her capacity to work miracles ever expanding. "But that means you'll have to work the Friday after Thanksgiving."

"Great-"

"Hannah, I have to tell you that if you're not in tomorrow..." she said, trailing off. Hannah imagined Jenny in her office, shaking her head and looking remorseful. "If you don't show up tomorrow, the department's going to replace you-"

She reminded Jenny, "I have been in the midst of a family emergency. My mother just turned up murdered."

"I know. I'm only the messenger. We've got murders to solve here in Gilford, as well. If Holder and the detectives don't have the right administrative support..."

"Okay. Understood."

"I should mention," she went on, though Hannah was distracted when Candice slid the glass door open and padded across the deck. "You're going to have to work on Thanksgiving."

"Not a problem," she said, sucking it up.

"Use today wisely, Hannah," Jenny advised before concluding their call. "I'll see you at the station *tomorrow*."

One day. Hannah had only one day to convince Cody that her father could be behind this.

If she could get Cody to execute a search warrant for 74 Center Point, then Hannah was hopeful that her mother's torturer could be put behind bars.

The sounds of liquid trickling over grass stole Hannah's attention, and she discovered Candice holding the jug of whiskey upside down over the railing and watching the contents stream into the bushes.

"Candice, what are you doing?"

Concentrating with her eyes fixed on what she was doing as she emptied the jug, Candice looked both determined and anxious. In fact, the girl's anxiety was palpable.

Hannah went to take the jug from her, but Candice jerked it away, glaring at her.

"What did you do that for?" she asked the girl.

When Candice didn't say anything, Hannah said:

"I know you were upset that Mary was drinking last night."

Candice's expression opened up a fraction, but she remained suspicious. Judging her apprehension, Hannah figured the girl was unwilling to let Hannah sweet talk her when Hannah was as guilty as Mary when it came to drinking.

"I shouldn't have bought those beers for Mary," she admitted.

"You shouldn't turn to that stuff," she agreed.

"You're right."

She softened.

"What would you like to do today?" Hannah asked her.

"When am I going back to Judy's?"

Hannah cocked her head and told her, "I'm not sure, but I can give her a call. Does that sound good?"

Candice frowned as though she didn't trust that a phone call would actually lead to a therapy session.

"Look, honey, I need to figure out where your sister is, so she can watch you today. I have a few things I need to do. You don't know where she is, do you?"

"I don't need her."

"Well, you need supervision."

"I can stay here."

"Alone? I'm not sure that's a good idea."

In defiance, she crossed her arms. "I'm not going to school."

"No, I know. The principal permitted you and your sister to take some days off."

"Are Daddy and Mary going to be arrested?"

It was chilling. "Why would you ask that?"

"Doesn't the evidence point to them?"

"Candice, do you have reason to believe they had something to do with Mom's abduction and murder?"

Candice poked in and out of her shell.

"Sweetheart," she began in a very gentle tone, as she ventured to touch Candice's arms. The girl looked fragile, like she could float away on a gust of wind. "I know someone took away your clothes." Hannah's voice faltered. She swallowed the lump in her throat and composed herself. "And I know they put you in the woods behind the house. Do you remember that? Do you remember someone taking your photo with those boys behind the shack?" She took Candice by the shoulders. "I need you to tell me who did that to you."

Candice leveled her gaze on Hannah and her stare pierced Hannah so deeply that she felt as though her youngest sister could see her thoughts.

The little girl said, "I wasn't born with the devil inside me. And I never let him in."

"No, I know, honey." Her heart ached for the girl. Did she think that's how Hannah viewed her? Did she think she was tarnished, having been victimized like that in the woods? "You have the purest spirit. I'm going to tell you something, but it has to stay between us for the time being, okay? Until I say otherwise." Hannah smiled, trying to instill hope in her half-sister.

Candice indicated that she could keep a secret, so Hannah told her, "Mom is alive."

Her eyes widened, but it didn't look like surprise or hope. She looked stunned.

"Don't be scared. She really is alive. But we can't say anything yet. Candice?"

Suddenly, Hannah heard the noises of a car's engine growling up the driveway in front of the house. She jumped up.

"That's got to be your sister!"

After rushing clear through the house, Hannah threw the front door open to find a black Audi idling next to her Taurus in the driveway, which caused her heart to leap up her throat. Furious, Hannah charged down the walkway, ready to confront whoever Mary had been with all night.

The passenger side door popped open and Mary climbed out.

Hannah wasted no time grabbing the teenage girl by her arm and escorting her towards the house, but Mary jerked free.

"Where the hell have you been all night?" demanded Hannah as she grabbed the girl's arm again.

"With a friend," she snapped, trying to jerk her arm free. "You're hurting me."

Hannah dropped her grasp and addressed the driver, "Get out of the vehicle."

"Why are you bugging out like this?" Mary asked.

"You didn't come home all night, and you're confused about why I'm bugging out?"

"I'm going through a lot right now," said Mary, a little snide for Hannah's taste. "My mom died."

"And there's a killer out there!"

Hannah barked at the driver again:

"Get out, now!"

"Come on, Bobby," said Mary, rolling her eyes. "Come meet my psycho half-sister."

Hannah glared at her, then watched an older man, who was not Walter Warfield, climb out of the luxury car.

"Who the hell are you?"

The man looked like he worked for the IRS. He was short, stocky, and stupid-looking with white-blond hair and an embarrassed face.

Mary was apathetic as she made a proper introduction. "This is Robert Krane, my friend. Bobby, this is Hannah Cole. She's not always this psychotic."

"Stop saying I'm psychotic." She turned on Bobby. "What were you doing with her all night?"

He glanced sheepishly at Mary so Hannah yelled, "He's four times your age!"

"Oh, don't get the wrong idea," Bobby started, but Hannah was already yelling at him.

"The wrong idea? She cut school the other day with your help. What idea should that give me?"

"You followed us?" Mary was irate.

"Save it," she snapped before yelling at Bobby. "She's fifteen years old! What the hell do you think you're doing, bringing a fifteen year old to a junky playground?"

"That was his brother," Mary cut in. "I was helping Bobby get his brother out of the park."

Bobby frowned and ventured to explain. "My younger brother, Mark. He's had a lot of problems. With everything that's happened to your mother, and I'm so sorry, by the way, but Kendra's disappearance caused Mark to start using again. I just wanted to get Mark off the streets."

Hannah felt her anger loosen. "So, you approached a fifteen-year old girl?"

He shrugged, admitting, "We kept crossing paths."

"It's a small town," Mary offered like that would explain everything.

"When I told Mary about my brother, Mark, Mary said she had an idea," he went on.

Hannah stared at her sister, and tried to analyze the story. Both Bobby and Mary seemed sincere.

"I should've never accepted Mary's help without speaking to her guardian, but she didn't seem to have one," he said.

Hannah asked, "Is your brother okay?"

Bobby lightened up and smiled at Mary. "Yeah. He had a rough night, but we got him into rehab this morning."

"So... It's common knowledge, our mother's... addiction...?"

He nodded.

"Alright," Hannah said softly. She told Mary, "I need you to watch your sister today. Go inside, please." Mary stalked over to the portico, but Hannah stopped her. "No running off."

"Yeah, yeah."

As soon as Mary let herself in, Hannah told Bobby. "I want all of your information. Full name, address, employer, your brother's name, and this rehab center. All of it."

"Ah, sure."

Hannah waited while he rummaged through his wallet for his card, after which he went into his Audi to find a pen and something to write on. He returned a moment later and handed the information over.

After briefly eyeing it, she asked, "Did anything happen between you two?"

He seemed to freeze up.

Hannah yelled, "She's fifteen!"

He stammered, apologizing and explaining that Mary looks and acts a lot older.

"Just stay away from her."

Bobby slunk behind the wheel and backed his car out of the driveway. She watched the Audi until it disappeared beyond the trees. At least some semblance of order had been restored with Mary's return.

As Hannah set off along the winding back roads that would take her to Sanbornton Mercy, anxiety crept into her gut like a shadow then abruptly crystallized into a stark pang.

She had one day and very little sway over anything. All of the witnesses were drug addicts. The victim was a woman who might have been so badly tortured that she would refuse to talk.

By the time she arrived at the hospital, the pressure had gotten to her, and Hannah felt suffocated. The walls were closing in and she couldn't feel the air in her lungs. She told herself to focus on putting her GLOCK into the glove compartment. Guns weren't allowed in the hospital. So, she found the gun in her bag, opened the glove box, and tossed it in, which jostled her flask into view.

God's answer to her anxious prayers.

Or was it the devil's answer?

She took the flask in her hands and stared at it, consumed by temptation.

Why had Candice's statement sounded so familiar?

The girl had said that she wasn't born with the devil inside her and she never let him in.

Hannah had been to two sermons and everyone around Sanbornton seemed to talk with God on their tongue. She couldn't place it.

Whether it was God's mercy or the devil's lure, Hannah drained the flask.

Whiskey burned its way down her esophagus and lit her stomach on fire.

She trusted that a familiar calm would follow, washing through her veins and relaxing her mind and smoothing the hard edges of her nerves.

"Sorry, Candice," she said under her breath before tucking the empty flask deep into the pocket behind the passenger seat.

Finally, she stepped into the cold afternoon. Gusts of wind stripped brightly colored leaves from the tree tops. The leaves fluttered down all around her. She kept her pace brisk, her heels clicking over asphalt, as she hugged a line of parked cars, making her way to the entrance.

The lobby looked less dismal than the last time she had been there when Mary had shot herself. Hannah shook off the grimace that had formed across her face remembering, and took a gander at the Thanksgiving decorations that lined the walls.

She noticed a police officer standing to the side of the receptionist's counter. At the counter, she announced herself, speaking with the young receptionist.

"I'm here to see Cody McAlister," she discreetly mentioned. "I understand he's with... *Jane Doe*."

The receptionist, whose name was Tenley according to the plastic name tag which dangled at an awkward angle on her blouse, waved the police officer over and met him at the side of the counter. A brief and quiet conversation ensued.

"He's going to radio Detective McAlister to come out for you," she said when she returned. "You can have a seat if you like."

Hannah stepped back, but didn't feel calm enough to sit. She hovered near a set of swinging double-doors that said *Authorized Personnel Only*, figuring Cody would come out of there soon enough.

Feeling eyes on her as she waited, she looked around and realized that the police officer had been staring at her. Good, she thought. She hoped she got strip searched and interrogated. No one should get through those doors otherwise. Cody could place a small army in front of Kendra's room as far as Hannah was concerned.

Cody burst through the double doors, and locked eyes with Hannah. He looked exhausted. There were gray circles under his eyes, his lips were pale, and his hair was matted.

"Hey," he breathed.

Hannah kept her voice low. "Has she said anything?"

"A lot," he told her. "But no smoking gun, yet. And the nurses keep knocking her out with painkillers so she can rest. I've only had a few moments to speak with her, and that has been when she's eating."

"Are you staying in her room?"

"Yeah. Me and Alvarez. He's another police officer."

"Is she stable? I mean, is she out of the woods?"

"It appears that way, but she's fighting off some nasty infections. Her wrist was cauterized just fine, and she had a set of stitches across her abdomen that held up, but her ear cavities... There have been complications, but I'm being assured that as long as she rests, she'll pull through."

"Good, that's good." Hannah took a moment to process the update, she wasn't sure whether or not it would be safe to trust a positive prognosis, though.

"You want to see her?"

Her eyes lit up. "Yes. Can I?"

"Yeah, that shouldn't be a problem." Cody got the lobby officer's attention and jutted his chin at the door, indicating he was going to bring Hannah through. Then Cody escorted her over. The officer met them at the door. "I'm going to take her in."

Knitting his brow, he pointed out, "I thought all orders were to keep this wing secured."

"Orders come from the top down," he reminded him, asserting he held a much higher position on the totem pole. As Cody pushed the door open for her, he asked, "You've kept this to yourself, right?"

"Ah, yeah." She reasoned that telling a nearly mute twelve-year old didn't violate the agreement. "How does she look?"

315

"Decent," he said, as they traversed the long, dismal hallway towards the ICU. "Nothing that'll break your heart. Her head is wrapped up to protect her ear cavities. Her wrist is wrapped, too. She has a few bruises on her face, but nothing alarming."

Hannah realized she had slowed her pace when the ICU windows came into view.

Cody shifted towards her.

"Hey, look," he said gently. "She's going to be okay. Before we know it, she'll be happy at home with her girls, cooking and using those piercing blue eyes of hers to glare at everyone in sight. That was a joke."

"Yeah." Hannah felt a sting of tears well up in her eyes.

He led her onward, and soon Kendra came into Hannah's view with nothing but clouded glass between her and her mother.

Alvarez was quick to slip out of the room when he spotted them in the hallway. Cody took a moment to speak with Alvarez, as she stared at her mother.

Kendra seemed peacefully at rest in her bed, though tubes and wires anchored her to a stack of machines.

Cody returned and placed his hand on Hannah's arm, indicating they could go inside the ICU room.

They passed Alvarez, who was now standing guard in the hallway. Hannah didn't hear Cody close the door behind her, as she slowly approached Kendra, the woman who had raised her, the mother she had turned her back on, and hadn't seen for eight years.

Overcome with emotion, Hannah suddenly felt like she was a million miles away from Kendra and from Cody, who had taken her hand in his.

Tears filled her eyes, blurring her vision, and a tidal wave of emotions spilled out of her.

The next thing she knew, Cody had his arms around her and was holding her tightly, as she quaked, sobbing.

Soon her emotions subsided and she urged him back.

"I need to ask her about something."

He furrowed his brow.

"It's about my father."

"She's doped up on painkillers, Hannah."

"I have to do this, Cody."

"What are you going to ask her about your father?"

"I just have this feeling that my real father had something to do with this, so I tracked him down. He lives right here in Sanbornton on the lake. His name is Walter Warfield."

He narrowed his eyes on her as though he wasn't following.

"I went there last night, to his house, and he had a bandage on his neck." She pointed to her own shoulder above her collarbone to show him where Walter had been injured. "If Kendra, I don't know, got a good hit in or stabbed him or something, and she can tell us that, then you can get a search warrant for Warfield's house. We can get him, Cody."

Out of urgency, Hannah had stepped in close, so he took a step backwards, studying her for a moment before he asked, "Why do you think your father had something to do with this?"

"The bandage," she stated emphatically. "And he said some things."

"He admitted it?"

"He *alluded* to it, and he seemed *smug*. And he acted like Kendra deserved to die."

"Hannah-"

"You've got to listen to me. I know he did this."

She did not appreciate how Cody was looking at her, like she had lost her mind.

"I've got a team on Dale," he reminded her. "With all the pieces we've gathered, he's our most likely suspect."

"No, no. It's Warfield. It's my real dad. Kendra's ex-husband."

"Hannah, it sounds like you've jumped to conclusions-"

"Listen to me-"

"This is coming straight out of left field."

"Cody, please. Please. Just trust me. Please get a warrant."

"Hannah," he sighed in a way she didn't find encouraging. "We both know how it works. I need probable cause to get a warrant."

"He said things to me."

"Tell me."

"Ah," she stammered, racking her brain. "He said that being a mother is a very important job. Ah... he said the world needs to expel devils... um-"

"None of that would constitute probable cause, Hannah."

"He implied he had something to do with her disappearance, Cody!"

"Keep your voice down," he reminded her.

She felt a hot rush of frustration shoot through her.

"Then never mind the search warrant," she blurted out. "Just go there. Talk to him. Poke around. You can rustle up some probable cause."

"Okay, look Hannah," he sighed again, but this time it was as though he was already regretting what he needed to say. "When I look at you, I see a person who's so desperate for her family to be innocent that she's blind."

Taken aback by his impression of her, she gaped at him.

"I know what I'm talking about, Cody."

"No, I'm sorry. You don't. You've gone off the deep end and I can't indulge this."

"Cody!"

"Keep your voice down," he warned her for the second or third time.

Hannah had to dig deep to gain control of her emotions.

He stepped in close and sniffed her breath. "Have you been drinking?"

She held his gaze, caught in a position she didn't want to be in, or have to admit. "I had to tell my sisters our mother was dead."

He shook his head. "It's barely one in the afternoon."

"What happened to 'no judgment'?" she challenged, though it was half-hearted.

"I can't watch you destroy yourself."

Hearing him, she was suddenly offended to the point of exploding. "My mother was nearly massacred! My long lost biological father is behind it!"

He stared at her, astounded. "Do you have any idea how insane you sound right now?"

"Why aren't you listening?!"

"Just stop. I've heard enough."

"You have to trust me on this. I'm begging you."

"For the sake of your mother, for the sake of this case, no, Hannah, I don't." He drew in a deep breath, desperately trying to find balance in a room spinning with chaos. "I appreciate your help and your concern and your passion, but... Ah, dammit. You're too close to this. I shouldn't have included you."

"Don't say that."

"It's tormenting you, Hannah. It's clouding your judgment."

"No, it isn't."

"Look, I'm sorry, but, Christ, I hate to say this." His face drew long. "You can stay at my house with the girls as long as you like, but as far as you and I..." He trailed off, shook his head, and mentally assessed whether or not he should finish his point. "We have to put things on hold until I close this case."

"What?"

"I'm sorry."

Her stomach dropped through the floor and her heart followed. "You're breaking up with me?"

"Not breaking up, just a break. Just until this case is closed."

He had destroyed her just like that. He had knocked the wind out of her, stealing all sense of hope that she had been clinging to.

When she spoke, her voice sounded as small as she felt. "Fine."

It was hard to look at him, but she made herself. "I still think you should look into Walter Warfield. He lives at 74 Center Point Road. On the lake." She insisted, "It wasn't Mary. It wasn't Dale. It was Walter Warfield."

"I'm sorry, Hannah."

"One last thing."

"What?"

"Did the police release the information about what happened to Kendra? About her hand and her ears?"

"No, and I would like to keep it that way."

She looked Cody dead in the eye and told him, "Walter knew about both."

"I don't trust your judgment right now, Hannah, and I don't trust your memory since you've been drinking."

It was a very long walk to the parking lot.

CHAPTER TWENTY-THREE

THE MID-MORNING sunlight, stark orange and blazing, cut through the trees and caused a terrible glare in Hannah's eyes, as she dashed from one tree to the next, clenching her GLOCK in both fists and aiming at the ground. With her back to the tree, she peered out, stealing a quick glimpse of Warfield's house.

It looked quiet. The garage door was down as it had been last night. There was no way to tell, as of yet, whether or not he was home.

Hannah locked her gaze on a huge tree up ahead. If she could reach it without being detected, she would be a good ten yards closer.

She scanned the trees and the nearby lake. All was still. She heard only the hollow hoot of a loon down by the water and the sounds of a chipmunk rustling leaves somewhere.

She took off running, her boots crunching over pinecones, and ducked behind another tree. Again, she peered at the house, as she caught her breath. From her new vantage point, she could see into a window that was located on the side of the house. She saw bookshelves inside, a domed ceiling fixture, a door frame, and the door ajar. There was no movement inside the room.

After ruling out entering through the garage, which was too risky, Hannah decided her best bet for breaking in would be to enter through the sliding glass door at the rear of his house. Other than that, her only option was to climb in through the window she was now spying through.

Part of her hoped she wouldn't have to literally break in. Sanbornton was virtually crime free. Maybe Walter had left a window unlocked and she would get charged with *entering* sans the *breaking* part. But then again, if she could find a shred of proof, Cody probably wouldn't charge her at all.

Her heart sank, and Hannah couldn't help but ride the emotional swell that came with knowing that a woman like her coming from a family like hers would never receive true love from a man like Cody.

When her heartache subsided, she dug deep, pulled herself together, and took off running towards the back porch.

Moving fast, she used long strides and pointed her weapon at the house in case Walter surprised her.

Walter had an affliction for *knives* and *blades*. But that didn't mean he didn't have an arsenal of firearms, as well. This was New Hampshire, after all.

When she reached the back porch, she scanned the terrain of sloping grass, the shore of the lake, and the windows lining the back of the house. The glare from the sun was working against her, but she saw no movement inside the house.

She strategized that she could run up the porch steps and try to enter through the sliding glass door in case it was her lucky day. If the door was locked, she could shatter the glass pane with the butt of her GLOCK.

She caught her breath and quickly raced up the porch steps.

She yanked on the sliding glass door.

Locked.

Damn.

She pressed her face to the glass, using her hand to shield the glare, and peered into the living room.

Walter wasn't there.

She cracked the butt of her GLOCK against the glass, but it only bounced off. She tried again, slamming harder, and managed a radial spider web of cracks. Three times the charm, she told herself, and whacked the glass pane with all her might again. The glass shattered and Hannah reached in, unlocked the door from the inside, and eased the door aside.

The heels of her boots crunched, grinding shards of glass into the wooden floor, as she entered. She listened, every fiber of her being on high alert for any sound. It was quiet but for a grandfather clock that ticked loudly from where it stood against a wall.

She looked around for a moment, getting her bearings as to which direction would lead her deeper into the house. She had already figured out which rooms she wanted to check. If he had an office, that could prove fruitful. She wanted to investigate his basement, as well. Surely, he had one, and if Kendra had been moved anywhere, that would be the place. Also, his bedroom could be useful.

Edging through the living room, she kept her gaze locked on a hallway that seemed to lead deeper into the house. Her gun felt cold and solid in her hands, and she kept her finger on the trigger.

If Walter Warfield was who she thought he was, she would not hesitate to shoot if he came at her.

When she neared the end of the hallway, she noticed his office to the right and to the left was a closed door. A basement?

With her gun raised, she quickly glanced over her shoulder to double check she was alone, then ventured to ease the door open as soundlessly as possible.

Stairs leading down.

Darkness below.

She stepped softly down one stair then the next, closing the door behind her as she went. She had to pause to let her eyes adjust to the darkness before descending any farther, so she used the moment to listen out. She only heard the quiet hum of a boiler somewhere below.

When she reached the bottom of the stairs, she felt around the wall for a light switch. It was too dim, and she could use the extra light. But she didn't find one in the immediate area, so she traversed what appeared to be a disheveled office.

There were stacks of boxes and tables holding papers, books, and miscellaneous items. Finding a desk, she perused the contents. From the corner of her eye, she saw there was another door. She spotted a light switch panel beside it.

Cautiously, she approached the door and slowly entered another room, which was quiet. She swept her gun through before turning on the lights.

Her heart skipped a beat when the room was fully illuminated and she could see what it contained.

In a word, the room was sterile.

A stainless steel table stood in the middle of the room. There were nylon straps dangling down from the sides of the table, the sight of which gave Hannah a very bad feeling.

At the far end of the sterile room was another table, but smaller. Hannah found a variety of surgical tools on this table and her blood ran cold.

Hannah examined the grotesque-looking tools that had blades of all shapes and sizes.

"Dear God," she muttered under her breath.

Sensing something was off, she whipped around and took aim at the doorway, but she was alone.

Letting out a rocky breath, she lowered the weapon.

It was then that Hannah saw another door. It was located next to the one she had entered through.

She wasted no time seeing what was inside the additional room. She found a black, pleather jumpsuit on a mannequin. Creepy. The mannequin's head was covered with a black, hooded mask. There was some kind of metal box where the mask's mouth should have been.

She jumped when her cell phone started ringing in her back pocket.

She cursed under her breath, fumbling to silence the loud ringing.

It was Cody's landline.

She answered the call and whispered, "Yes?"

"Hannah, it's Mary." She sounded choked up, like she was panicking.

"What's wrong?"

"Candice!"

"What's wrong with Candice-"

"I can't find her! I went to take a shower and when I got out, I- I- She's not here! I looked everywhere! I couldn't find her! I checked every room! I even checked outside. She's gone, Hannah!"

"Okay, calm down," she said quietly. "I'm on my way."

"Seriously, what is going on, Hannah? Mom is dead, and now Candice has gone missing?"

"We don't know she has gone missing. I can't drive to you if I'm talking."

Her cell phone sounded odd all of a sudden. "Hello?"

She checked the screen and realized she had lost cell service.

Hannah returned her cell phone to her pocket and turned for the door.

But Walter Warfield was standing in her path.

His dark, soulless eyes were locked on her, and yet, he looked amused to find his daughter in the basement of his house.

She took aim, but her hands were trembling.

"You're not going to shoot me," he said in a slippery tone. He quickly added, "We've only just started to get to know each other."

"What is this place?"

"Why did you break into my home?"

He was so calm it made her blood run cold.

"I'll ask the questions," she said with a shaky voice. "Did you blackmail those kids? Did you mutilate Kendra and leave her for dead?"

Cracking a smirk at her, he asked, "Is that what you think?"

"Why did you do it? Did you retaliate against Kendra because you were trying to cast the devil out of her? Is that how your demented mind works?"

"You don't know what you're talking about," he said calmly. "Now leave my home."

"No." She didn't like being two feet from him. If he wanted, he could grab her gun right out of her hands by the barrel. And if he did, squeezing the trigger would be no guarantee that she would hit him.

Taking one cautious step then the next, she inched away from the closet, keeping her GLOCK pointed at his chest.

"You've incriminated yourself, Warfield."

His expression changed as though he found that interesting.

"When I left here last night, you commented about what a shame it was that Kendra had been butchered. The police never released those details. How could you know Kendra had been disfigured, if you hadn't used those tools over there to torture her?"

"We all have a God that we worship," he said, dancing so far beyond her question that it made her head spin. "We all have a vision of heaven, and the just rewards that we're striving for."

"Start making sense or I'll have no use for you and if you're useless to me Walter, you are dead."

"You wouldn't understand."

"Try me."

"You can't stand in our way. Don't you see that, Hannah?"

"Tell me everything, now, or I'll shoot you in the leg and work my way up to your head."

From behind the back wall came a low, murmuring groan.

Her heart pounded hard against her chest cavity, as she tried to make sense of the groaning sounds, but her mind was reeling.

Her tone cracked, as she asked, "Who's that?" Then her heart leapt into her throat when she realized, "Candice?"

Moving quickly, keeping her gun aimed at him, she neared the wall and pressed her ear to it. Someone on the other side of the wall groaned as if in excruciating pain.

"Not everything went as planned," he explained.

"Who's in there, Walter?"

The groaning became louder and Hannah realized the person sounded male.

She ordered Walter, "Get him out." Then she called out, "Travis Danbury? Get him out now, or I'll shoot!"

From the other side of the wall, Travis groaned, "Help."

"I'm warning you," she said. "Get him out or I'll shoot you. I lost my mind a while ago, Walter. And the longer it takes you to do what I say, the more sense it will make to me to kill you." Hannah aimed her weapon at Walter's thigh, as she counted loudly, "Three. Two. One-"

He didn't move. He only stared at her. Then he laughed.

To Hannah's horror, she realized that she didn't have it in her to pull the trigger.

She couldn't do it. She couldn't look someone in the eye, no matter who they were, and shoot them. Realizing this caused a terrible sense of despair to burn through her.

Amused, Walter took his time getting around her as though this was a game he enjoyed. When he reached the wall, he pressed a specific spot and the wall swung inward by a few feet, revealing darkness beyond.

"Travis, I'm with the Gilford Police," Hannah shouted, her voice quavering badly as though she had been stripped of what little courage she had. "You're safe to come out."

Soon, a kid hobbled into view. His shoulders were hunched, and his eyes looked big and black—vulture-like—as he peered out at her, terrified.

Hannah noticed there was a snake tattoo on his forearm from his wrist to his elbow.

"Come out," she told him.

But as soon as he saw Walter, the kid dove back into the wall and slammed it shut.

"We've already won, Hannah," said Walter, filling her with ice-cold panic. "Good has beaten evil."

Wrestling with herself to be strong and fight—she was so close to waking up from this nightmare, she could taste it—Hannah mustered every last shred of courage she had, raised her weapon, and took aim at his head.

Candice?

The sight of her youngest half-sister scrambled Hannah's brain.

Candice was standing in the open doorway as if she had just come downstairs.

"Candice!"

A fresh wave of determination surged through Hannah when her brain registered that Candice hadn't been harmed.

Hannah—desperate to protect Candice, desperate to annihilate every threat, and desperate to put an end to this nightmare before her sister could be harmed…

Hannah pulled the trigger and shot Walter in the leg.

Walter fell to the concrete, grasping his thigh in pain and gritting his teeth.

"Shut up!" Hannah told Walter, as she rushed to Candice.

But her younger sister's demeanor suddenly became strange.

Hannah breathed, "Candice?"

The girl was staring down at Walter, as he writhed and groaned on the floor, and her eyes were misting over with tears.

Why was she crying?

"Sweetheart, let's get out of here," Hannah said, as she tried to take the girl's hand.

She shoved Hannah away from her and rushed to Walter.

What the hell?

Candice knelt down beside Walter and pressed her finger into his bullet wound.

As Candice twisted her little finger as deep as she could get it in the bullet wound and Walter screamed in agony, Hannah could not comprehend what the girl was doing.

"Candice, let's go!"

"We won," Walted told Candice, as she tried and tried to fish the bullet out of his thigh.

"I can't get it," she said, frantic.

He gently told her, "It's okay," as he took hold of her bloody hand and offered her a smile. "No one can take this away from us."

All of a sudden, Hannah reeled with disturbing, demented revelations.

Her mind began bending to its breaking point.

Candice had been the one with Kendra when she had been abducted into that van.

Candice had been the one in those photos used to blackmail the kids.

Candice had been the one feeding Judy St. Clair information.

She had been the only one who had seen anything.

Had she *pretended* to be traumatized? She was close enough to Mary to have known about the sexual power that her sister had over men. And *Candice* was the only one who Hannah had told about Kendra being alive.

The girl straightened up to her feet and stared daggers at Hannah. Quaking with rage, as tears streamed down her cheeks, her expression hardened to stone, Candice asked:

"How could you hurt him?"

Hannah felt her psyche fragment into so many pieces that she ceased to comprehend why she was there or what was happening.

As Candice began screaming at her, it sounded like a foreign language in Hannah's scrambled brain.

In her mind, Hannah was drifting into a lake of darkness.

She didn't see Candice pull one of Dale's guns from her pants.

She didn't see her younger sister aim the gun at Hannah's head, didn't see the girl's tears or her anguish, or hear her screaming accusations.

When Cody rushed into the basement, into the torture chamber, and Candice turned and aimed her weapon at him, Hannah was mentally a million miles away.

And when Candice fired her gun, again and again, at Cody, Hannah didn't understand.

She had sunk deep beneath the surface of her psyche. Ice water had swallowed her whole.

She didn't know that it was finally, completely, devastatingly over.

CHAPTER TWENTY-FOUR

TRACK & FIELD practice was Candice's favorite activity at the Sununu Youth Services Center. Of course, her youth counselor didn't refer to it as 'track practice.' The counselor liked to stand at the sidelines, fiddling with the zipper on her tracksuit, an eggplant number made of coated nylon that swished when she walked and included the juvenile detention center's logo.

The counselor always held a clipboard, but never looked at it or wrote a word down. Rather, she would squint through the winter glare and shout at the girls when they sprinted around her end of the loop.

All of the officers and coordinators who worked at the Sununu Center—a juvenile detention center for delinquent, criminal children—referred to this activity as 'fitness,' but *fitness* was too small a word in Candice's opinion. In her mind, this was Track & Field practice, plain and simple, same as the track practice she used to attend at the Sanbornton Elementary School.

The detention center's track was a quarter-mile loop, and had long-jump pits, high-jump apparatuses, and all the necessary equipment—mats for the high jump pit and batons for passing when the juvies were made to sprint one hundred meter dash relays. They even had shot-put balls.

Candice didn't mind that it was winter, or that snowdrift had covered part of the track. She didn't care that she would be locked up for twelve months. She didn't even really feel like she was locked up in the first place. It was damn perfect here.

She kept her knees up and her strides long, pumping her arms in rhythm with her hard exhales—*shoo, shoo, shoo*—as she came sprinting into the final stretch of the track. She was well ahead of the fray. Her so-called competitors were huffing and puffing far behind her.

Youth Counselor Driscoll started hollering at her, waving her clipboard and stomping her foot enthusiastically, as Candice tore past her, beating all the other girls.

"Push yourself, Candy!" Driscoll boomed, encouraging Candice to give it her all. "See if you can't catch up to the stragglers!"

Coming from anyone else, Candice would've despised the nickname, but Driscoll could call her any damn thing she pleased, as far as Candice was concerned. She just loved being out here, breathing in the sting of crisp winter air, looking at the gnarly trees dressed up in snow, and feeling her heart pound. This was her insurance that she would never look voluptuous and sexual like her sister, like her mother, like the devil's plaything.

She missed Walter.

His purity—he was mild mannered, pious, and chaste—contained qualities that her own father should've possessed. She missed how Walter used to read to her, those mystical bible verses she would try to interpret, figuring out the word of God.

Of course, Walter would offer his own interpretation, and they would engage in stimulating debate. Walter couldn't always see how the Lord intended an eye to be carved out of the sinner who had harmed the eye of another, but with Candice's patient encouragement, he soon got on board.

Most of all, she missed his warm hands, the care he took washing her in his bath during their weekly baptisms, which had been a ritual that he had suggested. He liked to steal away to his bedroom afterwards, while she dried off, then he would fix her milk and cookies and listen to her unload about the degradation at home.

He was a good man.

He had helped her execute God's will. He shouldn't be in prison now. Neither of them should.

Candice hooked around the curve of the loop again, and the sight of a few juveniles walking, they were so out of breath, inspired her to pick up her pace. Oh, she would catch up, all right, and Driscoll would be proud.

As she did, the images of tongues came to the forefront of her mind. The first time Walter had handed her a container, the gift of his commitment to her mission, she had stared down at the slimy lump. The disembodied tongue had been black with blood and full of veins that had reminded her of a spider's webs. Those heathens should've never tried to run her down with the van that night. It hadn't been part of the plan. But she had made them pay. She had made all of them pay.

An eye for an eye.

Closing in on the straggling girls, Candice locked her gaze on the back of the slowest girl's head and grinned. She quickened her pace until the toes of her sneakers threatened to clip the girl's heels. It was all about luck and timing. She would trip her. The thought of the girl spilling into dirty snow made Candice smile from ear to ear.

"Hey!" the girl squeaked the second Candice made contact. Glancing over her shoulder, her expression twisting into a frown as she understood that Candice had done it on purpose, she shouted, "Ms. Driscoll!"

But Candice was already sprinting off past her, kicking up dirt and snow with each punched stride.

That's how it was at times when the anger swelled up inside her. It was these people around her. She could see the devil in them. These weak people who let the devil in, and then did terrible things to each other as if it was the other person's duty to forgive them… These people made Candice sick.

Remember to forget was a phrase she had heard from Dale so many times, it turned her stomach.

Those ignorant cops… When the junkies had communicated the phrase, *remember to forget*—the one thing that she had permitted them to convey—the police should've linked it to Dale. Candice realized she had been naïve to hope that the police would actually be intelligent enough to draw the connection.

"Candy!" Driscoll waved Candice over, and when Candice looked at her counselor, she spotted Judy St. Clair by her side. "Visitor!"

Awe, hell. What did the bird-brain want now?

STARING OUT THE window and barely listening to Judy tell her about the upcoming hearing, which was scheduled with the Youth Diversion & Restorative Justice board to take place at the Laconia District Court, Candice thought about the foolish headline her stupid town had given to the crimes that Walter and her had committed—The Hermit Lake Tragedy.

The only tragedy she could gander was that people like Dale, Kendra, and Mary were allowed to go on living.

"Candice?" Judy asked, stealing her attention. The woman's eyes were as lit up as ever and locked on Candice, as though Candice was an enigma wrapped in a riddle that Judy might be smart enough to unravel. Judy wasn't. "Your family will be there."

"So?" she said.

Judy drew in a frustrated breath, studying her.

"Candice," she began, "the board is having a hard time with Warfield's statement. He's placing all the blame on you. It's damning. But at the same time, the district attorney doesn't believe you could've pulled off a crime of this magnitude. We can make a strong case for your immediate release, but you have to participate. This time is valuable, do you understand?"

Candice had stopped listening after the child psychologist had mentioned Walter. The man she had known and the man that Walter had turned out to be once behind bars didn't add up, but every time Judy told her about Walter, Candice refused to believe her. Walter would never utter a word against her. He just wouldn't.

"I can repeat myself if you don't understand," she offered.

"I understand."

"Then let's go over a few things," she suggested. "From my perspective, after your mother was abducted, you grappled with severe dissociation, night terrors, and classic symptoms of post traumatic stress disorder, having survived trauma."

"That's not a question," she pointed out dryly.

"Do you really want people to believe you faked those symptoms?"

To demonstrate, Candice let her gaze go soft, her mouth slowly drifted into a gape, and she suppressed her breathing. Judy glanced nervously around the visitors' center, looking for the guards before she leaned across the table and stared at Candice in disbelief.

Snapping out of it, the girl told her, "Night terrors are way easier."

It took Judy a moment to recover from having watched the performance. She asked, "How did you find Walter?"

"It's a small town."

"We need to establish he coerced you," she countered.

"He didn't. He listened and agreed. That's all."

"Candice." She needed to gather her thoughts before continuing. "Walter treated Kendra very badly during their marriage and it would seem he had intended to subject her to the same treatment, perhaps as a means to punish her for escaping in the first place. That's the argument we're going with to get you out of here. Can you tell me about how you two met?"

Candice didn't know if she wanted to get out of here, but she explained anyway. "At the church."

"The Church of God in Sanbornton?"

She nodded. "He was nice to me."

"So, he approached you?"

"Yeah, he was the first to say 'hi' and ask me about myself. He was my friend."

"And you spent alone-time with him?"

Candice glared at her.

"Candice, you obviously weren't with him when he harmed your mother. You're so far removed from this thing, it astounds me you've insisted you orchestrated it."

"But I did."

"How did you sneak away from your house?"

She snorted a laugh. "How did I slip out when my drug-addled mother was incapacitated on the sofa and my father was strong-arming Mary into committing ungodly acts with him in his bedroom? As if it was a real challenge." She rolled her eyes. "The devil lived in our house. He was lurking in the bottom of every beer can."

"You're referring to Dale's drinking," she stated for confirmation.

"Dale should be locked up, not Walter."

"Good," she said encouragingly as she made notes. "That's good. We can paint a picture for the board. Life at home was oppressive. Dale was drinking and abusing Mary. The incest drove your mother to use drugs when she discovered it. Walter had always meant to harm Kendra and when you opened up to him about life at home, it was exactly the reason he needed to hurt her in the name of God."

It had her blood boiling and she leaned in, speaking sternly, "I did this. *Me*."

Startled, Judy looked up from her notepad. "Why then? Why did you do it?"

"Everything you just said. But it wasn't Walter. It was me."

"Walter isn't innocent in this. He was the one and *only* one," she said for emphasis, "who actually committed these crimes."

"It was perfect, but you're all too stupid to understand," she said.

Judy straightened her spine. "You didn't anticipate anyone's stupidity. What does that make you?"

"Not as smart as I thought I was, I guess," she admitted with resignation. "The hand, the ears, the eyes that we never got to take. It was flawless. Mary was supposed to tell the police how Kendra slapped her across the face *with her left hand* when Mary told Kendra about what Dale had been doing to her. Mary was supposed to explain to the police how Kendra *didn't listen* when Mary confessed her twisted dynamic with Dale. Kendra had turned a blind eye. The police were supposed to hear Mary say all that, and realize that Mary cooked up the whole attack and got Dale to cut off those parts of Kendra in order to frame him later. Mary and Dale are supposed to be in prison right now, not Walter and me."

"You know what that sounds like to me?" Judy's expression had turned soft listening to her. "It sounds like a younger sister who really cares for her older sister. In a way, you avenged her suffering."

"I don't care about Mary."

"Would you feel that way if Dale hadn't victimized her?"

Candice fell silent. She wasn't unsure. But she stopped herself before she could go there. "Kendra should be dead. Dale and Mary should be in prison."

"What went wrong?" Judy asked as though she could pretend to be on Candice's side. "Why was Kendra dumped at the lake when she was still alive?"

"I don't know," she said angrily. "Her eyes were supposed to have been carved out and she should've been dead."

"Candice, I need you to consider that Walter may have gone against you and still is. You need to detach from him. We need to make the case that he did this, all of this. He isn't protecting you. You can't protect him."

"You think he left her alive on purpose? I doubt it."

Judy sat back in her chair and seemed to mentally ruminate about something. A smile spread across her wide mouth.

"What?" asked Candice, irritated.

"Maybe it's true what they say."

She rolled her eyes, but asked, "What's that?"

Judy shrugged. "That it was a miracle."

Candice stared at her for a long moment, realizing deep down a small part of her agreed. It *was* a miracle that Kendra had lived, but Candice wasn't sure what to make of it.

Judy became distracted by someone on the far end of the room behind Candice, and when Candice glanced over her shoulder, she saw Hannah crossing through the visitors' center.

Hannah, she thought, pressing her mouth into a hard line, as Judy rose to hug her hello. If Mary had been right about one thing, it was that Hannah should've never left. How could she abandon her younger half-sisters like that?

On Hannah's graduation day, Candice had spied their argument from under the refreshment table where she had tucked herself to play with the cottony cloth that hung down. Hannah had gotten in Dale's face, pointing her finger at his nose, warning him to stay away from Mary. She had sneered and spat when she told him that she knew he had plowed Mary with beer that night, the night of her prom, when the wee morning hours were still black as sin. Candice had only been four years old, but smart as she was, she understood why Hannah had been furious. She had understood her oldest sister's choice of words, and what they implied. *Don't you dare touch her*, she had warned.

But Dale had.

And if Hannah had never left...

Candice cringed to imagine how none of this would've taken place if Hannah had stayed.

When Candice had orchestrated Kendra's abduction, she hadn't been entirely sure what she would do with her mother.

It hadn't been until Hannah had the audacity to come home that Kendra's fate became clear in Candice's mind.

Cut her up and watch Hannah fall apart as the pieces of her mother came floating back.

Hannah had neared the table where Candice sat. She gazed down at her youngest half-sister and offered Candice a big smile.

"Are you excited for your hearing?" she asked.

Candice just stared at her.

"Can I sit?"

EPILOGUE

SOAKING UP THE sensation of the warm, winter sunshine on her face, Hannah stood in front of the bay windows of her new house, and looked out at the lake, its shore frozen with a thin sheet of ice, a dusting of snow drifting over. Icicles clung to the naked trees along the property, and the sky was a brilliant color of azure blue.

Wintertime in New Hampshire was beautiful.

Hannah had dressed that morning in a nice blouse and slacks, wanting to look her best at the Gilford police station when she took her exam. The blazer and high heels she wore should give her confidence. As long as she passed her test and got accepted into the Police Academy, she would be happy.

Staring out at the lake, she could almost forget her past and the horrible ordeal her family had survived.

Hannah feared to imagine what would've become of her, had Cody not shown up at Walter's that day. Would Candice have killed her? She would like to think not, but deep down she couldn't be sure. Instead of grappling with the dark possibility, she chose to focus on the fact that Cody *had* rescued her that day. He had taken the bullet that had been meant for her.

The shot had jarred her from the deepest recess of her mind that day. She had rushed to Candice, as Cody had laid motionless on the floor, the terrible stillness of his body breaking her heart.

Hannah had seized Candice and wrestled the handgun from her grasp, as her sister had fired and fired, bullets pinging every which way.

The horrible end to a horrible nightmare.

Hannah pushed it from her mind.

She turned when she heard footsteps behind her.

Groggy with sleep and bundled up in woolen sweats, Cody neared her and gave her a kiss good morning. As always, she melted into his arms for a moment.

He cradled Hannah from behind so they could both gaze out at their corner of heaven.

After recovering from a gunshot wound to his abdomen, Cody had sold his house and bought this one. Their new house was located in Gilford on Lake Winnipesaukee, close to the Gilford police station where Hannah could resume her position. Her department had been eager to add Cody to the payroll thanks to his valiant work on the Kendra Cole case, which had made him a Tri-State celebrity and hometown hero, but not more so than it had Hannah.

Releasing her, he asked, "Coffee?"

"I already made some. It's on the counter," she told him with a warm smile.

He cocked his head at that. "How early did you get up?"

"Early," she admitted with a smile. "I wanted to study a bit more."

Most nights, Hannah was able to sleep in their bed. She would curl up beside Cody and drift asleep, like she had last night.

Other nights, she slept on the floor. When she did, she often woke to find Mary watching over her. On those nights, Hannah would peer at her from beneath the blankets, her heart filling with such calm that she would doze off again, feeling safe.

Hannah joined Cody at the kitchen table where he was nursing a mug of black coffee and glancing through the local newspaper.

"I'm thinking about going ice fishing this weekend," he said, sliding the Sports section aside so he could gauge her interest or maybe he just wanted to look at her. Mary had given her another stylish haircut, this time cropping her hair high in a bob, which she had argued would make Hannah look authoritative. She had shown her how to use a flat iron and keep her tresses sleek with polish, mothering Hannah as she went about the tutorial. "You think Kendra would be up for that?"

"I think it sounds nice, yeah."

He rose from the table and refilled his mug in the kitchen.

As he returned, she noticed Mary helping their mother down the stairs on the other side of the living room.

Cody set his mug down on the table, crossed the room, and offered his arm to Kendra to assist her. When he did, Mary started off for the kitchen to make breakfast, her favorite meal to cook.

Their mother looked amazing and not just with respect to all she had survived. Her eyes were bright and lively. Her complexion glowed and she seemed to perpetually smile as though she felt elated to be alive.

Kendra had undergone two surgeries during her recovery. One to replace her kneecap, which had shattered when she had desperately tried to escape Walter Warfield's house. And the second had been to attach a prosthetic hand. She had seen a plastic surgeon as well, who had molded prosthetic ears to her head. By the looks of her, you would never guess her dark history.

This was the family now. Broken, but healing and so full of life that at times Hannah's heart swelled, filling with so much love that she thought it might burst.

After spending time with Judy St. Clair and undergoing a great deal of prodding, Mary had given her statement to the Sanbornton Police about Dale and all that had occurred in the shack between them.

As a result, Dale was currently in jail awaiting sentencing.

Twice a week, Mary went to therapy. Mondays after school, she spoke with Judy one-on-one and on Thursdays, both Mary and Kendra went together. Mary no longer blamed her mother. The Hermit Lake Tragedy had afforded her that much.

Dalton Gerrity, Blake Abbott, and Travis Danbury had not been convicted for their roles in the abduction, mainly because Kendra had insisted they, too, were victims. However, the kids had been placed under house arrest. Each of them lived with his parents, and were working on completing their community service hours and attending drug rehabilitation programs, which had been Cody's recommendation.

Not a day had gone by that Hannah didn't think about Candice. Her heart carried the distinct hope that one day she would truly know her youngest sister and have a relationship. Often, she drove to the Sununu Youth Services Center where Candice now lived. She checked in on her on behalf of Mary and Kendra, reporting back. In this way, she was still a soldier.

Nights when Hannah slept on the floor, Candice filled her dreams. Children absorb everything around them, the pain, the torment, the despair of those they love. Candice had watched Dale's depravity, how he had lured, manipulated, and abused Mary, and how his dark descent had driven Kendra to use drugs. Hannah understood why Candice had done it, why she had felt compelled, though she didn't agree with it. It was still a challenge to fathom. Dale had nearly destroyed everyone around him, one beer at a time.

Daddy soda.

Hannah hadn't touched a drop of alcohol since they found Kendra at the lake. Neither had Mary, and they wouldn't. They had made a pact.

Mary placed a serving dish of scrambled eggs on the table, as Cody passed out plates and utensils. When they sat, Kendra took Hannah's hand in hers, offering her prosthetic one to Mary, who closed the circle grasping hands with Cody.

Hannah smiled at Cody, squeezing his hand, then met eyes with her mother, who always managed to start each meal with a prayer.

"Dear God, thank you for this family. And for everything we had to survive in order to reach this very moment. We are blessed."

THE END

ALSO BY MIRA GIBSON

Thomas from the Sea

Who Killed Leeanne?

The Kensington Killers: The Complete Series
Lunatic (The Kensington Killers, Book One)
Crank (The Kensington Killers, Book Two)
Maniac (The Kensington Killers, Book Three)

The New Hampshire Mysteries: The Complete Series
Daddy Soda (A New Hampshire Mystery, Book One)
Rock Spider (A New Hampshire Mystery, Book Two)
Tar Heart (A New Hampshire Mystery, Book Three)

ABOUT THE AUTHOR

I write mystery novels, detective novels, sleuth mysteries, and psychological literary fiction! You can find me most days working on my computer in the sunshine of beautiful Long Beach, NY where I dream up small town characters and write dark mysteries that are filled with unsuspecting tenderness.

Find me on Facebook! **/MiraGibsonAuthor**

Visit MysteryRoyalty.com to learn more.

For questions and comments about this book, please contact www.mysteryroyalty.com